THE MEDICI CURSE

THE
MEDICI
CURSE

A NOVEL OF SUSPENSE

DACO S. AUFFENORDE

SCARLET
NEW YORK

THE MEDICI CURSE

Scarlet
An Imprint of Penzler Publishers
58 Warren Street
New York, N.Y. 10007

First edition

Interior design by Maria Fernandez

Author photo by Kimberly Campbell

Library of Congress Control Number: 2024949903

ISBN: 978-1-61316-641-3
eBook ISBN: 978-1-61316-642-0

10 9 8 7 6 5 4 3 2 1

Printed in the United States of America
Distributed by W. W. Norton & Company

For my family

Thus have you breathed your curse against yourself.
—William Shakespeare, *Richard III* [I, 3]

MEDICI FAMILY TREE

Fillipo de' Medici (1891 - 1966)
m. Maria Lazzeri de' Medici (1913 - 1942)

Marco de' Medici (1931 - 1993)
m. Silva Farnese de' Medici (1933 - 2000)

Aurora de' Medici Perruzi (1942 -)
m. Fulvio Peruzzi (1942 -)

Vittoria de' Medici (1968 - 2007)
m. Leo Rossi (1958 - 2023)

Francesca Perruzi Massimino (1968 -)
m. Claudio Massimino (1960 - 2023)

Anna de' Medici (1995 -)

Giana Massimino (1985 -)

Antonio Massimino (1992 -)

Paolo Massimino (1997 -)

PROLOGUE

n that Saturday night in late November, after
returning home from la serata inaugurale at the
Teatro dell'Opera di Roma, Vittoria de' Medici Rossi
crossed the foyer and headed toward the staircase. She
prayed that Anna was sleeping soundly. Vittoria's phone rang just as
she started up.

"The papers will be served in the morning," her lawyer said. "Where
is he now?" *He* being Vittoria's husband, Carlo.

"Sleeping it off in the study." Vittoria and Carlo had quarreled
before she'd left that evening—a hammer-and-tongs disagreement—
confirming that she was making the right decision for both herself and
her twelve-year-old daughter.

"Take Anna and get out of there."

A door upstairs banged against a wall—Anna's bedroom door! Vittoria's insides jumped.

"Oh, no! Anna must be having one of her nightmares. I have to go
to her. It's better if she sleeps through the night before we leave."

"Be careful," the attorney said.

Anna made a growling sound, and her feet stomped against the floor. The girl was indeed in the middle of a rampage.

"Sorry, I have to go," Vittoria said, then hung up and hurried up the stairs.

At the top, she stepped gingerly into the hallway. The door to Anna's bedroom was wide open. The young girl—bug-eyed—was now racing down the hall toward her mother. "Anna, it's me, Mamma."

"No, no, no," the girl said as she looked past Vittoria and scanned the hall. Fear rippled across Anna's face.

"It's okay, honey."

Anna stopped abruptly. "The witch is here."

Make no sudden moves.

"Please, Anna. It's late. I'll walk you to bed, sit with you for a while. It's just a dream. Everything will be all right."

Anna stooped over, as if trying to hide, and crept along the hall. When she reached her old playroom, she dashed inside and locked herself in.

Vittoria ran to the room and reached above to a groove in the wall where she had secreted one of many door lock pins.

"Where is it?" Anna asked in an eerie tone more chilling than ever before. Answering herself in a little girl's voice, she continued, "I don't know, don't ask me. Stop. You're hurting me."

"Sweetheart, please," Vittoria whispered. "Let Mamma help you."

A loud bang.

Vittoria struggled to unlock the door. Once it opened, she tried pushing her way inside, but the girl bore her weight against the door.

"Not him, no, no. Not him. I'm *not* going down there. I won't go. I won't. Get away, you . . . you . . ."

"Calma, andrà tutto bene, Anna," Vittoria said, hoping that the reassurance would calm her daughter.

". . . you witch," Anna shrieked. "Let go of me!"

"I brought you something fun from the opera tonight, tesoro," Vittoria said, hoping that the mention of a gift would free her precious girl from the nightmare.

To Vittoria's relief, her daughter went quiet. When the pressure against the door ceased, Vittoria entered, prepared to take the girl into her arms. But Anna bolted, shoved her mother, and ran toward the front staircase, clawing at her own arms. Before heading down, the girl stopped and turned around, her eyes wide with horror. One step back and she would fall. A rush of fear swept throughout Vittoria.

"Take your evil, you . . . you . . ."

Vittoria had to chance it and rushed to Anna.

The girl's expression changed from dread to anger, and her eyes homed in on the ruby and diamond necklace around Vittoria's neck. She pointed an accusing finger at the jewelry. "De' Medici blood!"

"Let's go to bed, it's late," Vittoria said in a gentle voice, trying to conceal her own distress as her daughter teetered precariously at the edge. Vittoria eased her way toward the girl.

Lightning cracked outside, followed by booming thunder. The lights dimmed, and the house went dark.

Then out of nowhere, hands grabbed Vittoria's neck, squeezing hard.

"Anna!" Vittoria sputtered.

The grip tightened.

Struggling to free herself, Vittoria gasped for air. She was dizzy, about to lose consciousness. In desperation, she swung her weight toward the wall adjacent to the stairs, taking the first step down. Thankfully, her daughter remained planted on the upper floor.

The hands loosened from around Vittoria's neck just as the necklace was torn from her.

Then came the shove.

Vittoria lost her balance and fell backwards. She reached for anything to stop the fall, but she found no purchase. Down the staircase she tumbled, her body pounding hard against wrought iron railings and wood treads. Lights flashed on. Recognition. Too late. Vittoria's skull met the cold of the marble floor.

De' Medici blood pooled across the porous white stone.

exit the Florence airport and start toward the Tuscan countryside and my family home, which I'll see for the first time since I killed my mother. I was twelve years old at the time, experiencing an episode of night terrors. Her death garnered a lot of media attention, because my mother, Vittoria de' Medici Rossi, was a well-known Italian opera star. I punch the accelerator on the Fiat 500 rental car and the engine roars to life.

The authorities ruled the death an accident. The official police report says she tripped and fell down the stairs after a night of drinking too much champagne.

For me, that night's a blur. Pieces have resurfaced over the years but not enough to reconstruct even a partial picture of what happened. I hope that my coming home will bring back the missing memories—for better or worse.

People say I coveted the Medici Falchion—a ruby-and-diamond heirloom that's been in the de' Medici family for hundreds of years. That I took it that night. But if that's so, where is the necklace?

Exiting the highway, I race along the narrow country roads and come upon field after field of vibrant red poppies. It's mid-May, and the flowers have burst into full bloom, adorning the landscape. The lovely buds dance in the breeze as if welcoming me home. I lower the windows to take in the fresh air and am greeted by its velvety warmth.

On the outskirts of Poggibonsi, a village located several miles from the small town of Colle di Val d'Elsa and not far from my destination, an old farmhouse comes into view. Two old men sit on a porch in rocking chairs. An elderly woman sweeps around their feet. The men act as if the woman isn't there. If I were her, I'd give those two a good swift sweep on their asses.

Behind me, an engine roars—a red motorcycle. Looks like a man, but his face is hidden by a helmet and black visor. I watch him in my rearview mirror. He speeds up, then brakes, weaving back and forth. The oncoming traffic is heavy, leaving no room for him to get by. I accelerate to almost eighty kilometers—about fifty miles per hour—to put distance between us.

Vehicles continue to whiz past from the opposite lane. The biker brakes, and I relax.

A moment later, he's practically kissing my car's rear bumper, playing his taunting game again. I grip the steering wheel hard.

"Che diavolo ti prende?" I shout. It feels so good to speak in my native tongue again, even if only to ask this asshole what the hell is wrong with him.

Tapping the brakes doesn't warn the guy off. Doesn't faze him in the slightest. My heart rate accelerates. Speed is exhilarating, but I'm not a fan of fatal car wrecks.

Fifty feet ahead of me, a large truck enters a narrow, one-lane stone tunnel that has cut slopes on both sides. A small roadside light blinks, indicating that I should stop.

When I slow down, the biker flashes his headlight. My grip tightens on the steering wheel.

The biker shifts from one side of the lane to the other. Traffic is too heavy for him to pass and avoid oncoming cars.

I grit my teeth.

A split second later, the biker accelerates, gets only a hair's-breadth distance ahead of my front bumper, and darts out ahead of my car.

Turning the steering wheel hard to the right, I barely miss hitting the man. The Fiat leaves the pavement, spinning 360 degrees as it slides down a steep dirt embankment. As soon as I work the brakes, the car fishtails, but luckily, it doesn't roll over.

The jerk doesn't bother to stop.

"Stronzo," I shout, shaking a fist.

My adrenaline surges, but I gather myself enough to check out my body—no injuries. I call emergency services and next the rental car company.

A middle-aged man runs up to my car, panting for breath. "Are you hurt?"

"All good. Just pissed as hell at that guy on the motorcycle. Any chance you got his license?"

"Sorry. Happened too fast." He looks the car over, points out a flat tire, and offers to help. I tell him that I've just phoned the police and the rental car company, and that a tow truck is on the way.

He stares at me for a long moment and then a strange expression comes over his face.

"Anything wrong?" I ask.

"You look familiar." He hesitates. "There used to be a singer who lived around here, but she died some years ago. Vittoria de' Medici? Are you . . . ?"

"Yes, I'm her daughter, Anna."

The man seems flustered. "You say the police are on their way?"

"That's right."

"You're lucky you were wearing your seatbelt. Others have been crushed when . . . You could've . . ." He gives a quick shake of his head. "I'll leave you to it." He waves and hurries to his car.

"Hey, can I get your name and number? As a witness?"

He just drives away.

Sixteen years have passed since I left Italy as a child. Unbelievable that this perfect stranger recognized me.

Forty-five minutes later, the police show up. The rental car agency delivers another vehicle. Two hours later, I'm behind the wheel of an older model Alfa Romeo Spider Veloce—the only car left at the agency in Siena. An unexpected benefit of this mess.

Before arriving at the estate, I reach Colle di Val d'Elsa, a fortress town from medieval times named by Dante Alighieri in his *Divine Comedy* and once ruled by the Florentine de' Medici family, my distant ancestors—so they say. It occurs to me that there may not be any food at the villa, so I decide to stop for a few groceries. Salami hanging in the window of a deli draws me inside the store like a magnet. There are so many varieties of cheeses and cold cuts. At first, it's hard to decide what exactly to buy. When the elderly woman rings me up, she looks at my face. Her smile fades and her hands tremble as she gives me the food. She also knows who I am.

A walk would do me wonders, so I head to the old part of town, the Borgo, admiring the old medieval architecture of brown and beige stone blocks that were used to construct the fortress, the cobblestone streets, and period buildings that have faded to pale oranges and yellows. It feels as if I've stepped into another century. Women hang wet laundry out to dry on small wrought iron balconies; others sit on rickety metal chairs smoking and enjoying seemingly pleasant conversations. Potted plants and flowers adorn the stoops and windowsills of homes—all connected like rowhouses in the city. A few cats scamper past me, stalking or running from what I don't know.

At a small café, I order a cup of dark chocolate gelato from a bored teenage boy who doesn't give me a second look. There's an empty wooden bench in the piazza. A place to sit and absorb the ambiance. Little kids are laughing and running around, playing silly games.

When a passing cloud obscures the sun, the light inside me dims. I've worked so hard to fight the darkness. But it always rears its ugly head.

According to the gossipmongers, before I pushed my mother down the stairs to her death, I ripped the Medici Falchion off of her, leaving cuts on the front of her neck. The police report says the other abrasions are consistent with her fall.

For centuries, people have claimed that the necklace is cursed, that anyone who possesses the jewel will suffer a violent death—Vittoria de' Medici Rossi being only the latest example. *Nonsense.* Why would I, a young girl consumed with phobias and plagued by walking nightmares, want such a thing?

The wind kicks up; debris skitters along the ground. From some-where, a woman shouts, "Vada via!"

Go away?

I search in the direction of the voice. No one is around.

A bell tower rings. A man dressed in black stands in the clock tower, a cord in his hands. Five bells strike.

A cold shiver races up my spine. I set the half-eaten cup of gelato aside and think, *Welcome home.*

2

t the entrance to the de' Medici estate, I'm greeted
by an imposing wrought iron gate—twelve feet high,
with sharp spires across the top and our family's
coat of arms, which is mounted inside the center
arch. Gargoyles that sit atop flanking columns give me a start. I
forgot about those, and about how those grotesques frightened me
as a child, although supposedly the creatures ward off evil spirits. I
clamber out of the car and push open the gateway. The metal hinges
creak and groan.

The drive to the villa is refreshing. The rocky, dirty road is lined
with tall, narrow cypress trees. Everything is in pristine condition, not
a gangly weed to be found. The lawyer for the estate was wise not to
release our beloved long-time butler and property manager.

An apple orchard stands to the far right, an olive grove on the left.
Beyond the fruit trees, low-lying hedges are sculpted into a maze. Once,
as a small child, I got lost in that maze. I screamed and cried, sure that
I was about to die, until my mother found me and held me in her arms.

She told me I should be making wishes and laughing—not crying. Her laughter warmed my heart. I'm still working on those wishes.

My breath catches when the car rounds the bend and the villa comes into full view—a classic Italian Renaissance-style mansion with arched openings, columns, and porches both upper and lower. A tower with a view for miles stands at the west end of the house. In the distance, vineyards rise and fall in every direction, with woodlands sprinkled to and fro as though painted into the landscape by a thoughtful brush. Atop a smattering of faraway hills sit neighboring towns, their protruding towers defensive structures built by the wealthy and powerful to spot approaching enemies and danger. But those pale in contrast to my mother's estate, and her house. *My* house now.

"All houses have souls, just like people," my mother once told me when I was a little girl of seven. "Most people's souls are good, but some are dark. Houses are the same way."

"That's bullshit," my father said. "Houses are wood and concrete and stone. Don't talk like that. You're scaring the kid."

"Am I scaring you, Anna?" my mother asked.

"No," I lied.

Later, when I heard my parents fighting—again—I thought that our house must have a dark soul.

The driveway meanders around until reaching the front of the villa, which ends in a roundabout with a water fountain at its center. I park the car, unload my luggage, and walk up the front stairs to the porch. A brass gargoyle knocker, matching those on the gate's columns, adorns the entryway; only it's tarnished now with a rich patina.

Just as I'm about to knock, the hinges on the door creak, and it opens. An elderly, expressionless man, maybe seventy-five, maybe older, appears. Dressed in a tailored charcoal suit, he's slightly bent, listing to his right. An earthen smell oozes from him—as if he lives in a cave.

"Buon pomeriggio, Signora de' Medici, e benvenuta a casa," he says in a gravelly voice.

No words of greeting ever sounded sweeter.

"Edoardo!" My impulse is to reach out and hug him, but I don't because he seems ill at ease. "I was so hoping you would be here," I say, speaking in Italian. His English was never that great. "And come on, call me Anna. Like you did when I was a little girl."

"Very well, Anna." He sounds as uncomfortable as he looks. "Your Italian is impeccable."

"Of course it is. I made sure I never lost it."

A large bluebottle fly darts out of the house, around Edoardo's legs, and then dive-bombs me. I step to the side and swat a hand in its direction. The insect veers off to the side porch and disappears into the shrubs below.

"Did you see that huge fly that just buzzed out of the house? Please tell me we don't have a problem."

He narrows his eyes. "I didn't see a fly. The house is pristine."

How could he have missed it? Not a subject worth pursuing. "It's so great to see you. It's been forever."

"I didn't think you would ever return." From his tone, it's not easy to discern whether he's happy or sad that I'm here. "My cottage is down the way, but I can stay in the servants' quarters downstairs, if you would rather not be alone."

My spine stiffens. "I've lived on my own for years now. I've got this."

"You're not afraid?"

"Should I be?"

"Come, let's get you settled in."

When we go inside, I set my luggage to the side and take in the grandeur of the two-story foyer, twice the size of most New York studio apartments, including any that I've leased. The scent of fresh-cut roses fills the air.

This moment is a step back in time: the magnificent crystal chandelier hanging from the ceiling; the wrought iron sconces on the walls; the bronze-colored silk fabrics hugging the edges of the windows; the circular staircase leading to the upper hallway that stretches from one end of the house to the other; the creamy white marble floors—the place where my mother must've taken her last breath. There are no residual signs of her blood. None. Of course not—the stained marble was replaced.

My chest suddenly hurts. My eyes clamp shut for a brief moment. Coming home was the right thing to do. Sure, the lawyer could've just sold the house, making my presence here unnecessary. But I'll never be right if I keep running away from my past. Running from the past hasn't worked.

Edoardo clears his throat. "Shall I show you around?"

He must be joking. This place was my childhood home. No, he's deadly serious. "Has it changed that much?"

"Not at all since you left as a child."

"I would've thought . . . well, never mind. I don't know what I thought."

"Nothing's changed, Anna. Let's get your things upstairs to your room."

"No, no, I'm fine. You look tired. Have you been waiting for me long? Of course you have. Let me drive you back to your cottage."

"Thank you, Anna, a kind offer. But I like to walk."

"You're sure?"

He gives a clipped nod, the gesture as familiar as it was many years ago. Yet, Edoardo seems like a stranger . . . which I suppose he is after so long.

When he leaves the house and hobbles down the front stairs, a wave of guilt washes over me. I can't let this elderly man walk home. He's gone to so much effort to get things ready.

He starts down the drive.

"Wait, Edoardo, I'm driving you." I go for my purse, which slips from my hands, causing the contents to spill. I quickly gather my things. Back outside on the porch, there's no sign of him. Nor does he answer my calls.

He couldn't have gotten far. I run down the road, shouting his name, and going farther than he could've walked with his slow gait. But he just seems to have disappeared into the thin Tuscan air.

I face the house. A murder of crows lands on the roof; they hop, flap their wings, and settle into their pecking order.

Where exactly is the cottage?

3

xhaling hard, I return inside and stop in the foyer. On the far side of this room and directly below the upper hallway is another corridor that spans the length of the house. An interior breezeway below the upper balcony leads to the large two-story living room. The area is palatial, with multiple seating areas. The case goods and tables are antiques, most made of dark mahogany. The couches and chairs are upholstered with rich brocade fabrics. And there in the corner of the room sits the grand piano.

So much privilege for the first twelve years of my life, and even during boarding school in America—and then I became the starving artist, because my father cut me off. Refused to use my own money to pay for my college . . .

"I'm not going to waste money on childish fantasy," he said. "You're no artist."

"How would you know? You have no taste. Never did, according to Mamma."

Rage clouded his dark eyes. "Don't go there."

"It's *my* money."

"And I'm your father who makes the rules. As trustee, my job is to save you from yourself."

The trustee who paid himself fees; that was all he got because my mother left him nothing else. "And you're using my trust fund for your own screwed up business investments and parties and women. Yeah, I know what you're doing. Don't you get that those girls are taking advantage of you? They don't give a shit about—"

"Enough!" His face turned beet red. "You're behaving like an irresponsible child. You want to fight? Take me to court. We'll see how far that goes."

"You're cruel."

Consultation with lawyers was a waste of time. No one would take on the case after reviewing the legal documents, not without a massive retainer.

Now my father is dead, and the entire estate is mine. But this new privilege will not be taken for granted. I hope I can do some good, or at least make some good art. Create something that will prove to the naysayers just who I am.

At the grand piano, I slide my hand across the fallboard's smooth surface, then lift it open and tap a few keys. The sound resonates throughout the room. It's so quiet here. Quite unlike the never-ending din of New York traffic. With one hand, I play a short jazz glissando. Its vibration reverberates inside my ribs, not with pleasure but with a wistful ache. It's only my excitement, my bewilderment at being home, and the rush of strange emotions twisting inside of me.

Windows and doors line the rear wall of the house. I open one of
the French doors and go outside to the veranda. The swimming pool is
blue and inviting. To the right of it is a flower garden with a pond and
a fountain. Beyond the formal gardens, a stone pathway leads through
fields and toward lush hillsides.

Is this place really mine?

A deep breath of fresh air is momentary bliss—until an icy gust of
wind cuts through me. The horizon is beginning to color with dots
of orange. Dusk is approaching, and the day's warm temperature is
falling fast.

Back inside, I secure the house, collect my luggage, and climb the
staircase to the second floor, passing several closed-off rooms. At the
end of the hallway is my old bedroom suite.

Nothing's changed. The pastel fabrics, furniture, my dresser with
a framed photograph of my mother and me. I glide a finger across the
glass of the frame—no dust. Atop my bed sit the same silk pillows. A
chair with a side table stacked with children's books, the same books
that I kept there those many years ago. A frosty feeling sweeps over
me. This place feels like a shrine to the dead.

No way am I staying in this room—a child's room full of nightmares. Can't take the chance.

Carrying my suitcase, I head to the other end of the house—my
mother's bedroom suite, which is decorated in deep reds and oranges.
Again, nothing's changed. Weird, because so much time has passed
that you would think the fabrics would've shown signs of wear, become
faded and moth-eaten. But, no. The linens are like brand new.

My breaths come hard. It's not the time to let my imagination get
the better of me. Of course. Edoardo has maintained the place and

has stored the linens. Which explains why the house and grounds are as pristine as the day I was whisked away.

Inside the bed chambers, I stop short when I encounter a full-length wedding portrait of my mother. She's wearing that horrible necklace—three tiers of rubies and diamonds—rocks made deep in the earth. My heart rate picks up a beat. *It's just a painting*, I tell myself. A very lifelike painting.

You were so beautiful, Mamma.

"Between us," I whisper to the painting, "the Medici Falchion doesn't impress me. It's gaudy and outsized. Who would want it?"

The lines of paint are immaculate. The lace on the wedding dress was exquisitely executed, the fabric almost palpable. My mother's bouquet drips from her arms in a way that seems to express a loss of innocence; a few of the flowers, which have turned brown, are falling to the ground. She's not smiling. What a strange depiction for what should've been the happiest time of my mother's life. An impulse to touch the face, my mother's image, sweeps over me now, but I don't reach out.

A closer look at the signature at the bottom reveals the name of the artist—Giuseppe Tringali. How puzzling. Portraiture has never been his subject area of choice, not that he made known to the art world. He and my mother must've been friends for him to have produced such a work. Could their friendship be the only reason he's offered me a fellowship to study with him this fall?

There's a loud metallic rapping of the gargoyle knocker. Then a woman speaking Italian calls out from inside the foyer, "Ciao! C'è qualcuno in casa?"

Oh my God, who is that? And how did this woman get inside my house? Because I'm sure I locked the front door. "Chi è?" I call out.

"Francesca Massimino, your aunt."

I let out a sigh of relief. This woman is not my aunt; she's my mother's first cousin. Born only a few months apart, the two women were more like sisters than cousins. In many ways, Francesca was like an aunt to me, once.

Inside the upper hallway stands an athletic-looking woman in her fifties who has just climbed the staircase, smiling happily. She's tall, with dark, silver-streaked, shoulder-length hair.

"Welcome home, Anna. It's so good to see you again."

"How did you get in?" I wave a hand through the air. "Sorry, that came out wrong. It's been a long day. You just really surprised me."

"Your Italian is perfect, cara."

"I made sure to practice it and studied the language in college. I didn't want to let it go."

"I hope you don't mind that I let myself in. When no one answered . . . Give me a hug, dolce ragazza." She holds out her arms.

Francesca Peruzzi Massimino—what's her angle? No word from her or any of the family in years, and now she's acting like a day hasn't passed since she last saw me. We didn't exchange one Christmas or birthday card this entire time. Unless, yes, unless my father hid them from me. And to call me a sweet girl . . . strange.

Not normally touchy-feely with others, it's not hard for me to hold back. When Francesca's happy expression begins to fade, I relent and let her hug me.

"I came by earlier and left you a bottle of our family's wine in the kitchen, some bread, a little dinner, and my phone number," she says, warmly.

"The door wasn't locked?"

She lets out an embarrassed chuckle. "No, you're right, I have a key. I should have said . . . but I didn't want to be presumptuous on your first day home."

"Why do you have one?"

"Your mother gave it to me years ago."

"And the locks haven't been changed since?"

She shrugs. "I guess not."

"I'm sorry to be rude, but may I have it? The key?"

An awkward silence passes. Then she reaches into her purse.

"You know, never mind, Francesca. I should have the locks changed. No telling who can get inside here."

She looks offended at my lack of appreciation. She's probably been helping Edoardo. "My apologies. Thank you for all you've done."

"You must be exhausted, Anna. I just wanted to welcome you. So, welcome."

My father always told me that I could be rude. It isn't my intention. She wants me to ask her to stay, but fatigue and jet lag have drained me of any sense of hospitality. I tell her that once I'm over the fatigue, I'll be in touch.

At the front door before she leaves, she stares into my face with misty eyes. "You look so much like her." Her pained expression deepens. "Sorry to hear about your father's passing, Anna. It's been a year now, has it not?"

"About that, yeah. But we weren't that close."

"I understand. Your father could be a difficult man."

"By difficult, you mean he was a criminal, Francesca?"

She considers me for a long moment. "I know nothing about that."

She's not a good liar. We both know if my father wasn't a criminal himself, he at least consorted with individuals of that ilk.

"I didn't like the way he treated your mother," she adds. "*That* was criminal."

4

ich, orange light spills through the foyer's windows. Everything inside the house now has a golden sheen—so enchanting. Drawn upstairs to my mother's suite again—now *my* room—I enter the adjoining sunroom. This space has always been a favorite of mine. My mother and I would sit cuddled up on a plump comfy couch and read stories together. Our favorite was Carlo Collodi's *Le avventure di Pinocchio: Storia di un burattino*, the beloved Italian children's story. I remember her lyrical voice as she sounded out the words, teaching me to read as a very young child. Now such a comforting memory.

Before I left New York, the lawyers were instructed to have the sunroom converted into an art studio. The couch is gone, as are all the other glamourous furnishings. Canvases of many shapes and sizes are stacked against the walls. There are several easels and a long table filled with paints and brushes and drop cloths and other art supplies. Never has there been such a perfect art studio.

A fresh start. In New York, my art didn't sell, not even after I earned my MFA degree last year. So, I scraped by working in art galleries, assisting a well-known but talentless sculptor, even doing nude modeling at the art school (so many creeps hitting on me, but I dated a couple of the more talented ones). No matter how desperate I became, my father wouldn't help me. His response was that I needed to learn responsibility. But his motivations were clear—he earned a bigger fee from the estate by preserving the amount of money held in trust. That meant making sure that college tuition didn't deplete the funds. I'm not certain yet how much is left, whether he managed to embezzle it all, because I'm waiting for the lawyers to send me the final papers. My mother kept everything sealed, her way of protecting me.

On my last day in New York, I put all of my old work on the sidewalk outside my apartment building and posted a sign that read: *Free art. Take one.* The paintings were gone in less than an hour. Maybe I'm not as poor an artist as a few of the gallery owners in Manhattan think.

I pick up a brush and swish it across one of the canvases—there's no paint on the bristles. I'm left-handed like Mamma. She used to say that made us more creative.

On impulse, I cross the room and enter a dimly lit stairwell. The cool-to-the-touch walls, worn smooth with time, are constructed of stacked sandstone blocks. Why not? I start down. The steps end at a landing and seem to go nowhere, but there are hidden passageways, used in the old days by servants and maybe to escape bandits or invading armies. Running my hands along the bottom of the wall, I find a seam, apply pressure, and a door pops opens, revealing more steps down.

Stay out of there! My father's voice rings in my brain.

But Mamma says I can—

Stay out!

"You're not alive anymore," I say aloud. "I'll do what I want." My pulse quickens. I find a light switch, flip it on, and continue. A faint musty smell touches my nostrils as I descend deeper into what must be the basement level of the house. Yes, it's a secret passageway.

Through a door is a private salon ripped right out of the eighteenth century—Louis XVI all the way, opulent and decadent. A large wardrobe with glass cabinets and shelves sits at the far side of the room. Inside are long dresses, wigs, and headdresses, some on hangers, some on mannequins. And Vittoria de' Medici Rossi's fabulous opera costumes. Accounts on the internet say these treasures mysteriously went missing after her death. Not so—she secreted them away right after she left the stage.

Framed photographs sit on the shelves. Most are publicity photos of my mother and cast members decked out in their costumes.

Of course. This was my mother's private sanctuary. What a thrill to have a part of her that no one else in the world has. How could I have forgotten about this room? I spent so much time with her down here, playing dress up, singing, dancing. But only with her. No one was allowed in this room without her …

"Don't ever go in there without me, Anna," my mother would say in the sweetest voice.

"But why, Mamma?"

"I have so many valuable things in here. You wouldn't want to break something. You know how clumsy you can be."

"I'm *not* clumsy," I would insist.

"Oh, don't be petulant, tesoro mio. Of course you are."

Was I? Not when I was awake. But during the night terrors . . . ?

While humming one of my mother's favorite arias, I open the case and lift the hem of a gorgeous blue-sapphire-colored gown. This dress isn't an opera costume. I hold the bodice close and have an urge to try it on but don't.

A few of the drawers below the shelves hold brochures and newspaper clippings from my mother's star performances. The rest of them are now empty but once held a vast trove of jewels.

My anger rises. Where did all the jewels go? I know the answer to that too. My father found a way to take valuables from this room. He probably sold them off for ten cents on the dollar, then gambled the sale proceeds away or lost them in one of his failed investments.

But there's one piece of jewelry he didn't sell: the Medici Falchion. He would've died to get his hands on that necklace.

Sitting on a table beside a couch is a photograph in a lustrous frame, now patinaed over time. It's a picture of my mother and me backstage at a theater house. I must've been three or four. I don't recall the play. But we were smiling, so we must've had a good time. My eyes mist with tears.

On a side wall hang rich oil paintings in gilded frames. They line the entire length of the wall. Five in total, and they all feature my mother from various performances. The detail and compositions are superb. The artist's signature is unmistakable—Tringali again. My God, the two must've been remarkably close.

Something makes me step away—shame, guilt. My attention is drawn to the wall beside the door. Painted on its surface is an elaborate floor-to-ceiling depiction of my mother in an operatic costume. She's wearing a kimono—Cio-Cio-San of *Madame Butterfly*. The background is a garden scene filled with cherry blossom trees, camel-lias, and azaleas.

An eerie heat slinks across my arms; beads of sweat rise on the nape of my neck.

The eyes in the painting have changed focus. *No way.* I step closer and stare up. They *are* different. A vague, undefinable anxiety fills me. I'm not sure I'm ready to live in this house.

Time to leave the parlor and head back upstairs.

A sudden impulse causes me to stop near the landing that seemed to go nowhere. Using my phone's flashlight, I study the surrounding walls and find another door, behind which is a small, empty closet. The middle of a stairwell is a very odd place for a vestibule. The light from my flashlight catches what must be secret spy holes that look down into my mother's parlor. These holes are where the eyes in the painting are.

So who was watching who? And why?

Shining the flashlight through the cutouts, I peer through them.

Stay out!

Half a dozen people, no more, a dozen, are down there. Everyone is scantily clad and wearing masquerade masks. I don't recognize anyone. They're laughing, drinking. A couple is engaged in oral sex; the woman has a tattoo on her chest.

I gasp, draw back.

The vision is gone.

Stay out!

5

pstairs in the studio, a warm gust of air sails through a now-open casement window. The glass rattles against its frame as the window gently rocks with the wind. Yellow roses climb a trellis set against the house and the breeze brings their intoxicating fragrance inside.

I'm reminded of the summer trips throughout Europe that my mother and I took together. We visited elaborate gardens as well as the major museums, the opera houses, and theaters. She knew this world, especially the juicy stuff, like who had one too many girlfriends—anyway, that's how she put it. In the art world, she knew who the real artists were and who the frauds were. Her stories intrigued me, got me interested in art at a young age.

I tap my fingers on the windowsill, thinking back to when I was age ten. We'd just left a play. We stopped in the open-air gallery of the Loggia dei Lanzi in the Piazza della Signoria in Florence to look at Benvenuto Cellini's ghastly bronze sculpture of *Perseus with the Head of Medusa*—a gruesome decapitated head held high for all to see. My mother seemed unaffected, almost to revel in its grotesque-ness. I was horrified that someone could cut the head off another. When I nudged her, she explained that Cellini was an arrogant man who openly admitted that he could do as he liked, that his murder of an underhanded rival, Pompeo de' Capitaneis, was just. Because Cellini's art was so brilliant and admired, his scandalous misdeeds were overlooked, even pardoned. She smiled and said that art had triumphed. I wonder if this was her way of showing the world that she could do as she liked. She wore the Medici Falchion that day. I'm an adult now, not so innocent myself, but still I'm flabbergasted at this memory. Who tells a child such things?

While I rest my arms on the windowsill, a couple of honeybees fly toward me, in search of nectar. I don't freak out. Maybe it's the mesmerizing whirr of their fluttering wings that soothes my phobia.

The bees scatter. Another insect flies at me. Not a honeybee, not a fly, not exactly a beetle, but a bug with a loud buzz and an aggressive nature. I slam the window shut with such force that it's a wonder the glass doesn't shatter. Then it springs open again.

Too late. The insect makes its way inside and flies crazily around the room.

"Get out!" I shriek and compound my silliness by giving the command in both Italian and English. Evidently, the bug doesn't under-stand either language, because it comes at me again.

I run to close off the bedroom, grab a blank canvas, and race around, swatting frantically at the intruder. Its angry buzz grows fiercer. I swing left then right, practically obliterating the canvas.

The insect divebombs me relentlessly and then tries to invade my left ear. I swat until the bug is off me, or so I think. Then I realize it's still on me, creeping down the front of my neck. One wrong move and it'll sting me.

I snatch up a large paintbrush and, with one precise whack, swipe the insect from my neck.

The insect's wings flap erratically, and then the bug spirals to the floor. I leap forward and squish the bug with my shoe. Its body crunches like brittle plastic.

So much for open windows.

With a piece of tissue, I squat down to pick up the black, red, and yellow carcass. A strong smell similar to that of a stink bug emanates from the corpse. Its black stinger remains intact.

This bug is more than familiar. One of these stung me when I was six. I've hated insects ever since. Especially this particular kind, which I named a devil bug.

I throw the remains out the window. The honeybees have returned. The lovely scent of roses wafts inside my studio. I'd like to leave the window open but don't dare. As soon as I start to shut it, I'm assaulted by an odious smell.

Something else around here is dead.

6

nce I've unpacked a few items the following morning, I head downstairs and inside the living room. The area is bright now that the sun is up. Everything looks so fresh, like a new coat of paint has been applied to the ceiling and walls.

At the piano, the fallboard is closed.

I lift the cover and play Claude Debussy's "Clair de Lune"—my mother's favorite.

"Very nice, Anna." The unexpressive yet loud voice makes me flinch. "You play like your mother did."

Edoardo stands at the entryway. "Oh, it's you. I mean that in a good way." He seems unaffected. "Thank you for the compliment, Edoardo, but I don't come close to playing the way Mamma did." True, I inherited some of Vittoria de' Medici's musical genes—my undergraduate minor was classical piano—but I wasn't good enough to major in music. My voice is decent, and that made me popular at karaoke bars, although that's in part because I get a little too wild after a few drinks.

"I came by to check on whether you needed anything," he says.

"Yes, actually. Thank you for asking. Screens on the windows to keep the bugs out. One of them got in and attacked me."

"I'll see to it. Anything else?"

On the wall to his right are portraits of the women in our family. As a child, I paid little attention to these. Now I'm intrigued. "Tell me about the paintings of my ancestors. Wedding portraits, I assume, even though none of them look happy."

"Yes, well . . ."

"Is it because they're all wearing the Medici Falchion? The same wedding dress? Are they afraid because the women in my family are doomed?"

"Don't speak that way. *You* are not doomed."

"I don't want to be. But weren't they?"

He doesn't reply.

I point to one of the paintings. "That's my . . . grandmother, no, my . . ."

"This is your great-grandmother, Maria Lazzeri de' Medici."

"What's her story?"

He seems to ponder this. "Her story. She was the wife of Filippo de' Medici."

"That's it?"

"In those days, that was pretty much it for a woman, as one might say."

"So, she and Filippo are my *grandfather*'s parents."

Another nod. "Their son, Marco, was your grandfather."

"Right. And Aurora is their daughter. My great-aunt Aurora is Francesca's mother, which makes my mother and Francesca cousins. So how did my great-grandmother die?"

"Anna, why would—?"

"How did she die, Edoardo?" These are questions that never occurred to me to ask as a kid. After I left Italy, my father wouldn't talk about my mother or her family. I had to sneak around to find out anything, listen in when he didn't know, and even then, I didn't learn much.

"Automobile accident."

"Specifically."

"She . . . she broke her neck."

"Was she wearing the necklace? The Medici Falchion."

Reluctantly, he nods.

I point to the next portrait.

"Valentina Bardi de'Medici. Your great-great grandmother, who was married to Giuliano de' Medici. She was thrown from her horse while on a caccia alla volpe, an exhibition hunt. She died instantly. And yes, she was wearing the necklace."

"Riding a horse?"

The next painting is of Silva Farnese de' Medici, my grandmother, who was married to Marco. She wears the same dress, same necklace. I swallow hard. My recollections of my grandmother Silva are vague. For good reason, I was really young, maybe five or six, when she died of throat cancer. Though I have a distinct memory of her contagious laugh, which brings a smile to me now.

I ask about the portraits of women from prior generations. All died young; all died of of an injury or illness related to the head or neck.

"They truly are cursed, aren't they?" I say more to myself than to him.

"Rubbish," he says.

"They look so unhappy. Why would these women allow such paintings of themselves to be made? I would've ripped mine to shreds."

"It's just the style of the times, nothing more. You're an artist, you know how tradition goes."

I run my fingers along the frame of Grandmother Silva's frame, and then, overcome, I touch the necklace. The texture of the paint is smooth, the sensation cool to the touch. Thinking about how these women died fills me with an overwhelming sense of pain. Something stings my finger, and I quickly retract my hand.

"Are you okay?" Edoardo asks, but he doesn't move from his spot.

A bubble of red surfaces on my finger. A papercut? Blood? Paint? I wipe the moisture off on my jeans and lean closer to the portrait but don't see any evidence that the paint is smudged. Nor is anything particularly sharp on the canvas visible. Maybe the edge of the frame? When I check, the wood is smooth.

Light beams splay inside from the back windows. One lands on Silva's wedding portrait and illuminates the painted rubies and diamonds. Edoardo seems unfazed.

"Thank you for the family history," I say. "Dark as it is."

We go quiet.

"By the way, Edoardo, the door down to the basement is locked. My key won't open it."

He hesitates, looks unsure, then says, "Nothing but old junk down there."

"There must be keys around here someplace."

"I'll have a look around. How else can I help you, Anna?"

"Weren't your quarters downstairs?"

"Yes, but we never locked the door."

Then who did?

"Oh, now that I think of it, Edoardo. There's something more I would like to ask." He looks at me oddly. "Did Mamma have costume parties?"

"She liked to entertain."

"Edoardo, I asked about costume parties."

"Who remembers? It was so long ago."

Except, he's forgotten nothing. That's all too clear.

7

fter spending my first week in Italy relaxing, exploring, and recovering from jet lag, I text Giuseppe Tringali, introducing myself and asking to meet. He replies right away, giving me directions to where he's staying at the moment. Says to meet him at noon.

It's a perfect day for a drive to the village of Pietrasanta, a small town that attracts artists from around the world. Situated between the Versilia coast and the Apuan Alps, the region has plenty of the Carrara marble that sculptors covet.

Tringali and I have never met, but I've seen his photographs online and find him at the Church of Sant'Antonio Abate, standing in front of the Ferdinando Botero fresco *Paradise and Hell*. He's not hard to recognize—a striking resemblance to a modern-day Leonardo da Vinci without the beard. His expression is stern—almost scowling.

"You know, when I first saw you," he says, "I thought you were Vittoria for the briefest moment."

Except, how could he see me? He hasn't taken his eyes off the Botero painting. I look up at him; he towers over me, although I'm five-eight.

He gestures *con esuberanza*. "Wasn't Botero incredible? His boldness of colors, just *splendido*. But not so ridiculous that we see the work as cartoonish. His characters, grotesque and over-sized, speak to human fear. And the devil himself, notice how he exudes knowledge. At the same time, he's demonic, he evokes fear, controls it. It's in his eyes." Tringali considers the painting for a while longer, his brows rising and lowering. In a weird way, he seems to be patterning the devil as depicted in the artwork.

"I never understood why Botero painted a baby in hell," I say.

Tringali looks at me with narrow eyes. "Escaping torment, of course. Tell me, does it appear that Hitler's head has been sawed off? Some say yes, others say no."

"If that's all he suffered, it's not enough."

A warm smile replaces Tringali's stern expression. "I like you already. I also like the artwork you submitted—no, like is the wrong word. Potential. You have great potential. You're not good yet, but you have potential. Admirable that you recognize the need for a mentor like me. Come, let us take a walk."

He leads us to an open-air café, where we order lunch. He speaks only about his own art. I do manage to get him to talk about the architecture of the marbled village, but he always returns the subject to himself. His conversation is enthralling, I admit, like having the ear of one's favorite professor. Then he waxes eloquent about what my duties will be when we begin working together—a lot of setting up easels and cleaning brushes and making coffee, the subtext clear.

When lunch ends, I say, "You painted the portrait of my mother, and Juquetta Lucchesi painted the portrait of one of my grandmothers. Both hang in my house."

"Do you like them?"

"They're . . . It's puzzling. The women seem so austere, sad really."

"Juquetta died three years ago. Talented enough, but to spend one's life painting portraits, that's such a bore. Promise me you won't do that, Anna. No, of course, you won't. You're not the type."

"Yet you painted my mother's wedding portrait and a few others that I found in her parlor."

He waves a dismissive hand. "I did that for Vittoria, but if you think those are portraits, you're quite mistaken. They are emotional interpretations. Psychic extrapolations. Now, Juquetta painted portraits. Her studio was near mine in Capannori, a stone's throw away. She was a colleague and a friend, though we had a bit of a falling out after she refused to model nude for me. Happened the day after she turned sixty. Yes, that put a strain on our friendship. She was beautiful and voluptuous like you and your mother, even at that age. Such a shame."

What a thing to say.

"I resented the fact that she wouldn't let me make her immortal with my art," he says and looks me over with an appraising leer. "I could make *you* immortal."

A long glare conveys my message clearly. There's not a chance I'll model for this man, apprenticeship or not. When an artist becomes a subject, they lose credibility. "What do you know about the Medici Falchion? That's not a matter of public record. All the women in my family wore it. You painted my mother wearing it."

Those eyebrows elevate, then fall. "Why ask me? It's *your* family's heirloom. I'm sure you saw your mother wearing it quite often. You probably tried it on yourself."

"Mamma died when I was twelve. It's not like she ever told me anything about it, other than the necklace is a family heirloom. And she refused to let me try it on. You think because of the curse?"

"The Medici Falchion is a powerful amulet—not a cursed object. That's what Vittoria believed. Some are strong enough to control and use its power. The weaker ones are at the necklace's mercy." He takes a sip of coffee, gazing at me over the rim of the cup, then sets it down.

"You're saying Mamma was one of the weak ones?"

"Not at first. She became a star through her strength—her ambition, her ruthlessness, qualities that too few admire. She credited her success to the necklace's powers. But the poor woman got complacent and gave into the conventional, and that weakened her."

What bullshit. "By conventional, you mean . . . ?"

"Marriage. Children. A life away from art."

That foolish statement deserves no response. His tone was so blasé, yet the asshole just accused me of turning the person I loved most into a weakling.

"You really didn't know your mother, did you, Anna? But as you said, you were just a child. I do wonder . . . would *you* be strong enough to control the necklace? You were always such a sensitive child."

I throw some euros on the table and stand to leave.

"Where are you going?"

"Nice meeting you, Mr. Tringali. Thank you for your time."

"Wait. We need to talk more about your studies."

Unsure why, I sit. "I'm not certain it's a good idea for us to work together."

"It's conversation, Anna, which you brought up. See what I mean about being sensitive? You can't be easily upset like this if you work with me or anyone else. Not if you want to succeed in the cutthroat world of art. Get used to it, the world is a critic. Some are favored, others not. As for art, I'm exactly who you need. Now, let me tell you about my recent projects."

He launches into a ten-minute monologue about how his "unique" and "exquisite" paintings are changing history. How he's resurrecting art by combining Renaissance tradition with postmodernism. That deep, rich colors can portray the gloom of present-day man. His lecture is tedious, informative, and a walk through the halls of graduate school. My passion is to paint landscapes with subjects, paint what I see, create something new. I want to experiment. But expecting to change the direction of the entire art world, that's ludicrous.

We spend the rest of the day exploring the area together. The man likes to hear himself talk, though his academic knowledge is astounding. Keeping him on subject isn't hard, as long as the subject is art and himself.

When it's time to go, we take the scenic way around and down a short strip of the coastline. The sun is setting, the colors vibrant—the only time he actually quiets. We sit on the beach. I take my shoes off and dig my toes into the sand.

After the last shades of red slide from the horizon, he says, "Your mother was exceptional."

"My mother *was* cursed," I blurt out. "And I'm told I was her executioner."

Where the hell did that come from?

He scoffs. "You're an artist at heart. All the greatest artists are executioners. And they suffer. Without suffering, there's no artistic expression. Enjoy the summer and start work with me in the fall—if you have the fortitude."

"I'll get back to you," I say, not sure whether I'm responding to his offer to join him or whether I have sufficient internal strength.

As I drive home to the villa, I can't stop thinking that I'll never be right in my heart or head unless I find that necklace—cursed or not. If I really took the jewel from my mother and hid it during my nightmare, it's still there in that house. It's got to be. But recalling the details of a sixteen-year-old dream? I couldn't tell anyone what I ate for dinner a month ago.

How can I possibly recover *that* memory?

8

he following day, I go for a long walk on the property grounds and trailblaze up a hillside to its summit. The hill ends in a steep descent. Sitting down on a boulder, I get lost in the view. Lush green and blue undertones mixed with dusty browns and tans color the foothills that seem to continue on forever. It's breathtaking, sublime. I'm filled with peace. Tranquility.

A bird of prey flies over me. Its line of flight draws my attention to the opening of a cave along the face of the sheer cliff. Recently, some friends in the States, experienced spelunkers, took me caving, but I'm a neophyte. I wouldn't think of going in there alone.

After about an hour, I head home.

As I pass the water feature in the flower garden, a rank smell fills the air. The carcass of a young female capriolo. The small European roe is floating in the water.

My stomach turns. I consider waiting for Edoardo, but I can't bring myself to force an old man to clean this up, nor can I leave the animal there. Besides, it couldn't weigh more than thirty-five pounds. So, holding my breath, I pull it out by its hind legs and lay it on the ground. It's been shot, and not cleanly. The worst of it is that some asshole left this poor creature to die a painful death.

I drag the remains toward a field of high grass.

Out of nowhere, a swarm of insects descends upon the dead animal—those devil bugs.

I shriek and drop the dead roe's legs. Some of the insects veer away from the carcass and divebomb my face and neck. My screams and flailing arms do nothing to dissuade them.

I run.

Nearing the house, the insects suddenly peel off, as if a hunter has called off the dogs. I make it inside unscathed, I think.

My head spins, the vertigo lifting my skull.

Through the French doors I watch in horror as the ghastly insects descend upon the carcass and devour the carrion in less than a minute. Nothing is left of the roe except its skeletal remains.

Can't be. Shakily, I move away from the door and slide down onto a chair. My stomach twists and clenches as dry heaves threaten.

Gathering myself, I take a hot shower, where I spend a long time scrubbing off the touch of death from my hands. After a light dinner, I head to a plush living room couch where I sip Cognac that I found in a liquor cabinet and try not to think about that poor roe and those awful insects.

None of that seems real.

Eventually, the warm glow from the alcohol settles my mind.

How pleasant it is not to be married to my phone, constantly checking messages. It's so peaceful now. Maybe I really can live here, surround myself with all the beauty. Then my eyes land on one of the female portraits. I scan them all. Their grim faces horrify me. When the light in the room flutters, so do the eyes in the paintings. I cross the room for a closer look. My skin crawls. Their eyes follow me. But I know that it's just an artistic technique. I look closer at the paintings and scoff at my unfounded anxiety.

I return to the couch, take a long sip of the brandy, and lean forward to set my glass on the coffee table. As soon as I straighten, my throat constricts. The pain is intense. I gasp for breath, trying not to panic. I'm paralyzed, and not only with fear. An invisible tentacle wraps around my neck, strangles me.

Impossible.

Why can't I stop choking? My ears ring so loudly that they hurt. I collapse onto the couch, gagging and struggling for air, on the verge of losing consciousness.

"Anna, do not go downstairs!"

The ringing in my ears won't stop. My brain threatens to burst through my skull. My entire body is without feeling, I melt into the cushions while fighting to remain alert. Fighting to stay alive.

9

ost in the ether, I run haphazardly toward the breezeway and down the hall. All the lights are on. Who turned them on? The basement door is open. Who has the key?

A loud *boom* reverberates throughout my entire body.

"Who's there?" Stupid to call out and give my location away. I'm alone. Helpless as the child I once was. There's only one place to hide.

I race downstairs, and there it is—*that door*! Going through is a poor choice, but I can't help myself and slink over to it. No one would think to look for me inside there. The entryway is locked.

The door at the top of the stairs slams shut. My heart skitters.

I run in the opposite direction and steal away into the parlor through a secret door. How do I know about this? Even now I feel as if I'm disobeying rules, entering the forbidden sanctum.

"Anna." The word is elongated, the voice taunting. "Get out!"

I begin laughing like the madwoman I must be.

10

hen I wake, I'm in my bed. It's morning. The last thing I remember is lying on a living room couch, choking. I throw off the covers; I'm fully dressed.

Downstairs on the main level, the lights are off, and nothing is out of place.

The momentary relief turns to panic. Did I have a walking nightmare? Has my biggest fear come true? Did I have the kind of dream that turned me into a killer? No, I refuse to believe any of this. My worries are only from the stress of coming home.

I brew some coffee and sit down at the kitchen island. It's not safe for me to be in this house, not if this happens again. But where is it safe?

The labyrinth is a place created for contemplation, for thought. Not a place to fear, it's a place to clear one's head of troubling thoughts. Many churches have them in courtyards. Peaceful—unless evil invades.

As I walk along the interior of the maze, my mind quiets, and I focus on the bushes, the orchards, the blue skies above. I'm suddenly angry. At myself. At having been forced to endure a life with a horrible father. But mostly for what happened to my mother, and at her for letting it happen. She was supposed to protect me—she should've protected herself.

"I didn't do it," I scream, but I don't really believe that.

I jump over the bushes and jog around the villa to the backyard where I left the remains of the dead roe. There's no sign of it, not even the skeletal remains that the bugs picked clean. Not a single bone. Maybe predators dragged it off. But there's no trail, no tracks or marks left behind.

Back inside the house, I decide to paint. It's the one thing that relaxes me, frees me. And after lunch, I'll visit some relatives. Maybe they'll make me feel safer.

Isn't family supposed to keep you safe?

11

ignore Fulvio Peruzzi, the proprietor and chief wine-maker of the Peruzzi Winery, stands just inside the winery. Great-Uncle Fulvio is holding a corkscrew and is about to open a bottle of wine—Chianti. He's a tall, wiry man with a weathered face and deep expression lines on his forehead and around his eyes, which his straw hat fails to mask. He must be in his eighties by now.

"Zio, ciao!" I cry out, raising my hand to say hello and ask him what he's drinking, but we both know very well that he only drinks Chianti. I remember him calling it God's juice. As a young child, I giggled when he said that. It never tasted like juice even watered down.

"Bella, bella ragazza," he cries. "Come here, give me a hug."

He hugs me so tightly that my ribs feel like they're going to crack. When I groan, he releases me.

"I'm so happy to see you, Anna. You've grown into a beautiful woman, and your Italian is perfect."

Smiling, I say, "I've watched a lot of Italian television over the years."

We laugh and chat for a few minutes, catching up. Then he invites me inside the house to see his wife, Aurora—my great-aunt, my grandfather's sister. She and Francesca are making bread. I've missed Aurora. She was so kind to me when I was a kid.

Aurora gestures to the pastries on the kitchen table. "We have fresh rags, Anna. You used to love them as a child. Please, let's sit and enjoy some." She smiles so kindly that I'm charmed.

Rags are flat, twisted cookies made of sugar and butter and spiked with brandy. One of my absolute favorites. I join them at the table and take one of the sweets. "Delicious, just as I remember, Aunt Aurora."

Her smile grows even broader.

"No wedding ring," Fulvio says in a brusque but somehow endearing tone. "You're not married? Why not? A girl your age should be married."

I have to stop myself from laughing. "I haven't found the right person yet."

"A pretty girl like you?"

Yeah, a pretty girl accused by the gossipmongers of matricide. I wonder if that means no man is right for me.

"Leave her alone, Papà," Francesca says, waving a hand at him. "Anna is a young woman. In America, they marry older nowadays. And did you forget my daughter isn't married yet either? She's much older than our Anna." Giana, her eldest, is ten years my senior.

Fulvio flashes Francesca a look of disgust. "Anna, you should come back one day soon and say hello to Antonio and Paolo, your old playmates. Both work with me in the vineyards now. They're not married either. Paolo is too shy, and Antonio isn't shy enough."

"So they haven't changed a bit," I say. Antonio, two years older than me, would've been called a class clown, except he was too good-looking. The girls had crushes, and the boys mostly followed him. Paolo, a class behind me in school, had his brother's good looks but was an introvert—Antonio's opposite.

"Oh, believe me, they aren't boys any longer," Fulvio says. He holds his arms up and pretends to flex his biceps. "Strong handsome men now."

"Stop, old man," Aurora says. "Anna, we're so happy you finally decided to come home where you belong. I'm so sorry about your father." She shakes her head woefully. "Your mother's house has sat empty. Such a shame. It's so beautiful and should be enjoyed. You'll have a nice home there."

"I'm not sure I'll be staying," I say. "I might sell it."

"Oh, no, it has to remain in the family!" Aurora says.

"Mamma grew up in that house," Francesca says. "Her father built this house when she married and had to leave."

"Which is so lovely," I say. "Warmer than my mother's . . . than my place. I'm not used to something so large and cold."

When Aurora's father—my great-grandfather—died, what is now my house passed to Aurora's brother, my grandfather.

"I have a question about the house. I can't get in some of the rooms. Does anyone have a set of keys to the whole house?"

"Like I told you already, only the front entryway," Francesca says. "Maybe the management company your father hired can help."

"They gave me everything they had. Which is only the key to the front door."

"I'm sorry, we can't help with that," Aurora says.

"I know I sounded unappreciative the other day, Francesca. I'm sorry. Jet lag, the excitement . . . no excuse. What I'm trying to say is, I want to thank you for keeping watch on my place."

"My apologies, I took you by surprise," she says. "You could've taken me for a stranger, someone who might harm you."

Conversation stops for a moment.

"Your mother had beautiful clothes, furnishings," Aurora says.

Do they know about the clothing in the parlor? Maybe they protected her things from my father, the public.

"Some of the outfits are probably back in style," she continues. "Retro, as you young people like to say." She studies me. "You look about the same size as your mother was when she was your age. You should enjoy what you can. She would've wanted that."

I nod, unsure that'll ever happen.

"You meant the world to her," Aurora continues. "More important than even her career. She loved you so much."

I feel my cheeks warm. "Thank you for the kind words. But speaking of the house, I wonder if I could ask you a few questions about our family history. And about the Medici Falchion."

Aurora crosses herself.

"Anna, it's hard for your Aunt Aurora to speak about this," Francesca says. "As you see, she's a very devout Catholic."

"Because of the curse?" I ask. "Because of what it did to my mother? And to me?"

Now Francesca looks flustered. "Anna, we don't believe—"

"Please, enough," Aurora says. "I believe."

Francesca looks warily at her mother and firmly says, "The so-called curse is just a silly urban legend, Mamma." To me, she says, "If you're thinking the necklace had anything to do with your mother's death, stop. What happened to your mother was a terrible accident. Nothing to do with a curse. And don't blame yourself, if that's what you're doing. No one knows exactly what happened."

"Except everyone blames me, right?"

"No one knows what happened," Francesca insists.

"Vittoria's death was very hard on everyone—mostly you, Anna," Fulvio says in a sympathetic tone. "Your mamma was a nice girl, and what a superb voice. But we don't like to speak of the loss. Let's speak of happier times. No, let's make the present happy. Anna, you must stay for dinner. I'm sure you remember what a fantastica cook Aurora is. Francesca? Not so good."

"Papà," Francesca playfully scolds.

"All right, fine. She cooks okay. Getting better with the years."

I glance at Francesca who is taking the joke in stride. To Fulvio, I say, "Maybe another time. I'm still settling in, but I appreciate the invitation."

"Another thing, Anna," he says. "Just don't stay cooped up in that house. It's not healthy. Get out and enjoy the countryside. Come here, drink some wine. I'll put you to work in the vineyards too. You and my grandsons."

I grin at Fulvio and promise to take him up on the offer someday soon. Wine drinking, for sure.

Aurora insists that I visit soon to learn how to make Tuscan bread. Although I'm terrible in the kitchen, I agree, not wanting to offend them. And I do need to be around people.

I say my goodbyes and head outside to my bicycle, which is parked against the wall of the winery. I stop to tie my shoelace and hear Aurora call my name. When she reaches me, she's a little winded.

"Aunt Aurora?"

She grasps both of my arms. "You have to believe this: your mother's death was only an accident. You didn't do it on purpose."

My stomach drops. "Didn't do it *on purpose*. Which means it's true that I pushed her?"

"Anna, you were so young, only twelve. You weren't so well after that. You'll only make yourself sick again if you think this way. Or if you think about that necklace. It would've been better if you never left Italy. It was unkind of your father to take you away from your family, the people who love you the most." She steps away and touches her crucifix. "You did nothing wrong. You were only a child. Just be careful in your house. You're alone."

"But the necklace—what happened to it?"

"Be thankful it's gone. That you . . . You're safe now that it's gone."

"Aurora, any memory of my taking it or of anything that happened that night is gone."

"Just let it be."

Before I can say more, she turns and hurries away to the house. As I get on my bike, I hear loud voices back in the kitchen, but I'm too far away to understand what's being said. I'm startled when the discussion bursts into a full-fledged argument.

I pedal faster. Aurora believes the Medici Falchion is cursed. She also believes that the villa is unsafe. They all do.

12

ack home, I head to the kitchen, open a bottle of Barolo, and pour myself a glass. Fear will *not* consume me. No matter what my relatives believe. Down the hallway, I venture inside the study. The room smells of old, leather-bound books—a comforting aroma. I slide my hand across the spines, reading titles ranging from European history to Dante to Shakespeare to Umberto Eco.

I set my glass down and begin opening desk drawers. Inside the center one is a set of keys. Of course.

The fourth key gets me access to the basement. There's no odious stench—why I expected one, I'm not sure—but only the expected dank, musty smell. I head down, gripping the banister with one hand and carrying my glass of wine with the other.

Just before I reach a turn, the air pressure changes and the door at the top of the staircase slams shut.

A misstep causes me to stumble, and wine sloshes on the wall. Thankfully I don't fall. I've got to do something about the air conditioning system in this house.

Continuing down, I navigate a full turn and then, at the bottom, a quarter turn. I feel along the wall, find a light switch, and go inside a vast room. A large wooden antique dining-room table sits in the center. Atop it is large stone bowl. A knight in armor with a sword in its right hand stands in a corner. The walls are adorned with sundry items, including crossed swords above a large tapestry of my family's coat of arms—a shield with a gold field and six balls, five red and one blue with three golden lilies painted on its surface. Many opine that the five represent bitter red oranges, a symbol of the family's trade with the East. Some say they're red pills, reflecting the Medici background in medicine. Still others believe they're bezants, Byzantine coins, symbolic of the family's wealth and banking. As a child I leaned into the tale that my ancestor, Averardo de' Medici, a commander of Charlemagne's army, slew an evil giant, Mugello, who was terrorizing the people of Tuscany, and that the balls represent the dents in Averardo's shield.

The armor always fascinated me as a kid. Many times, I pretended that there was a real knight inside and that he protected me. I would boss him around, scold him for not doing as I told him. Even let him taste my lemonade once, poured it through his helmet, actually. My mother wasn't pleased. Thankfully she never told my father.

Now, with the tip of my index finger, I touch the sword's blade. A sting causes me to jerk my hand away. Droplets of blood surface from a small slice in my fingertip. No way should this sword be this sharp, not unless someone has made sure to keep the blade honed.

Why would Edoardo do this?

I suck the wetness from my finger, tasting its metallic salt, and then press two fingers together to stanch the bleeding.

On the opposite wall are a couple of rooms. One is a large cellar stocked with bottle upon bottle of various wines. The collection is remarkable. I pick up a bottle—1959 Chateau Petrus. Liquid diamonds. I return it to its slot and find several more French wines, then run across the Italians.

A bottle of French wine—a Petrus Pomerol Grand Cru—from a nearby rack has my name on it. Why? I use my phone to check the price—four thousand dollars. My head spins. Really? I start to replace the bottle on the shelf but stop myself. If this has my name on it, why not drink it? To celebrate my homecoming.

I leave the cellar carrying my glass of Italian wine and the bottle of French. Down a long hallway on the opposite end of the house is a large, open area. An enormous tapestry hangs on the far wall behind what must be my mother's parlor. The artwork depicts a sword fight taking place outside a village. In the main square, townsfolk and fancy-dressed people surround an object. Upon taking a closer look, I gasp. At the center is a guillotine. A woman is about to be beheaded. Another woman's head sits in a basket. I clamp my eyes shut and turn away.

On the adjacent wall, more family portraits hang—this time of the male side of the de' Medici family—fathers, brothers, husbands. Each subject has his name engraved on a placard that's attached at the bottom edge of their frame. The first portrait is of my great-grandfather Filippo Rossi. Unlike any of the women in the family portraits, he looks happy. Right beside the portrait of Filippo is a painting of his son, Marco. He looks happy too.

How revolting that the men in their portraits seem elated, while the women in theirs look tortured. Disgusting, but not surprising.

Next to my grandfather's portrait is an empty frame. It dawns on me that this was to hold my father's portrait. Maybe it was painted and discarded. I wouldn't be surprised if someone in the family did this after my mother died.

The next wall over, the heads of boars and deer mounted on plaques are affixed to the wall—gruesome, but a testament to my family's hunting prowess—and their thirst for blood, as evidenced by the horrified expressions those animals wear. Not much different from the women. My mouth goes dry. I sip my wine. These will have to go.

A massive boar's head with the largest tusks I've ever seen on a wild hog is mounted above a door, almost as if protecting what lies beyond.

As soon as the door opens, the scent of cedar engulfs me—a storage closet. It takes a moment for my eyes to adjust to the darkness. When they do, I drop my glass of wine. The bottle I've placed under my arm comes loose and rolls across the floor inside the great room behind me.

From the shadows, I see scintillating green eyes, staring at me, judging me.

My mind is playing tricks again. Except I'm sure I'm not dreaming this time.

I want to run, but I'm frozen in place. Finally, I thrust out an arm, which collides with the wall. Clumsily, my hand scrabbles around until it finds the light switch. The room illuminates.

There, along the rear wall, stands my mother, wearing a wedding dress—the de' Medici wedding dress.

13

amma!" I shout angrily. Searing pain shoots down my legs. I step away, about to run. But something stops me. Probably the accusing stare that radiates from her emerald-green eyes.

No! Mamma's dead!

The bottle of wine that had previously slipped from my arm bangs against a wall in the great room. I flinch and the truth falls into place. This isn't my mother, it's a wax replica. So lifelike, yes. I draw in a deep breath.

"Foolish girl, stop acting like a child!"

I walk to the mannequin and feel its arm. The skin is weirdly natural—soft, supple. Must be an added layer to the plastic frame. I scratch a nail over it and pull at its exterior. The substance gives and snaps back into shape—synthetic. The hair, which is fixed exactly as in my mother's wedding portrait, also feels real. Maybe it is. The makeup—some kind of permanent paint—is perfectly applied. The eyes, green glass, are translucent and reflective. No wonder they glowed.

Why is this figure wearing the wedding dress depicted in every one of the female family portraits?

I touch the dress. The lace is delicate, old. I want to rip this gown of misery to pieces.

The one item missing is the Medici Falchion.

The history of this figure comes to me. Right after my mother retired, having just played the starring role of Floria in *Tosca*, she had her likeness made for a museum in Milan. My father disapproved. My parents quarreled. Only eleven at the time, I was so fearful that I ran and hid in a nearby closet, fearful that my father would become violent, that he might hurt my mother, that he might hurt me for listening in.

"It's cheesy," he shouted. "You're not some pop singer or country star. You're not even an opera singer anymore. It's self-indulgent. Narcissistic."

When the yelling kept getting louder and my mother sounded afraid, I ran into the room and screamed, "Stop!"

She laughed in my father's face and walked away, which she often did to end an argument. He was livid, demanded that she trash the figure. But she only hid it from him. She said she enjoyed living with herself too much to part with the likeness. Our little secret.

I leave the storage room and retrieve the wine bottle—that it didn't shatter is a miracle.

Something on the other end of the basement clanks hard, like a heavy object has dropped to the floor.

I jolt. Someone else is down here.

"Hello?"

No one answers. I hurry to the other side of the basement. The knight's scabbard and sword have fallen to the floor. Nothing else appears out of place.

My finger barely touched that blade. Nothing moved. How did that cause the items to fall?

I return the bottle to the wine cellar, and I put the knight back in order. As I start toward the stairs, I see it—*the Dungeon Door.*

I can't . . . I won't go down there. No! Stop!

My father's voice invades my mind. It was him. He did this to me.

"You'll learn to listen," my father said. He shoved me inside the dark and stared down at me. "Five minutes. Don't move from that spot." The recollection of a key turning, clicking, and cranking, casts a lingering shadow of despair that seeps deep into the marrow of my bones.

Turning away, I hurry upstairs to the kitchen, where I rest my hands on the island and take deep breaths. The fine hair on my arms stands on end. I can't take a chance. I'm afraid of myself, afraid of what I'll do if I have another nightmare. On shaky legs, I hurry back down the hall and lock the basement door.

I clamp my eyes shut and envision the figure. My dead mother—she's living in the basement. No—it's not a *she,* and it's not *living.*

Everything will go to the museum in Florence or Rome—all of the wedding portraits except the one of my mother. The dress, that green-eyed figure. Those dead animal heads. The tapestry. If the curators don't take this junk, I'm sure a house of horrors will.

Maybe Aurora wants the portraits. Last resort, it'll all find a new home in the trash.

I laugh as I imagine what people would think seeing those lifelike legs sticking out of my garbage bin. With my history, they'd probably send the homicide squad.

When my laughter subsides, unease washes over me. Will I sleep knowing that thing is downstairs in a basement closet? And . . . that door.

14

uring the following days, I spend most of my time in the art studio working on a café scene. Tringali is the subject; I'm painting him as a centaur—an uncontrollable, barbaric force. I'm happy that I can find some humor in life.

Sunday morning, I'm awakened by an insanely loud rapping from the gargoyle knocker. Its echo reverberates throughout the entire house. The sound reminds me of a brass cymbal toppling over and pounding across a stage floor. I roll to my side. The clock reads six A.M. I can't sleep now, so I throw off the covers and search for my robe.

More pounding. I hurry from my room, make my way down the staircase, and open the front door just as a hand falls from the knocker. A man stands on the stoop, holding a large bottle of wine, a magnum. "Good morning," he says with a smile.

Recognition seeps in. "You're Paolo Massimino. Giana and Antonio's little brother."

"Sì, I'm Paolo, but I like to think they're *my* siblings." He says this good-naturedly, even though I seem to have offended him by profiling him as an afterthought as compared with his elder sister and brother. He's changed from the scrawny kid I used to know. Now he's tall, with the muscular physique and rugged complexion of a person who works the fields and lifts heavy barrels of wine.

He holds the bottle out to me. The label reads *Peruzzi*.

"Grazie, cugino!"

His eyes dance happily, exactly the way they did when he was a young boy. He hesitates, looking almost embarrassed. "My mother and grandmother are making bread today. They'd like you to join them. It would really please them if you do. Oh, and you're also invited to dinner."

"I'll only make a fool of myself if I step one foot in the kitchen. I'm a total disaster when it comes to cooking, baking. Everyone will think I've gone soft, turned too American, which I have."

"I'll tell them you're too busy to bake. Dinner is at five. It's the grandparents' anniversary."

I tell him that I'll see him there and thank him for the invitation, at least the one for dinner.

Just before dusk, on the drive to the dinner party, I detect something odd about the vines growing on the land that I lease to the Peruzzis. As an artist, I've studied nature, and now as the owner of vineyards, I've made it my business to learn what I can about the variety of grapevines grown in this region. Something isn't right. These grapes aren't as tightly clustered as they should be, and the berries are too small. It would be tragic if their harvest failed. Then it hits me.

Arriving a little early, I find Francesca arranging the garden table, which is adorned with flowers and beautifully set.

"Ciao, zia Francesca."

She smiles.

"I just noticed something on my way over. Are there new varieties of vines growing on my land? The land my father leased to you?"

Francesca's shoulders straighten, a combination of surprise and annoyance. "You can tell grape varieties just by looking?"

"I'm a visual person, and truthfully, I've studied a little."

She forces a smile. "The boys are growing a few new varieties, that's all."

"But that's not legal. Is it? I thought the regulations in our region are really strict, don't allow new varieties in the area. I'm just concerned because I read that one bad plant could destroy everything around, especially if it carries a blight. Fulvio should be worried too."

"The lawyers cleared it, Anna. Everything has been inspected, and the plants—Cabernet Sauvignon and Cabernet Franc—are growing quite nicely. No problems. The boys monitor those vines like they're newborn babies."

"Anna, piacere di vederti," Giana says. Her presence breaks the tension. "You, too, Mamma." She has her mother's medium frame, but unlike Francesca, she has short, curly hair. She stands with a rigid posture, like the admiral of a fleet.

We exchange condolences over the recent deaths of our respective fathers. Claudio, her father, passed from cancer just over a year ago.

He was a quiet man who faded into the background, deferring to his assertive wife, Francesca, and to his outgoing children, Giana and Antonio. Paolo is more like his father.

I tell Giana about how different life is in America and ask her what she's been doing.

"I own an art gallery in Rome," she says.

"A very successful one," Francesca adds.

"I just learned about that because I just followed you on social media," I say. "I don't know why I never thought to do that. Anyway, you rep some awesome artists."

She grins.

I can easily envision this woman running her own business. But art? The Giana I knew was an athletic child without patience for creative activities like drawing or cutting out designs with construction paper. "Very cool. Do you paint now?"

"No, never. I don't make art, I sell it. My job is to discover the right artists to rep and make a profit. I love being an entrepreneur. Sounds a bit coarse, but to each their own."

"You represent Giuseppe Tringali, I assume?"

"Why would you assume that?" she asks with a sour expression.

"Sorry, I . . . Because he's a family friend? Or was? He painted portraits of my mother, and since our families were so close—"

"I wouldn't represent that has-been even if he made decent art, which he doesn't anymore. In my opinion."

"I haven't seen him in years," Francesca says. "He and your mother had the relationship, not us. We weren't important enough."

"Which hasn't stopped him from pleading with me to show his work in my gallery," Giana says. "He's a pompous ass, and I cater to the younger, more contemporary crowd. Anna, tell me more about your life and your art."

I give her the run down, about my college years and grad school studies, my MFA, and my odd jobs as a struggling painter. That my father was a jerk for not helping me.

"Send me some images of your work," she says. "No promises."

"Of course. That's very kind of you to ask."

"And expect candor from me," she adds. "No one needs to waste time if things aren't as they should be."

"Candor is a blessing. It's the only way a person can learn."

Francesca folds her arms. "Your generation never wants to hurt one another's feelings . . . and the silence, the mincing of words, all that only ends up causing problems. People should speak their minds."

"Very brave of you to return after so many years," Giana says, ignoring her mother. "If I went through what you did, I don't think I would ever have come back. You must—"

"Tranquilla, Giana!" Francesca says.

So much for speaking one's mind.

Giana raises her hands. "My apologies, Anna. I certainly didn't mean to offend you. I told you I'm a candid person." She looks at her mother as she says, "I only mentioned Anna's bravery as a compliment."

When Aurora calls, Francesca leaves. But not before giving her daughter a portentous glance.

"You didn't offend me, Giana," I say. "I like blunt people. I'm one myself. Which is why I'm going to ask you, what do you think of the Medici Falchion and all the talk about its curse?"

She looks intrigued. "Did you find the necklace, Anna?"

"No. But I would like to know where it is."

She folds her arms. "Okay, so about the necklace and this 'curse.' I guess it depends on how you define *cursed*." She looks down at the table and leans over to straighten some drooping flowers. "Or do random, horrible coincidences become curses because people need to explain everything? Most people are more afraid of the unknowable than they are of curses."

"What coincidences? The way the women in the family died?"

"Yes that. And our mothers' friend Emma."

"I've never heard of her." Giana seems to be implying that Emma's death was somehow related to my mother's necklace. I can't believe Mamma would've loaned the jewel to someone else. Or was Emma's fate altogether different and yet somehow just as tragic?

Before Giana can respond, Francesca calls her inside.

"One of these days, I'm going to completely rebel," Giana says. "Those old women think I'm an indentured servant." She lowers her voice. "You know, since you arrived, the necklace has become a hot topic again. Rumors are that you hid it and that you've returned to claim it. I'm sure you're aware."

I scoff. "People can be such gossips. Not just around here, everywhere."

There's a brief, awkward silence.

"So changing the subject," she says, "I understand the paperwork is in place to sell your north vineyard to my brothers. Before your dad passed, he was working out the details with the lawyer. I can't tell you how happy you've made those boys. Antonio and Paolo have wanted that property for years."

The one they've already planted the new varieties on. "Well, I'm sorry, but there's been a mistake. My late father clearly acted out of turn."

"But your father agreed to sell, claimed he was your agent. What I understood from our lawyer is that everything would be settled as soon as your mother's estate closed."

"My father had no authority to make any such deals on my behalf. The property is in my trust and can't be sold by anyone but me. Like I said, I'm really sorry, but my father shouldn't have done this. It's not fair to your brothers or to me. But quite frankly, I'm not about to sell my property."

"Not my fight."

Francesca reappears, frowning at Giana. "Enough of this talk. You'll spoil the night. And Anna is our guest."

So they really don't see me as part of the family.

Giana clasps her hands together and looks away, her signal for a truce, or at least a way to stand down from a battle that isn't her concern. Francesca slides an arm through her daughter's, and the two go into the house. I presume that Francesca wants to tell her daughter to watch her tongue. After a few long moments, I follow them inside.

Who was Emma? But what I'd really like to know is whether her death had something to do with the Medici Falchion.

15

he Peruzzi family and their guests gather on the spacious loggia. The long, rough-hewn wooden dining table sits on the other end of the porch near the kitchen. There are maybe fifty people present, friends and family. But I don't fit into either category, and I don't belong here. I feel the same distance from others that I've experienced most of my life. There's something else—unlike my life in the States, the people here know about my past.

Champagne corks pop, glasses are filled. Fulvio taps his flute with a spoon. The guests quiet and gather near.

Fulvio raises his glass to Aurora. "To my lovely wife of sixty years. And to another sixty."

Aurora playfully nudges her husband's arm. "Fulvio expects us to live forever."

"May you both live for eternity!" Giana says.

Everyone cheers and clinks glasses.

Fulvio extends a formal introduction, warmly welcoming me home. Now, despite the cordial greetings when I met a few of these people informally, I detect unease, even hostility from some.

Raising my glass, I say, "Fulvio and Aurora, your marriage is like a wonderful painting that captures eternal beauty."

Fulvio, obviously pleased, nods to me in gratitude.

A solemn Paolo walks to the older man's side.

"Where is he?" Fulvio asks, loud enough for me to hear.

"He's not answering my texts," Paolo replies.

The tension in the space between grandfather and grandson is palpable.

Aurora says, "Let's eat."

At the table, Paolo and Giana take seats that flank me. The three of us make small talk. The question of Emma weighs on my mind. But it's not the time to ask about her.

The first course, primo, was gnocchi—delicious. The secondo, now being served, is wild boar with Pappardelle al Cinghiale—my appetite momentarily wanes as I think about those boar heads mounted on my basement walls.

The rumble of a motorcycle heading down the driveway grows louder as the vehicle approaches the party. Then a red bike comes into view. Pulling to an abrupt stop in the gravel, the driver cuts the engine, flips up his visor, and pulls off his helmet. With a showy flourish, he kicks the stand into place, hops off the bike, and with a raised chin shakes his long hair into place.

Unbelievable. This man is the asshole who ran me off the road. Seriously? My second cousin Antonio?

"Where have you been?" Fulvio bellows at him.

Giana looks my way. "My brother is such a flake."

After hugging his grandmother, Antonio whispers in Fulvio's ear and then comes toward us. Without asking permission, he picks up his sister's glass of wine and takes a large sip. "Buona sera, Anna," he says, grinning at me like the mischievous kid he used to be. People really don't change.

If he's expecting me to smile, he's mistaken. What I want to do is get up and punch his lights out. "The day I arrived here, a man on a red motorcycle ran me off the road. Almost killed me."

"Antonio, no," Paolo says. "Did you really do that, fratello?"

Antonio looks offended. Not innocent, just offended. He walks around to my side of the table and nudges the woman beside me, so that he can share her seat.

"Not enough room," she says and again starts speaking with her friend.

When he looks at me, Giana scoffs. "Seriously, Antonio?"

He shakes his head. "Ah, le donna!" he says playfully. He finds an empty chair and squeezes it in between Giana and me. "We've gotten off on the wrong foot. If by chance I was the one who caused you to run off the road, it was inadvertent. Can we please start over, be friends like we were before?"

"Sure, yeah," I say. "So, you work at the winery with your grandfather?"

"That, and at my gallery," Giana says. "Antonio splits his time . . . when he feels like working."

"Sono ferito," he says feigning wounded pride. He picks up his neighbor's glass of wine and takes a sip without her knowing it. In response to my frown, he puts a finger to his mouth and shakes his head. "Don't worry, we're good friends," he whispers. "Tell our cousin the truth, Giana, that I make the gallery a success. I charm the rich customers into buying that junk. Especially the women. Right, mia cara sorella?"

"Yeah, yeah. Antonio helps me a lot with the gallery exhibitions, promotional events, and he's good at closing deals. Takes a certain charm and persistence. Paolo is the real winemaker, the real dreamer with clear vision."

"When we were in school, Antonio used to run past us girls at lunch and steal our Pan di Stelle cookies—our favorite dessert," I say. "We only got them on Fridays. I remember one of the girls, Alessia, she was ready for him. She stuck out a leg and tripped him just as he was coming for hers."

"Which was very mean of her because I always gave them back."

"Half eaten," Paolo says.

"What happened to her?" I ask.

"She's a judge in Milan now," Antonio says. "Just as mean, I hear."

Aurora announces dessert—a choice of custard or zuppa inglese, a rum-soaked sponge cake stained red with Alkermes liqueur and topped with pastry cream.

Antonio heads toward the dessert table, passing Fulvio, who grasps his arm, stands, and whispers into his grandson's ear. Antonio reaches into his pockets, pats his pants, then heaves a big sigh, a confused expression on his face. Then the two men have what looks like a heated conversation.

Fulvio frowns, gives Antonio an aggressive push, and roars, "Antonio, sei un idiota! My gift to Aurora!"

Someone gasps, and then a few embarrassed murmurs bubble up among the guests.

"It was a diamond ring," Giana whispers to me. "The sixtieth is a diamond anniversary. My grandfather spares no expense for occasions like these."

The tension is almost tangible. Undoubtedly, I'm not the only person who fears Fulvio will strike his grandson, but Aurora says, "Family is what's important. I don't need anything else."

Most guests relax and start talking again, but the muscles in Fulvio's ancient face remain taut. Antonio kneels down, clasps his hands in prayer, and begs his grandfather for forgiveness. And from where I'm sitting, it looks as if the younger man is crying real tears. After some moments, Fulvio pats Antonio's shoulders, tells him to stand, and says that of course he's forgiven.

Giana elbows me. "He always puts on some show like this to get himself out of trouble. Our grandfather still falls for it. But I'll tell you, it's a damn good thing that ring was insured."

"How do you put up with him?"

"Antonio?" She looks over at him admiringly. "I guess I enjoy his stupid charm." She looks back at me. "We give him a bad time, trash talk the hell out of him, but he really is a good sport. Don't get me wrong, I'm not suggesting that you two hook up. But he would be a nice friend to you. Loyal."

When Antonio rejoins us, Giana biffs his shoulder. "So what happened to the ring, you stupido?"

"The box fell out of my pocket on the ride home."

Paolo rolls his eyes.

"Have you seen our vineyard yet, Anna?" Antonio asks. "Your father did us a great service by selling it to us."

I don't respond. No need to spoil anyone's dinner.

The rest of the night is pleasant enough. Antonio continues his playful, almost flirtatious banter, while his sister keeps needling him about all his crazy antics.

"Your jokes are disgusting," she finally says to him. "You act like you're hitting on your own cousin."

"You forget, we're second cousins, practically strangers," he says. "And if I was, it's perfectly legal in every country of the world. With you, it would be repulsive with anyone. But that would never happen with us even if *you* were a stranger."

Giana punches him hard on the arm. Despite his muscular bicep, he winces. "That hurt, Giana."

"Good. If you don't behave, I'll tell Raffi." She glances at me. "Remember your little friend Raffaella Bianchi? They've been a couple for years."

Raffaella Bianchi was a nice girl. One of the kids who didn't shrink from my daydreaming and flights of artistic fancy.

"Giana likes to hear herself talk. Raffi and I broke up."

"For the twentieth time," Giana says. "Antonio, stop annoying Anna. Or I'll tell her how you cheat on Raffaella. How she cheats on you."

He swigs the rest of his wine and stomps away, only to make his way inside a group of young girls.

"Where is Raffi tonight?" I ask Giana. "Isn't her family close with yours?"

Giana shrugs. "God knows where Raffi is. She's into this extreme urban exploration. Abandoned warehouses, condemned sites. Takes pictures for her social media posts." Giana mock laughs. "Anything for a like. Sorry, I'm being paged by the elders again."

From across the veranda, Francesca waves at her daughter.

The woman keeps watch over her grown children as if they were toddlers. What is she so afraid that they'll say?

16

t midnight I thank my hosts, say goodnight to others, and leave the anniversary dinner party. I'm slightly buzzed on the wine, but not so much that I can't drive safely, and certainly not hammered the way I often left parties in New York. The evening was actually enjoyable. Giana and I rekindled our relationship. And Paolo was still shy after all these years. But once he started explaining the winemaking process, he lit up and wouldn't stop. He's the first person I've ever met who could make esoteric concepts of chemistry and botany understandable. I hope he'll forgive me when he learns that I'm not selling him my vineyard.

My villa is completely dark. I need to remember to leave lights on when I go out. This isn't a well-lit apartment in New York where safety lights automatically come on at night. Inside the foyer, I turn on the chandelier and stare up at the dark hallway. The house is eerily calm. As I'm ascending the stairs, electrical motors grind and vibrate, and the lights go out.

The circuit breaker panel is in the pantry.

I stumble and reach for the railing, foolish not to have used it when I started up.

Once my phone's flashlight shines, I relax and make my way toward the control panel. Something on the floor is slick. The light from my phone reveals that the floor is flooded with water, which is flowing from the kitchen.

A loud thud echoes from the living room. Then crackling.

What the hell is that?

I hurry inside the room, only to find someone lying crumpled on the floor. My heart skitters. "Edoardo!" His body is jittering; he's convulsing.

"Edoardo!" I shout.

His eyes open wide. "Stop! Don't come any closer."

"I'll call for help."

"No, don't. Please."

"But you're hurt." Just as I start to ring emergency services, my phone suddenly feels burning hot. Too hot to hold; I try bouncing it in my hand. It's like fire. I can't . . . I cry out in pain and drop it.

When I look over at Edoardo, he's now on his feet and approaching me. "Thank you for your concern, Anna. But as you see, I'm quite well."

My jaw goes slack, and my brain spins while I struggle to comprehend. How can he appear so normal after what just happened?

"Storms are expected over the next week or so," he says matter-of-factly. "It's the season. I came to make sure the generator is functioning. My mistake, I didn't notice the water on the floor. And please accept my apologies if I frightened you."

My heart is still racing. "You fell . . . in the water. You were . . . I thought you were about to die." I rub my forehead, begging reason to return. He fell, he's embarrassed. "No, Edoardo, you took a fall, you need to get checked out."

"Not a concern. Just a slight bump. And I didn't slip. There was an electrical short—an appliance. The toaster, I believe."

"Well, that sure doesn't explain the water on the floor," I say sarcastically. And what about the fact that he slipped in water and isn't wet in the slightest. "Wait. You got an electric shock?"

"As you know, water and electricity don't mix. A pipe is leaking from underneath the sink in the kitchen. Don't worry, I'll clean this up, have the pipe fixed in no time."

I start to get some towels to soak up the water, but before I can take a step, he says, "Anna, freeze!"

I stop.

"There's an electrical short somewhere in the system. I'll fix it, I'm good with these matters. Just go to bed, let me handle this. No reason for you to get electrocuted."

"Yeah, but the electricity went off. Are you sure it's just a short from an appliance? The toaster was working fine this morning. I had to plug it in, but there wasn't a problem."

"I've arranged to change the locks. The locksmith will arrive in the morning. Won't take him any time. Get some rest." Before I can ask him to explain what a locksmith has to do with an electrical short and water on the floor, he walks away, saying he needs to get some tools.

Something is off.

"Someone has been in this house. Edoardo, tell me what's going on." I catch up with him. "Tell me, please."

With sadness in his eyes, he reaches out and touches my forehead with an icy hand. I'm suddenly lightheaded.

"For you own sake, I wish you had never come back, Anna."

What did he just say?

The next thing I know, I'm waking up in my bed.

17

orning light wakes me. I throw off the covers and head downstairs, carefully watching where I step. Everything is in pristine order. Eduardo must be okay. Still, how baffling.

I'm in a bit of a stupor until the locksmith arrives midmorning. The presence of another person grounds me. I show him the entrances to the house. When I ask about *that door*—the Dungeon Door—down in the basement, he says he can't touch it. Too old, too complicated. When I ask for a referral to someone who is an expert in antique locks, to my annoyance he shakes his head.

Not long after he leaves, I get a call from Giana, who invites me for lunch.

It'll be good to get out of this old place. Because I'm still distressed over Edoardo's accident, if that's what it was.

How can everything look so pristine but underneath be falling apart?

We meet at a small café, where Giana recommends sharing the fried zucchini flowers, along with an antipasti tray.

"You were going to send me photos of your work," she says. "I haven't received anything."

"Sorry. I haven't sent them yet."

"Do you have any on your phone?"

I hesitate. I left my paintings on a New York sidewalk, but I haven't been able to convince myself to delete the pictures from my phone.

"Let me see," she insists.

Am I that transparent? No matter. I locate the images and hand her the phone. "Some people say I'm not there yet. Others think I might not ever get there, that I'm wasting my time."

"Just who are these so-called experts?"

"Professors. Gallery bosses. Giuseppe Tringali thinks that I have talent, and if I study with him, I'll—"

"To hell with Tringali. He just wants to get in your pants. Like he tried with our mothers, the creep."

"He seriously—?"

She holds up a hand and takes a long time scrolling through the photos—the art that *I* don't believe measures up.

"I wouldn't lie to my cousin—some of the people are correct. You're not ready. Others are wrong. You do have talent. A great eye for color, and you're technically proficient. You've always had talent, Anna, even when you drew pictures for our mothers and me as a child. But your work is bottled up—like you're trying to keep secrets from the viewer. You can't do that. Art requires that the artist hold nothing back. You're communicating through the eye, not the mouth. Remember that.

She's right about my holding back, but that's hard to admit.

"You have to let go, if you want to discover yourself, Anna. Face the truth about who you really are. That's when you create great art that sets you apart." She hands me the phone.

"And how does an artist do that?"

She laughs. "If I knew the answer to that, I'd be an artist myself. But I wouldn't worry too much. It's nothing that you can't figure out or be taught."

Nothing I haven't heard before. Should I be encouraged or devastated? Secrets have lurked inside me since I was twelve—no, even before that. But how do you reveal secrets to others when you don't fully understand them yourself? "You mentioned someone named Emma the other day."

Giana's eyes darken. "Sure you want to talk about this? It gets gruesome."

What artist hasn't seen the gruesome? To keep her going, I nod encouragingly.

"It happened before you were born. Our mothers and their friend Emma were going to a party for a bunch of opera singers. They called it a sing-off. Emma was Vittoria's younger understudy, always eager to impress her. Vittoria drove the convertible that day, my mother was in the front passenger seat, and Emma in the back. On a lark, Emma stood up to sing. Just as she got to her feet, a delivery truck full of wood planks passed them. Boards of lumber came loose, and one flew out and decapitated her. Terrible."

My hand flies to my mouth.

"Your mother was so distraught that she missed a month of performances. The opera house had to bring in a singer from Milan as a replacement."

"No doubt." I pause. "And the Medici Falchion? Why was Emma wearing it?"

"According to my mother, Vittoria let her wear it for the ride."

"Seriously?"

Giana shrugs and takes a sip of her wine. "It must be hard being in your mother's home."

"What does your mother have to say about my mother's death? They were so close."

"Very little. And I wouldn't bring the subject up with her. She won't talk about it. She gets angry whenever it's mentioned. You saw how she reacted when I started to talk about it the other day. Same for Aurora."

We spend the rest of lunch gabbing about Giana's gallery and clients. After we finish, she looks at me amused. "You know what, Anna, I'm going to help you. One of my clients, Giorgio Bellagamba, is hosting a party the middle of June at his home in Rome. I want you to come. Artists and important patrons will be there. But I must warn you . . . Things can get a little wild."

"I've done wild before."

"We also have a tradition. We pick an artist to create something in real time. Sometimes the product is genius but more often it's crap, you know?"

"Sounds fun."

"You're family, so I'll make sure to feature you."

"That's very kind of you."

"Oh, and an old photographer friend of our mothers will be there. You want to get her going? Tell her you don't believe the Medici Falchion is cursed."

18

uring the rest of the afternoon I slap paint on canvas.
When I'm satisfied, I go relax by the pool, where I
eventually doze off.

"Wake up, little sparrow," a voice says.

My eyes fly open—Antonio Massimino. He makes an unabashed
show of checking me out—all of me. "You've certainly grown up."

I sit up and throw on my coverup. "What brings you around . . .
cousin?"

He shucks off his shirt and extends his hand to me. "Let's take a
swim."

"You don't believe in invitations, do you?"

"Like you said, we're cousins. Do I really need one?"

I shrug. "Why not?" As soon as I've slipped off my coverup, I turn
back around only to find him tossing his pants on a chaise lounge. He
didn't bother to wear underwear on this unexpected visit. At the edge
of the deep end, not looking my way once, he dives in. He keeps his
distance; I keep my swimsuit on.

"Hey, my sister told me that you're coming to the art party in Rome," he says, resurfacing and shaking the wet from his hair. "It gets a little wild."

"So she told me."

"What do you Americans say? Sex, drugs, and rock and roll?"

"Maybe American *old people* say that. And don't forget, I'm Italian, dude."

He grins, but clearly considers me an American. "Just be sure you wear something spectacular and sexy, Anna. That's easy to take off."

"My clothes are staying on. Will jeans work?"

"Dress up for the photos. You'll be all over social media. And don't worry, you're riding with us."

"Who exactly is driving?"

He chortles. "Not me. Paolo says he'll come along too, which is a first for him, because he doesn't like wild. The man is a winemaker and doesn't even drink much wine. Great at spitting, though."

I can't help but laugh. "So you're saying that your kid brother, Paolo, acts like a grownup?"

He splashes water at me. "Who the fuck wants to grow up?"

19

n the weeks leading up to the art party and as the weather warms, Antonio, Paolo, and I spend time together swimming in the pool. We also dine out and visit the surrounding villages. Giana is right. Despite our rocky start, I enjoy Antonio's company—he's fun, with a good sense of humor, and more knowledgeable about the artworld than he and his sister had let on.

In my free time, I paint, work out, and wander around my property. The thought of the Dungeon Door is never far from my mind, but I can't muster the nerve to go near it, not alone. Maybe it's better that the key is missing. But I can't deny that I'm bothered by that.

After packing my clothes for the weekend trip, I head down to my mother's parlor and open the case where her gowns hang. I come across a slinky, deep-plum, full-length, sleeveless dress. The back is bare, with rhinestones set in a single strap that drapes from one shoulder down to the opposite hip. The tag is still inside. I don't recognize the designer, but the name is Italian. I look at the size—same as me. I hold the dress against my body. This dress is perfect for the party.

Saturday morning, the Massimino brothers and I set off for Rome. The drive takes about two-and-a-half hours. We listen to music, and Antonio entertains us with funny and sometimes outlandish stories, many about his grandfather Fulvio. We arrive that afternoon at the small boutique hotel where we're staying, not far from the Colosseum.

I shower, put on makeup, and roll my hair into a twist. What would my mother think about me wearing her dress? Sometimes she could be generous with her clothing and jewelry. Other times, not so much. I never could predict. Once, I was backstage at the opera—a special day—and when I touched her dress, she slapped my hand hard. I forgot about that until now.

I slip on my shoes and slide the garment over my head—it fits like a glove—and then apply the last coat of my lipstick.

The brothers meet me in the hotel lobby.

"Wow!" Paolo says—a very emotional response for him.

"Sexy!" Antonio adds. "Glad you took my advice. But that dress is so tight, it won't be easy to take off."

"Which is one reason why I chose it."

The men are wearing nice shirts and jeans—very expensive jeans, but still *jeans*. "Am I overdressed or are you guys underdressed?"

"Neither," Antonio says. "You're in Rome. People go as they want. And you're the featured artist."

"*Featured artist*? Please. Honestly, I think Giana only meant that she'd introduce me to a few influential people."

"No, no," Paolo says. "Antonio is telling the truth . . . for once. And by the way, you really are a spectacular sight." He places his hands on his heart and then extends an arm to escort me. Antonio extends another.

Paolo drives us to the party, which is located at a private residence in a gated community near the Vatican Gardens. The sun is setting, and the lights of Rome are beginning to sparkle.

A muscular man greets us in the porte cochere. He wears a white, tight-fitting bodysuit that leaves nothing to the imagination. A parking valet arranges to take the car.

"Coats, bags, purses, wallets, accessories," he says in an even, yet commanding voice.

"I'll keep mine, thank you," I say. "I'm a New Yorker at heart. Trust issues."

Antonio places his arm around me and pulls me close. "It's a requirement. Your things will be perfectly safe, locked up. Rome is a big city, but not New York. At least, not in a place like this." He places his wallet and phone from his back pocket onto the pseudo-mime's tray. Paolo does the same.

"How will he keep them straight?" I ask.

"He has an eidetic memory," Antonio says. "Trust me."

The man lowers his eyes to the tray and waits.

When Antonio gently nudges my arm, I place my small purse alongside the brothers' wallets. The man walks to a safe and deposits the items—sort of like a coat check.

In the large living room area, the furniture is pushed toward the walls, leaving an open space in the center of the room. An imposing fixture designed to resemble a tree stretches across the ceiling, its branches metallic strips, the leaves light bulbs. Its trunk slides down a wall to the top edge of a fireplace. How cool.

Antonio was telling the truth about the evening's attire, I'm not overdressed. Some guests are dressed formally, others wear beach wear.

When Paolo catches my eye, he raises his brows with disdain. He looks like a fan of Rembrandt walking through a Basquiat exhibit.

A woman wearing a translucent lime-green body suit with nothing underneath appears with a tray of drinks. "Mind the green stems," Antonio whispers to me. "Those cocktails are laced. Like, with Molly."

I take a glass with a green stem. "When in Rome."

Paolo passes, but not Antonio. We toast and take a sip. The drink is refreshing, tastes like an expensive champagne.

Some minutes later, just a few I think, I'm already feeling the effects of the drink. My skin ripples as if feathers are gliding across it.

A petite, redheaded woman in her mid-fifties steps in front of me. "Hello Anna, I'm Carra Rivelli. Giana mentioned you would be here."

The brothers excuse themselves and head off in opposite directions. Antonio walks over to a woman whom I immediately recognize as my old school friend, Raffaella Bianchi. She's tall now, lithe, and looks like she belongs on a Hollywood movie set. Raffaella was a cute girl; but I doubt anyone would've predicted she would grow up to be so strikingly beautiful.

"Wonderful dress," Carra says to me and slides her hand down my arm. I can't decide if her touch is provocative or maternal. "A Milan label, no?"

A cold shiver races up my spine. "I picked it up in a vintage boutique in Southampton, Ms. Rivelli. That's a city in New York." I lie because this woman is so presumptuous—and because people might judge me for wearing this dress.

The woman smiles. "Call me Carra, please. And I know where Southampton is. Also Montauk, Cape Cod, and Carmel, California." She hums as she looks me over. "In case you don't know, you're wearing a one of a kind dress, a Mezzasalma. The rhinestones along the strap are cut quite distinctively." She gazes at me.

What an odd woman.

"Giana says you want to know about Emma's death and the necklace. I'm surprised no one ever told you."

"Why would they?"

Carra gives me a skeptical look. "After Emma was . . . let's say decollated, the necklace flew off and fell into Francesca's lap. We thought that meant Francesca would be next, but your poor mother . . . I'm sorry. I'm being insensitive. Your mother's accident happened first. Since then, well, as you know, the necklace disappeared, and there have been no more tragedies . . . not that we know of."

She doesn't believe for a second that my mother's death was an accident.

"You know very well they say I pushed my mother down the stairs."

She takes a deep breath. "So they say."

The ecstasy has most certainly kicked in, and this woman's face seems to stretch, and despite the gruesomeness of the subject matter, I want to hug her for being blunt. "Tell me more about Emma's death."

"I was supposed to ride along with the women that day. I was about to get into Vittoria's car—literally—when I got a call from one of the tabloids. I was urgently sent out to photograph a rock band arriving in Siena. Boring, but that's what I did earlier on to make extra money, work as a paparazzo. If I had gotten in that car, maybe I would've been the one wearing the necklace that day."

What? Why were these other women even allowed to wear the necklace? When I wasn't even allowed to touch it, much less try it on.

"Vittoria sometimes let her friends take turns trying on the necklace, if she was in a good mood," she continues. Carra's a mind reader too. "I never did, though." She pauses, leans forward and straightens the strap on my dress.

I hadn't noticed that the rhinestone band was slipping from my shoulder. Was I leaning so much to cause it to slide? I want to be annoyed at her presumptuousness, but I'm grateful.

She lifts her chin, then takes me in from top to bottom. "Your mother was wearing the Medici Falchion when I photographed her in the dress you're wearing now."

"I told you, I bought this—"

She laughs. "Oh, come now, Anna. No shame in wearing your mother's dress—no matter what happened." She steps to my side and, without asking, adjusts my dress "There's a tag showing on the back. Check the designer, if you haven't already. You'll find it's Mezzasalma. Mezzasalma means half-cadaver, you know? Shall I remove the tag?"

My mind zooms in and out of reality, odd thoughts springing to life. Why the hell didn't I remove the tag? Because I thought about doing so, but only tucked it in, almost as if cutting the damn tag off would cause my mother pain.

I suddenly feel as if the necklace is dangling from my neck. A touch of my throat finds only bare skin. Is this dress tainted? No, don't think this way. Carra is waiting for some reply. Weird. "No thank you," I say, forcing out the words. "Cutting tags devalues a dress."

She laughs. "Do yourself a favor, Anna. Don't look for the necklace. And if you have it, get rid of it."

"Everyone is so quick to believe that I killed my mother so I could rob her of the necklace. Poor Anna, she killed her mother and took the necklace."

"Didn't you?"

"That's what everyone says. But where are the witnesses? And I don't have the necklace, if that's what you want to know. Nor do I believe in superstitions or curses. The evil in this world is manufactured."

"That's what your mother wanted to believe. Relax and enjoy your life. I wish Vittoria and Emma had lived to enjoy theirs." She leans in close and whispers, "I've always wondered why, if Francesca tried the necklace on so many times, she's lived so long."

No wonder Francesca cringes at the mention of the necklace.

"Oh, God," she says. "Here comes trouble."

20

wo middle-aged men walk up to Carra and me. The shorter man blocks my way. The taller one says, "You have the most extraordinary lines and curves."

"Meet the Twins, Anna," Carra says with a sly smile. She leans closer to me and whispers, "Twins, I hardly think so. It's only their gimmick."

Whatever these guys are after is beyond me. "I didn't catch your names. You are?"

"The Twins," the shorter man says, "We know about you, even though you've lived abroad for so many years. Mostly because of the scandal."

"And what gives you the right to bring this up at a party?" Carra asks.

The shorter man ignores Carra and looks only at me. "Your mother's murder, Anna. Your father pushed her down the stairs. The police couldn't prove it was homicide. Maybe they were bribed. People say your father took you to America to run from the law."

Whatever mellow high my drink was supposed to provide has vanished. "What a relief, I thought I was to blame."

My response seems to amuse these scandalmongers.

Of course people have spread gossip through the years that my father was the culprit. I've wondered about this myself. But Edoardo came in right after the fall; he saw me at the top of the stairs, and my father wasn't there, so I'm told. And my mother's lawyer, who's died since—he spoke with her on the phone only a few minutes before she died, and he says that my father was already asleep.

But was he?

The shorter man makes a halfhearted slashing gesture across his own neck, then flicks his fingers as if tossing off a piece of dirty lint that's not there. These two have no compassion. They're acting as if I wasn't related to my parents.

"Don't be such pigs," Carra scolds. "Anna don't take them seriously. They think they're artists because they transgress. That hasn't been a thing since the 1990s. They're just a couple of old codgers trying to act cool. Embarrassing." She walks away with a look of disdain.

The tall man leans down to me. "Ignore my twin. He's fascinated with the macabre. People always obsess over celebrities like Vittoria who die young. James Dean, Marilyn Monroe, Princess Diana, Janis Joplin, Jim Morrison, Jimi Hendrix—your mother was an operatic rock star around here. And there's nothing more exciting than a dead rock star murdered by her husband."

"I've heard enough," I say, trying to get past the two men.

"Before you flit away, have you ever modeled?" the short man asks.

"For artists?"

"I am an artist, not a subject."

"You would be perfect," the taller man says. "My twin and I are thinking of doing a live show with nudes—body piercings and tattoos—you know, sculpture in the flesh."

"I'm sure it will be groundbreaking and the video will go viral," I say. "But you know what? I think the art would be far more groundbreaking if you were *my* subjects—I've always wanted to paint my own version of ashcan art. And what better models than twin pieces of trash."

They appear dumbfounded. It feels good to shut up these pompous fucks. Before I can leave, Giana joins our little group.

"I don't know what they've said, but whatever it is, ignore them, Anna."

"Then I suppose the vise grips are out too?" the taller man asks, touching me with his clammy hands. I pull away.

"Vice grips if you twins are the nude models," I say. "And I know the perfect location to attach the devices. I'll need to size them. I'm assuming you two are extra smalls?"

This finally gets them to move along.

"Well done, girl," Giana says. "I can't stand those clowns. Artists . . . Present company excepted. My problem is, they sell. Now come on. Let's see what my brothers are up to."

We join Antonio and Paolo and are served another drink—one of the green stemmed glasses.

Raffaella Bianchi walks over holding hands with a man I don't recognize. "Mio caro amico!" she cries and gives me a bear hug, two kisses, one on each cheek, and then a broad smile. "Oh, Anna, it's been so long. Why didn't we keep in touch?"

"I . . . I really don't know." How do you tell a former friend that your past was too painful to hold on to?

"We'll change that now," she continues. She takes her companion's arm and pulls him forward. "This is Luca. Luca, meet my friend Anna from America."

We exchange greetings.

"Who were those weird old guys you were talking to, Anna?" Paolo asks. He clearly doesn't come to these parties.

Antonio laughs. "The famous twins."

"A couple of creeps," I say. "They asked me to be a nude model in a live show where they would pierce random parts of my body. I countered with the suggestion that I would paint *them* nude with certain not-so-random parts of their anatomy fastened in a vise."

Everyone laughs.

"It's actually a huge compliment that they asked you," Raffaella says. "They're really famous, and they only use beautiful women in their art. I would love to model for them."

"Why don't you volunteer?" Antonio asks.

"Because when I suggested it, you got jealous. How convenient you forgot that. Like you always do."

Antonio glowers at her for a moment but then cracks a smile.

"I say go for it, Raffi," Luca says.

She reaches up and gives her current boyfriend a long kiss on the lips, while he caresses her lower back.

I'm not the only one who's intoxicated. Just how many of those green-stemmed glasses has she had?

When Raffaella ends her sloppy kiss, she faces me and affectionately touches my arm. "Anna, you look more like an American model to me. You know, more curvaceous than the Europeans. I mean that as a compliment. Okay, maybe that's just a stereotype. What I'm saying is that you're beautiful, Anna."

"Bravo for curves," Antonio says.

Giana calls for everyone to gather in the middle of the room. "Tonight, our topic for artistic exploration is the expression of love and its opposite. We'll feature one artist and one human subject."

"Love and its opposite?" I whisper to Raffaella. "Isn't *hate* the opposite of love?"

"The opposite of love is indifference," Raffaella says as she glares at Antonio in a way that "just friends" don't look at each other.

"Anna Rossi is the artist," Giana says. "Raffaella Bianchi is the subject."

I look at my old friend. "I didn't actually think . . . Did you know about this, Raffi?"

She smiles sweetly.

Antonio says, "Good luck," then leans over and kisses Raffaella on the lips—nothing platonic about that. He turns to me, but before he can even think about targeting my lips, I reach out a hand and shake his. Luca, the supposed boyfriend, stands with a silly grin plastered on his face.

None of my business.

Raffaella slides her arm through mine, and we step forward. My hands feel as if they're about to leave my wrists. Unlike the twins, I've never done performance art.

"Make it great, my artist friend," Raffaella says, pulling me closer. "And we'll be on the cover of the premier art magazine and splashed across social media. Trending big."

I nod, although my knees have gone weak.

21

he man in the white jumpsuit lays a large canvas across the floor. Everyone hushes. He squats down and smooths out an edge, then rises, and performs several front flips across the cloth. Gleeful chatter erupts at his performance, though no one applauds.

Giana greets Raffaella and me, then says, "Paint meets human canvas."

"Wait a minute. Raffaella's just the model. I thought . . ." I gesture to the canvas on the floor. "I thought I was painting on that."

The crowd boos. Was I speaking so loudly that everyone heard me?

"That would be boring," Giana says. "Raffi is your canvas."

I glance at Raffaella, who's beaming as if she's just won the lottery. She already knew this.

Antonio starts applauding and the rest of the crowd join in.

Raffaella and I are taken to a bedroom. She strips naked without a hint of embarrassment. They give me a tight-fitting white bodysuit that's fortunately opaque. I'm tempted to object to this Las Vegas lounge act, but I'm too loaded and too curious to spoil the night. More than that, I want to impress this crowd, dilettantes though they may be.

Back in front of the guests, Giana places a mask over Raffaella's eyes. I now understand why the door attendant confiscated our personal effects—no smartphone cameras or other recording devices. Raffaella smiles at the audience, her body exposed. Giana's assistant provides me with latex body paints and some brushes. I start work on Raffaella's front side, the drugs and alcohol helping me to ignore the audience and my friend's flawless anatomy.

My self-consciousness threatens to overwhelm me, but within a few minutes my instincts take over, and my hands move almost involuntarily, yet with purpose. Down her chest and torso, I paint colored lines that transform into jewels, while using the lines of her body to complement my every brushstroke. The performance feels both erotic and creative. How cool is it that I'm able to paint with a finer detail on her body than I would ever have imagined possible.

Every so often, people mumble and titter. Occasionally, someone gasps. My would-be mentor, Tringali, quietly praises me from somewhere in the room. He's actually here? How unexpected.

When I finish with Raffaella's front side, I make sure that she remains forward facing so that no one in the audience can see what I'm painting on her back. These people want to know the real Anna de' Medici Rossi. Well, that's what they're going to get.

Once finished, I set down my brushes. Giana announces, "Love and its opposite." Raffaella has no clue what I've painted on her—the *opposite of love* side.

When she turns around, many of the guests gasp while others murmur in awe.

Loud applause erupts.

It takes me a moment to realize that the clapping isn't mocking but rather genuine praise.

Carra takes photographs. The professional photographer was allowed to keep her camera. Tringali makes sure to bomb as many of the photos as he can.

Raffaella can't possibly realize that she's about to be the subject of Carra's next iconic image. Maybe one of the photographs will even make the front cover of a good old-fashioned magazine.

I'm surprised that my childhood friend seems more than okay with being painted up and photographed nude, but what do I really know about Raffaella?

"Wait a minute, there's one more thing," I blurt out. "A finishing touch."

Raffaella turns her back to the crowd, and I paint more on her décolletage and chest.

The crowd fidgets as they wait. I hear snippets of various conversations about what I've already painted on Raffaella's back.

People continue to buzz and discuss the composition on her back.

Finita! "Raffaella, please turn around."

She complies, and when the crowd sees what I've added, they go silent. Every single person in the room looks shocked except Carra, who continues to snap her photos.

"What is it?" Raffaella asks, confused.

Carra shows us her camera screen, and when Raffaella sees what I've painted, she runs out of the room. Giana and Carra go after her.

Antonio hands me a fresh drink, one with a green stem. "You're a formidable talent. And a very weird person, Anna."

Feeling pleased, I take a big sip.

Paolo, who's standing with us, lowers his head.

Antonio, who doesn't miss his brother's reaction, elbows him. "Never mind my brother, Anna. The detail is incredible. Fantastico! Especially done so fast. More than that, it's clever and smart and terribly fascinating. Certainly provocative, your shoving it in people's faces."

He really can pour it on.

Paolo and I look at each other; I want his approval, recognition, anything. "Tell me what you think, Paolo?"

"You seem to like bugs. You were afraid of them as a kid."

"I still am. That's why I paint them. To deal with my fears. Art is meant to spark thought, to allow us to reflect on ourselves and the world around us, to push boundaries, making us see life in new and unconventional ways. I think I made you feel something."

He regards me with a pained expression and looks away. "Yes, but it's a little too gruesome for my taste. Painted for shock value."

The insult that he struggled to avoid was a result of my pushing him, and in essence what he tried not to say is that I prioritized shock value over depth and substance. That my work lacks the complexity, that it's without lasting value.

On Raffaella's back, I made it appear as if her skin had been ripped open, with her internal organs dissected and shredded. From those wounds, horrid red, black, and yellow insects—devil bugs—crept out. On one of her shoulders was an image of an embedded knife.

Gruesome, yes. But the painting had infinite depth for me.

When our eyes meet again, he says in almost a whisper, "I'm sorry I offended you."

"You didn't. Art means different things for different people. For me, it isn't meant to be a beautifully wrapped gift tied up with a pretty, red bow . . . well, not always. It should be provocative. If my work scares you, or anyone else, then I've met my objective."

He says nothing.

"So I take your opinion as the highest compliment, Paolo."

"I wasn't talking about the grotesque wounds and bugs."

"No. You weren't, were you?" He meant the last embellishment that I'd added after the applause—the final touch. I painted the Medici Falchion around Raffaella's neck. To show these people that I'm not afraid. To show them that I don't believe in curses.

"You upset Raffaella," he adds. "She's very superstitious."

Antonio waves a dismissive hand. "She'll get over it when she realizes that adding the necklace is sure to make headlines in the art world and beyond. She wants the world to know her, like they do you, Anna. To be famous, like your art will be. Someday. Check out her social media, her sad attempts to be an influencer. She doesn't understand that she's just the canvas, not the art or the artist. But your adding that necklace on her body, now that was a great kindness to a girl of such limited talents."

"That's harsh," I say.

"It's the truth. The great news is that you'll get your name out there sooner than you ever expected."

The shorter twin passes us. He grimaces in horror and swats at insects that aren't there. Tringali comes over and warns me that kitsch and controversy don't make true art. "But I'll change that when you study with me."

A woman shrieks from a back room.

"Raffaella!" Antonio says and takes off.

Paolo and I follow, and when we reach the room—the kitchen—we see Giana and Raffaella driving away.

Giorgio, our host, secures the back door.

"What happened?" I ask him.

"She's struggling to breathe. Giana is rushing her to the emergency room."

"I'm sure it's all in her head," Antonio says. "The girl is a drama queen."

My cheeks burn as a wave of guilt hits me hard. What was I thinking? I wasn't. I was under the influence—still am. Not once did I consider Raffaella's feelings. I was defensive, self-absorbed, and imperious to paint that necklace on her.

"Let's celebrate Anna's triumph," Antonio says. "I know a few hip places."

I rub my forehead. "After what I've done to Raffaella, I don't think I want to—"

"You didn't do anything wrong. Even if you believed in curses, it's a picture, not the necklace itself. People make such a big deal about artistic freedom, and you exercised yours. You're so cool. Let's hit some clubs. This is your first time in Rome as an adult."

I finally accept. The truth is, I didn't do anything wrong. And I'm not ready for this night to end.

As we wait for the car, Paolo checks his wristwatch—dress attire for him. "I'm exhausted," he says, yawning. "I think I'll pass. But you two go have fun."

Is it that, or have I just fully disgusted him?

"You'll need to call for a ride," he continues. "Neither of you can get behind the wheel."

"Fine by us," Antonio says and gives his brother a playful shove. "Go get your beauty rest. We can take care of ourselves."

Paolo drives away and Antonio uses his app to get us a car. Some minutes later, we pass the brightly lit Colosseum. The ruins of the theater are beautiful lit up, maybe because men and animals are no longer being slaughtered there for the amusement of others.

Roaring rings in my ears. I'm really high from the last drink.

Antonio moves closer to me, so close I can feel his body heat. He places his arm around my shoulders. I tell myself that he's just being friendly, that he's impressed by my work, but my body says more.

"Are you and Raffaella a couple?" I ask. "Or do you want to be? Don't bullshit me, Antonio."

He whispers in my ear, rubbing his lips across my neck.

After a night of clubbing and too much alcohol on top of the drugs, I wake up to the sound of a phone ringing and realize Antonio is in my hotel room and bed.

He listens to the caller, frowns, and responds with multiple okays, before saying, "Yes, I'll be right there." He disconnects the call, throws off the covers, and stands. "Raffi is ready to leave the hospital. All in her head. She realizes that the painting will get her a lot of new followers. See, no harm done."

Except, there was harm done. I made a terrible mistake sleeping with a man when I was intoxicated, sleeping with a man who was involved with another woman. After Chase hurt me, I promised myself I would never behave like this. So much for promises.

22

utting his phone away, Antonio approaches me, clearly expecting a pleasant send off. When he bends down close to me, I hold up my arm to fend him off.

Fortunately, he steps away.

"We were high," I say. "No reason to make anything more out of what happened."

"You're sorry it happened?"

"No, I enjoyed it, so don't make me sorry. And you're in love with Raffaella."

"No, we broke it off."

"Is that the first time you broke it off?"

His look of embarrassment answers for him.

"Go to her. And tell her I'm glad she's okay."

He actually seems hurt by my rebuff. But I'm not about to fall for a bad boy again, much less a second cousin—legal everywhere in the world or not—who is more interested in his motorcycle and his reflection in the mirror than in anyone else. If that weren't enough, he's taken.

I roll over and try to go back to sleep—impossible. It's 4:30 in the morning, too early to start the day, but I get up, dress, and go out for a walk in the dark.

The streetlights cast long shadows. An occasional car drives by, their headlights blinding. A siren sounds in the distance. A jogger two blocks away crosses the street at an intersection and disappears.

I roam past museums and churches and stores—closed. On the outskirts of a park, a sign identifies the location as a historical site, one of the largest catacombs in the city, with an underground basilica constructed toward the end of the fourth century. That fifteen thousand people are buried below ground in this very spot. That the catacombs are open to the public.

Europe is a living, illustrated history book, its pictures the ancient architecture that I, alive and well, can walk past and be a part of. I don't feel like a tourist, but neither do I feel like a native, which leaves me wondering what I am to this country.

A breeze sweeps over me as I look at the church grounds. It isn't exactly a park, but it's inviting enough with the grass—an oasis in the city.

Someone speaks, and I jump. A middle-aged priest, wearing a long white robe, stops when he reaches me.

"Sorry, you caught me off guard," I say.

"My apologies. Is everything all right?"

"I'm just an early riser out for a walk."

"Tourist?"

"I'm Italian but have just returned after living in the States for many years."

"Oh, I see. You've come for sunrise mass."

I'm Catholic, sure. But after my father took me to America, I stopped going to church. "I would love to see the catacombs. I know it's early, but . . ."

He gestures for me to follow, starts off, and stops when he realizes that I'm not behind him. An old tower, part of the church, looms behind him. He doesn't speak, only waits patiently. Finally, I do follow.

He guides me along a path and down some stone steps. We traverse a narrow hallway where the skulls of humans are entombed in the walls. How odd that a person—or a part of one—can end up as a wall.

"Who were these people?" I ask.

"Everyone and anyone. Priests and servants of the Church. Paupers. Criminals or those who repented. Pagan Romans interred here because of overcrowding and a shortage of land." He sounds so matter of fact.

A skull falls from the wall only a few feet away, startling me.

The priest bends over and picks it up. His demeanor remains casual, as if this happens often. He holds the skull at some distance, as if far-sighted, and examines it, presumably to determine if it's broken. He pats his robe, then lets out a frustrated sigh. "I don't have my glasses."

"May I?" I ask, extending my hands.

He looks at me oddly, but he gives me the skull. I examine it. "No breaks or cracks." I pause. "Think this head belonged to a female? Or a child? It's small, and the jawline isn't strong."

His eyebrows rise.

"I'm an artist. I paint figures, so I've studied anatomy." I return the skull to him, and he replaces it inside the wall. He raises his hands to pray, and I do the same. When he stares over at me, I close my eyes.

A haunting murmur echoes throughout the underground. I bring my hands to my chin and squeeze my eyelids.

"Something wrong?" he asks.

I gaze up at him, surprised that he's looking at me. "Yes, no. I thought I just heard my late mother's voice. She was a professional opera singer."

He scrutinizes my face. Oh God, he must realize that my mother was Vittoria de' Medici Rossi.

"Mystical experiences are not unusual down here," he says. "This is sacred ground, once a refuge for Christians, a place where martyrs have come to rest, to hold up the walls of faith."

A loud buzzing stirs my insides. "Do you hear that humming?"

"You're not the first to be frightened. Follow me."

"But what was that?"

"Dripping water echoing off the walls." He explains that when droplets of water hit the rock formations just right, there's a ringing sound, like a dull bell. Or even a cricket.

What I heard wasn't simply dripping water droplets or the chirp of crickets.

"You're clearly troubled . . . Ms. Rossi, is it?"

"You know who I am?"

"I know the story of your mother. Care to talk about it?"

How do you tell a stranger, even though he's a priest, that you're haunted by the knowledge of what you're capable of?

My silence is answer enough. He guides me to a narrow hallway several yards ahead of us. A plastic barrier restricts access, but we pass through it. The light is quite dim with only emergency signs illuminating the way. Unlike the path we've been on, this floor is rough, rocky, and damp. We reach a set of iron bars blocking access to an alcove. The area beyond has large boulders and smaller rocks, with piles of rubble, strewn about haphazardly. A fine layer of dust coats the entire area—even the bars of the gates.

"We closed this area off after two workers died when a wall collapsed," he says. "Such a tragedy for them and their families. Cracks in the floor began to appear right after. No one expected the rock to give way. But as you see now, there's a large chasm. The floor is weak and continues to deteriorate."

Dangerous, for sure.

"Around the corner, there was once a lovely spot to pray." He points to an opening in the wall to our right, about ten feet in. "A marvelous rose quartz pillar is around that bend. It's a blessed sacramental that melts troubles away. Pink represents our relationship with God and His unconditional love, which requires nothing in return except faith."

"You figured out who my mother was," I say. "Do you believe in curses?"

He exhales hard. "Just as objects can be blessed, they can also be cursed if evil touches them. If you have such an item, you can do only one thing—destroy it."

I nod. We both know he's heard of the Medici Falchion—its notorious history, steeped in darkness and death. "May I see the pillar?" If anyone needs to melt their troubles away, surely he must understand it's me.

"If you get hurt . . . You'll have only yourself to blame."

"I'm willing to accept that. I think you know my story, what I live through every day."

He goes to the stone wall beside the gate, feels around in the middle, and pulls out a flat rock that's just under a foot square. Hidden behind that façade are smaller stones embedded in the wall. He pulls some of them out, pushes others in. A mechanism clanks, and the gate opens.

"That's very cool," I say.

"A puzzle lock, an ancient security technique. You can go inside a short way, but when the wall breaks right, stop and don't go an inch farther. If you lean forward and look around its corner, you'll be able to see the quartz inside the cavern. Use your phone to light the area. Stay close the wall. Agreed?"

"Yes, agreed. But aren't you coming, too?"

He shakes his head.

Slowly, I step inside. Seems safe enough. Ten paces in, I come to the break in the wall. I stop, lean forward, and shine my light around the corner. The quartz pillar is a translucent, scintillating pink. The single glowing column stretches at least twenty feet high and measures three feet around. Mesmerized, I'm overcome with a feeling of peace. Wow, so unexpected. I would never have thought for a moment . . .

The humming returns. It sounds as if someone is whispering in my ears, urging me on. It feels as if I'm lost in the ether, a heavenly dream. Pink glitter paints the air. If I just keep going I can leave it all behind. If I can just touch the pillar . . .

"Stop," the priest warns. "Time to leave."

Instantly, I snap out of it.

I follow him into the basilica, where he walks behind the stone altar. Only two other people are present, nuns in full habit. I take the bench a couple of rows behind them. The stone seats are ice-cold and I immediately begin to shiver, losing the blissful feeling from just moments ago. The priest conducts a traditional and quite elaborate service in Latin and Italian.

When the nuns kneel, I do the same. When they fold their hands in prayer and bow their heads, I do the same. But when it comes time for communion, I sit.

The priest stares at me.

Again I lower my head, close my eyes, and envision my drawing of the Medici Falchion on Raffaella's neck. Doing drugs last night, sleeping with Antonio . . . so stupid. But adding the necklace to the body painting? I'm ashamed now. I don't wish Raffaella dead, and I didn't paint what I did for fame or to shock. It was only an expression of what lives inside of me. The truth is that I can't live without finding the necklace.

The humming grows near. A cold breeze sails across my neck. I gasp and fall to my knees.

"Anna."

No one is there.

23

ow that I've put the bizarre weekend in Rome behind me, I spend a few weeks immersed in my painting, reaching for an inner calm. Paolo and Antonio call multiple times, trying to get me out of the house. Both invite me to have lunch or dinner with them and some of their friends. I want to join them, but decline. Today feels different. I've been avoiding this, dominated by my fear of night terrors, but I can't live like this a day longer. It's time to be brave and resume my search for the Medici Falchion. I'm determined to explore the attics and tower of my villa to see if I can actually find the necklace. Call it an instinct, maybe a lost memory, but something tells me that the damned thing is here just waiting to be found. And it's pure torture.

The sweltering attic space is completely devoid of anything, even cobwebs. The floorboards and walls don't contain any crooks or crannies large enough to secret a closet or storage spot.

Gazing at the olive grove through a small circular window, I take a moment to stretch my arms and neck. What a magnificent view, more magnificent than I remember.

Something large and black bangs hard against the window, leaving a long crack in the glass. My nerves jangle, causing me to stumble back. Tentatively, I approach the window again and peer down into the motor court. Perched on the edges of the fountain are a dozen crows. One spins around and around in the swirling water—obviously dead. That bird crashed into the window, I'm certain of it. I'm sickened and relieved at the same time—relieved because the bird wasn't some figment of my imagination.

Outside at the water feature, I shoo the rest of the birds away. Some caw, a few swoop toward me. Others fly to the ground and pace, picking at the rocky drive. Crows have excellent memories. If you taunt them, they'll never forget, nor will they forgive you. Nevertheless, I shout at them, swinging my arms until they all fly away. The murder lands on a large branch of a hazelnut tree, where they sit in a row and stare down at me. Nuts tumble to the ground and bounce and roll.

"It's not my fault," I shout up at them. A few jump and resume their spots. Odd creatures.

Scooping the dead bird out of the water by its legs, I note that its beak is deformed. Blood drips from its head, and its neck dangles to the side as if it's been snapped in two, as if the poor thing was a victim of the Medici Falchion. As I throw the carcass into a nearby field, I'm left wondering what sent the crow careening into the window. It was no small crow, but a mature one. Could it be that it was old, disoriented, and so chose to end its life rather than suffer the torment of a slow, sickly death?

The wind gusts; leaves rustle in the trees. The murder caws loudly, a panicked call—or a warning? Who cares? I run inside the house and sink down into a living room chair.

Piled on a side table is a stack of old magazines from years ago, before I was born. I sort through them until I reach one toward the bottom of the stack. The cover features my mother wearing the Medici Falchion *and* the same dress that I just wore to the art party.

My mind is a jumble. Like I'm a broken vase, desperate to fit the pieces of myself back together.

Edoardo must've put these out in the last few days. Because I don't recall ever seeing them before. But why would he do that?

My phone, which I left on the coffee table, dings. It's a text from Giana, telling me to check Carra's Instagram page. Carra has posted photos from the party—and of Raffaella as my human canvas. An article on the event has been published. When I see what I painted on my friend, I shudder.

In Casole d'Elsa, there's a newsstand located inside the confines of the old fortress. It's near the Verrocchio Art Centre.

The seller, an older man, looks at me askance. "I know you."

Oh, God. Again? "I don't think so."

Without my asking for the magazine, he turns toward the shelf and selects the publication that features a picture of Raffaella and me on the front cover. "I knew it was you."

Paralyzed, I wait for a compliment, or even a criticism, of my artwork, but it never comes. So I shake it off and pull out my wallet.

"You should never have come," he grumbles.

"Excuse me?"

"You've brought the curse with you. I saw that horror you painted on that girl. People say the paint was tainted, possessed with evil."

"That's in no way true. And for the record, I don't believe in curses." Slapping the money onto the counter, I take the magazine out of his hands. "Keep the change."

"Emma was my sister. Your mother murdered her."

Blood rushes to my head. "I'm sorry for your loss. But my mother had nothing to do with that. Neither did a stupid piece of jewelry. It was an accident."

"That's not what we say around here."

I turn on my heels, grab an afternoon single-shot espresso, find a small table, and turn to the article. Raffaella's back is depicted in sharp detail. But the part of the painting featured most prominently is the Medici Falchion. Did I really paint that, or was it my renegade hand? Am I so starved for attention, so arrogant and desperate, that I took the obvious path to notoriety? Maybe Paolo nailed it the night of the party when I pushed him to speak his mind.

The article goes into a great deal about my mother's death. More rumor and speculation over how she died. Sickening, even though there's little mention of my possible role in her death. The article also quotes Tringali, who proclaims that I'm already his student.

"Omigod, you're her," someone says, a tinge of awe in her tone.

I look up to find a college-age woman with purple, blue, and pink hair, along with nose and eyebrow piercings, standing near me. Her clothes are splattered with paint speckles, so she's probably a student at the Verrocchio Art Centre.

"I like your hair," I say. "I wore a similar style a few years ago, when I was working at a gallery in the East Village . . . in New York City." I don't say that I reverted to my natural color because I was done playing the stereotypical role of an artist and finally ready to become one.

"There's so much to love about your work," she says. "So beautiful, yet so tortured. What I would give to work with Tringali. He comes by the school occasionally and guest lectures. Brilliant."

Nothing pleases me more than the young woman's compliment. I smile and thank her, not puncturing any bubbles about who Tringali is or isn't. I haven't made up my mind.

"The article talks about the necklace and stuff," she says. "Do you have it? Ever wear it? You must, because you painted it so realistically."

"Seriously? You're asking me that? I thought you were interested in art."

She doesn't take my not-so-subtle hint to drop the subject. Her eyes blaze with intoxicated curiosity. "I love art, but I'm dying to ask, did the cops figure out what really happened that night? Your mother, the necklace . . . I'm so sorry for your loss." She barely takes a breath before continuing. "Everyone says you have the necklace. Because if someone else stole it, wouldn't they have sold it? Been caught by now? Unless they tore it apart and sold the stones. Think of all those cursed stones—"

I stand so abruptly that I bump into the tabletop. "You have a good life. And focus more on your art than the shit you read on social media or in the tabloids."

She gapes at me, not comprehending her insensitivity. Maybe *she* is a good protégé for Tringali.

As for the girl's unanswered questions? The Italian police don't share evidence stuffed away in their files. In this case, there is no evidence. Unless my father committing me to the psychiatric hospital right after my mother's death counts.

So just where *did* I put the necklace?

24

ack at the house, I toss the magazine inside a kitchen drawer. I know what I have to do. If the necklace is here, it's on the other side of the Dungeon Door. I can't explain why, but I'm certain of it.

Steeling my nerves, I head down to the basement to revisit that dreaded door.

The Dungeon Door differs from the other doors down here—it's constructed in the Gothic style like the others, but its arches extend upward toward an apex that's higher. Its façade is more intricately carved—cherub heads, gargoyles, sea creatures, birds, even sunflowers. More like an exterior doorway hung on a church, it's not generally one that's found in an Italian Renaissance house. Heavier, too, than any of the other doors in this house. A simple knock on its surface reveals that.

The keys on the keyring won't work, that I'm sure of because unlike the other locks in this house, this one is a ward lock, quite old, and it clearly requires a unique skeleton key. One that has bits that will move past the unique internal obstructions of the wards and move the bolt to open the lock.

Maybe the door is stuck because it hasn't been opened for some many years. I try the handle, twisting with all my strength. No good.

Down the hall leading to the other side of the house, there's a small, unimpressive bedroom—Edoardo's quarters. I slowly push the door open. To get inside, I climb down five additional steps and am greeted by a drop in temperature. Who would live down here?

A metal bedframe holds a skimpy old mattress; to its side is a table; across the room, there's a bureau for clothing; and along the back wall stand a chair and small desk with a single drawer. No pictures on the walls, no personal effects anywhere. A quick search reveals that there's nothing inside the furniture, in the desk drawer or the cabinet, or under the bed.

In this glamorous villa, how could a loyal employee be forced to live in such a dismal space? No wonder Edoardo prefers his own cottage.

A chill floats over me. My presence here is an invasion of this man's personal space, empty as it is. I'm leaving.

I have a vague sense of where Edoardo's cottage must be, somewhere along a tree-lined path. It's the only way he can disappear from sight so quickly. With time on my side, I'll search until I find it. At the bottom of the front porch, I look up to see Edoardo walking toward me, not more than thirty feet away, with his stooped-over gait.

When he reaches me, he bows politely. "What can I do for you, Anna?"

"I'm looking for the key to the basement door, the one that looks like it belongs in a church."

"It's not safe in there, Anna. Nothing to see."

"I own this house, and I don't like being locked out of any of it. So if you don't mind, I think you have something that belongs to me."

He gives a firm shake of the head. "You'll only find a dangerous cave. Please don't wander in there."

"The key, Edoardo."

"No one except your mother had it. Not even your father. That's how dangerous it is."

"That's odd, because my father was able to open it. He shoved me inside there."

Edoardo regards me with a pained expression. "That was a long time ago. What he did, I'm deeply sorry that happened to you. There was no controlling him. I did what I could."

"Oh my God, of course. More than once, you let me out of there. I remember that."

"I should've done more to stop this."

"I'm sure you did what you could. Thank you for helping me." I want to embrace him, but something, perhaps a coldness in his gaze, holds me in my place. "If you let me out, you must have a key. There must be more than just one around here."

"There's only one key to that door. I don't have it."

"Then where is it?"

He looks off into the distance, his resolve weakening. "Your mother kept it inside her journal."

"Where's the journal?"

"I don't know."

My anger surges, but it's not the time to explode. "Edoardo, tell me the truth. You're trying to protect me, but it's only hurting me."

"I don't know where she hid it."

Our eyes meet. He's telling the truth.

"She used to hide the journal from your father."

"And from me?"

He shrugs.

"Maybe I learned that skill from her."

His expression turns stone cold.

"Were you at the villa when my mother died?"

"If you're asking whether your mother was wearing the necklace when I arrived, the answer is no. It was already gone."

So, my father told me the truth. "Do you believe the necklace is cursed?"

Crows in the nearby nut trees caw. A puffy gray cloud moves over us, casting its shadow. Edoardo appears older, his face darker. A crack in the cloud's lining lets blinding light through; I have to look down at the ground to avoid the sun's burning rays.

I cup my eyes to shield them and look at him for an answer.

"I don't believe the Medici Falchion is cursed," he says. "I do believe that, perhaps, people, by their bad actions, have cursed the necklace."

If my mother kept a journal, it might be in one of the bookcases in the study. There, I thumb through book after book. One is a leather-bound version of Edgar Allen Poe's *The Mask of the Red Death*. Fitting. The journal isn't on any of the bookshelves, in the secretary's drawers, the chests, or side tables. I try the desk but find nothing. It's not in the study.

Continuing my search upstairs, I scour the bedrooms, closets, even my mother's parlor, but I find no journal. By day's end, complete exhaustion has set in.

The following day, I repeat my search, plundering closets, checking behind paintings for secret alcoves, looking behind the books that line the bookshelves and in any other potential hiding place. Down in the basement, I check every inch of every room, even inside that cedar-lined storage room where my mother's life-size figure is stashed. I don't flip out at seeing it, although I can't say that I'm at ease with its presence in this house either. Discouraged, I trudge back upstairs, pour myself a glass of Chianti, and head back to the study.

Seated at the desk, a quick search for specialty locksmiths reveals that there's no one in the area. Doesn't matter where they live, I've got money enough to pay for them to travel here. I need to make a list, start phoning and asking for referrals. The center drawer contains not one writing utensil. The side drawers to my left—nothing. When I pull on the top drawer to the right, it won't open. Odd. It wasn't jammed yesterday.

Grasping the handle, I give it a hard yank. It opens but only half an inch. There's paper inside, so there must be something to write with as well. I wriggle the drawer up and down and side to side to loosen whatever is holding it closed. No good. Annoyed, I stand, grasp the handle with both hands, and pull as hard as I can. The drawer flies out. I spin and catch the box before everything falls to the floor.

"Mamma mia!"

Once I have a pen and some paper, I try to slide the drawer in place. It won't go in. "Uffa!"

Squatting, I look inside the cavity and see what the problem is. A flimsy piece of wood, which will now have to be re-glued, has lodged itself into the side of the internal structure. When I try to prop up the dowel, it breaks off entirely, and a weather-worn, dark-brown leather book slips down.

Not a book, the journal!

"Evviva! Che bello!"

The journal's thick front panel is gold embossed with the de' Medici coat of arms and reads *Vittoria de' Medici*. The pages are filled with her lovely writing, her penmanship old-style cursive, much of the lettering calligraphic. That was Mamma—everything was art. The words are in Italian and French. I flip through more pages and discover that she's recorded our family's history. Dates for births, marriages, deaths.

One page has a reference to my great-grandfather Filippo de' Medici and his wife, Maria. For the generation following that—my grandparents' generation—Marco de' Medici is listed as the oldest child and Aurora de' Medici (now Aurora Peruzzi) second. But there's another entry, for a child named Edoardo Bortelli. His birthday falls slightly earlier than Marco's.

Edoardo? Our Edoardo?

My God, does this mean that Edoardo, the caretaker, is my great-uncle? But his surname is different, and he's so close in age to Marco that they couldn't possibly have the same mother.

I sit back a moment, then reread the page.

Siblings don't have to have the same mother. If this journal is accurate, Edoardo would indeed be my mother's uncle, my great-uncle—and the first-born child. If so, everything should've passed to him. Or not. Inheritance laws in Italy have only changed in recent times to recognize the rights of those referred to as "illegitimate" children—if they're recognized by the parent.

I take a sip of wine and ponder more.

Maybe my mother loved Edoardo so much that she considered him an uncle, despite the circumstances of his birth. Then it hits me, and I shudder. If Edoardo really is the firstborn, and if by chance I didn't kill my mother, then who's to say that he didn't kill her? His standard of living as compared to that of the de' Medicis and the Peruzzis is dismal. He would've had a motive to take the necklace.

But if that were truly the case, wouldn't he have fled long ago?

An entry several pages forward stops me cold: the words *Medici Falchion* and the description, "The Medici Falchion, a ruby-and-diamond necklace, is one of the royal jewels from the Medici-Bourbon line."

A history of the descendants from Giovanni de Bicci de' Medici (born 1360) follows on the succeeding pages. When she gets to Cosimo I de' Medici, who was born in 1519, she makes special note that he fathered an illegitimate daughter, Bia, who was born in 1537. Her mother's identity was kept secret. Cosimo and his mother so adored the child that he commissioned a jeweler to make a necklace—what later became known as the Medici Falchion—to be gifted to Bia on her wedding day. When Cosimo's wife, Eleanor of Toledo, learned of the gift, she became enraged. Bia died unexpectedly at age five, supposedly as a result of a fever. But written in the journal is a different history: that Eleanor's spies poisoned the child. Eleanor took possession of the necklace. And so began the deadly fate of the de' Medici women. The necklace was coveted for its beauty and magnificence and changed hands by theft and concealment, eventually finding its way into the Bourbon line of succession.

Eventually, King Louis XVI of France gifted the Medici Falchion to his wife, Marie Antoinette. Not long after, the French Revolution started and Marie Antoinette was sentenced to die by guillotine and was beheaded. Afterward, the Medici Falchion was lost for a time. In the following decades and centuries, our family somehow regained possession.

"Assurdo!"

I laugh aloud with joy. "Oh, Mamma. What a tale you weave." And I thought my imagination was out there. I sip more wine and sit back.

My mother used to call me a princess, but that was dress-up, just play. She wasn't only a performer; she was a creative writer too. Because if there's any chance that I'm descended from royalty, my relatives next door would be shouting as much from their rooftops. And where's our palace? Better yet, shouldn't we be lording over Casole d'Elsa from inside the ancient fort? It's easy to make up some ridiculous stories.

I return to the journal and discover a poem. Looks like the writing of a young girl. Yes, quite a fantasy, Mamma.

> *Breathe, breathe*
> *Can you breathe so deep?*
> *The rose is beautiful*
> *Its fragrance becomes deathly sweet*
> *And I breathe until I can't*
> *Until comes the sting of that terrible bee*
> *Oh, what a treat*

My mother knew about those devil bugs when she was just a child too. But to call their sting a treat? Was she crazy? I quickly turn the page. Now she writes about visiting her late mother's resting place and how it gave her comfort. How she felt safe knowing her own mother was near.

No place for me to look for that kind of comfort. Mamma was cremated. My father scattered her ashes without me. How dare he?

I turn the page to find another entry about the necklace. This time, the script is in Latin—required classes in my boarding school for five years. *Nitimur in vetitum.* "We strive for the forbidden." Then another entry in Latin as well that translates to: "The forbidden must be kept hidden from others, placed upon sacred ground."

"What a load of crap," I say aloud. Am I reading the movie script for a bad remake of *Raiders of the Lost Ark*?

Another page depicts a peculiar drawing. Like doodles. I trace my finger around the objects, some circles, some squares, looking for meaning. Then it strikes me. Maybe this journal is a book of clues as to where the necklace might've been secreted away from my father.

Did my mother have such a place? Could I have known about it? If I really took the necklace, I might've hidden it in the same place. A thought percolates, undefined, like a word you know but can't think of.

On the inside cover, the thick binding is loose at the outer corner. I gently grasp the edge of the cotton and loosen it more, only to discover an empty slot that contains the unique impressions of a skeleton key. Edoardo was telling the truth. But where is the damn key?

Progress has just led to another dead end.

Encouraged, I stuff the journal inside the center drawer, push it to the back, and head down to the basement. I stop in front of the tapestry and study it. In the upper-left corner, a peasant woman appears to be running away from the town center with other villagers. But she's the only one looking back—at the guillotine. Red, white, and gold threads appear around her neck—a representation of the Medici Falchion. That, I'm certain of.

There's a sharp stabbing in my neck. I tell myself it's only psycho-somatic pain.

When I turn to leave, the hulking figure of a man appears. I shriek and take a swing at his face.

"It's me," Antonio shouts, barely dodging my punch.

"What the hell are you doing down here?"

"I knocked but you didn't answer. The door was open, so . . . Everyone else is going to Siena for dinner. I've already eaten, so I thought I would stop by and see how you're doing. You've become such a recluse, cousin. You're not still upset about Rome, are you?"

I smirk. "No. It's just that . . . Never mind. Help me take down this tapestry, will you?"

25

he first of July, I receive an invitation from Paolo to tour his family's wine cellar, which is, as I've been informed, not open to just anyone and never to the public. We climb inside the smallest work truck I've ever seen, barely room enough for two. We leave the windows open to enjoy the warm summer breeze. The ride is delightful until we turn onto the dirt room that cuts through the vineyard. The air immediately fills with dust. But the view is worth a little dirt up the nose. Mature Chianti grapevines with rich canopies of leaves and full clusters of grapes are nature's work of art. Fulvio spares no expense in the upkeep of his vineyards. Each stake stands upright, every plant is evenly spaced, and the vines are firmly attached to the wires.

At the end of the long row, we turn onto another dirt path that leads toward the hillside. There, we park in a grassy area and head to a steel entryway that looks more like a bomb shelter.

Antonio is waiting outside. He disarms the security system and, once inside, turns on the lights. The air smells musty. The floor is made of massive stone slabs. Off to the side sits an old freight elevator that appears to be operated by a hand crank.

We head down earthen steps. Around a corner, we pass through a door, and finally reach a spacious barrel-vaulted room. The area is immaculate; the air clean and controlled. Along the circumference of the room are massive casks. On three sides, hallways extend as far as the eye can see.

"This, I hadn't expected," I say. "Amazing."

"I'm glad you like it," Paolo says. "But I've got to say, it's real easy to get lost in here."

What of the caves beyond the Dungeon Door? If they're anything like this, they aren't so scary.

"My brother is a wimp," Antonio says. "Fulvio closed off any dangerous areas and tunnels long ago. The caves were used during wartime to escape from enemies or to hide valuables. My grandfather knows the stories."

Indeed—a place to *hide valuables.*

"That's so cool," I say. "How long has your family been making wine?"

"Forever," Paolo says. "Fulvio has had many an offer to buy the vineyards and winery from large corporations."

"No chance he'll ever sell," Antonio says. "We take pride in keeping what's ours in the family."

That irks me. I step forward and shove his shoulder.

"What the hell was that for?" he asks.

"Don't you think I feel the same about my property? The vineyards that my father tried to sell to you behind my back?"

"Anna, I'm sorry. I didn't mean anything. Your father led us to believe we had a deal. He said he had your power of attorney. How could we have known that he wasn't telling us the truth? No one knew."

"My brother is telling you the truth," Paolo says. "And we're sorry. But I hope you'll consider honoring your father's wishes. We're winemakers, and the vineyards are precious to us. You don't make wine, Anna. You make art."

His beseeching eyes make me feel sorry for him. Unlike Antonio, winemaking is Paolo's life.

"I don't want to hurt you guys, but I can't sell. Those vineyards have been in *my* family forever."

Antonio raises his hands. "Can we discuss business another time?"

"Good idea," I say, but know that I haven't heard the last of this.

"The first vintage from our new vineyard will be in your honor, Anna," Paolo says.

If this is Paolo's peace offering, it works, despite the fact that he said "our" vineyard. "If you're serious, I'd love to take a stab at designing the label. No obligation to use it."

Antonio biffs his brother in the head. "Great idea."

Paolo nods, but I can tell he doesn't love the idea. Maybe there's a way to satisfy everyone—perhaps a long-term lease.

We start down a stone passageway, both sides of which are double layered with smaller barrels. Paolo describes the vintages stored in the different areas—the year and whether it was a mediocre, good, or great harvest. We soon find ourselves inside a room lined with rows upon rows of bottles, stacked to the ceiling.

"The beauty of storing wine in caves," Paolo says. "Preserves the wine for decades, maybe even longer." He launches into a discussion about how the Romans in 80 BC mined salt and chalk below Reims, France. How they used those caves to store their champagne. How hundreds of years later, the local winemakers decided to use the caves for storage again, and how, without proper cellaring, you'll never make the perfect wine.

"It's an art," Antonio says, kissing his fingers. "That's another reason why our family is so amazing. So many of us are artists—present and past."

We proceed down long corridors that never seem to end until we reach an empty room. Paolo announces that this is where the brothers will store their new vintage. I find a red Sharpie in my bag, walk to the wall, and begin drawing graffiti on the pale stone.

Antonio comes alongside me. "What are you . . . ? Fulvio won't be happy that someone is tagging the wine cellar."

I hold up a finger. "Step back. It's a little gift for you. Spur of the moment, the best kind."

After some long minutes, I turn around with a satisfied smile.

"That's brilliant," Paolo says, eyes wide—exactly the reaction I'd hoped for.

I drew the words "Il Sangue di Anna," which I discreetly wove into a picture of grapevines. It isn't apparent at first, but I also spelled a word in English using the vines—that word is *blood*. The grapes, too, resemble droplets of blood. Why? Because it's my family's blood and toil that has fought to protect their lands, which has now allowed the brothers to produce their wine. That's my family's tradition—to protect what belongs to us.

I look at Antonio. He's completely impassive. Paolo winks at me. Unlike his brother, he gets it, and seems unruffled. Perhaps he takes solace in the fact that eventually the bottles will cover the ink; or maybe he actually likes what I've drawn. Makes no difference. I've made my mark. I like the sound of Il Sangue di Anna. English translation: *The Blood of Anna.*

We start back through the winding tunnels. Something behind us crackles. I glance back. "You guys hear that?"

"No ghosts down here," Antonio says, nudging me. I playfully nudge him back. Paolo joins in.

Antonio makes a howling sound. "There might be werewolves, though."

"Antonio thinks he's cute," Paolo says.

"I am cute," Antonio says, and we continue the horseplay.

I hear it again, sounds like wood cracking. The brothers aren't bothered.

Again, there's a series of distinctive and rhythmic noises, resonant and hollow thuds, creaking and scraping—a rolling sound.

I turn around. "Hey!"

"Maledetto inferno!" Antonio pulls me to the side. "Anna, watch out!" We smash our bodies against the wall. Paolo jumps on top of a small vat opposite to us.

Two large casks roll toward us, picking up speed. They collide and bounce. One bumps my leg. The other runs over Antonio's foot. He yelps. The barrels ricochet off the walls and clunk to a stop.

"Fucking hell," Antonio says.

"How's your foot?" I ask.

"I bet I've got a broken toe." He rips off his shoe and feels his foot.

"What a wimp," Paolo says. "You look just fine."

"Yeah, yeah," Antonio puts his shoe on. "I guess you were right, Anna. But there are always weird sounds down here."

But rogue casks?

"Don't listen to him, Anna," Paolo says. "Barrels, bottles, shelves. Everything is constantly settling down here."

Antonio looks at one of the rogue casks. "Good stuff. If Fulvio sees this, he'll go totally insane."

The brothers roll the barrels back to where they belong. I'm no expert, but the cradles these two casks sat in don't appear undisturbed or damaged in the slightest. So how did they get out?

Paolo seems to understand my concern. "Things shift. Once I saw an entire shelf fall. What a mess that was."

"Weird."

"Nah. It happens. We live on a revolving planet."

Antonio roars with laughter. The brothers play fight with each other.

I glance down a dark corridor, something flashes by. My eyes are playing tricks on me. Knowing that doesn't prevent my stomach from tying itself in knots.

I've got to get out of here.

26

owards the middle of July, Antonio invites me on a weekend sailing trip off the island of Elba, says we'll be staying in Portoferraio. On Saturday morning, he picks me up in one of the winery's trucks—we're making a delivery along the way. But that's fine. After we unload the wine, he announces that we're cutting over to Volterra and then Cecina, and on our return drive, we'll stop in Pisa to climb the tower.

"I don't think I've ever had my own private tour guide," I say. "You know you don't have to go to all the trouble."

"No trouble at all. I'm just reacquainting you with your birthland. That's what a friend should do."

I feel myself blush. "Antonio, we're going just as friends."

"Don't worry, I'm not looking for a repeat of our night in Rome."

I don't know whether to believe him—he is a guy—but I'll make sure there's no repeat.

After a long drive, we stop for lunch at a beachside restaurant in the coastal town of Cecina. The host seats us at a table with a view of the ocean. The crystal-clear, emerald-green water laps against the shore. The sound of children's laughter draws our attention to the sand. A family of four runs along the surf, kicking and splashing water at one another.

"Isn't it just . . . well, heartwarming," he says.

"Yeah, I love the ocean."

"I mean the family. I want six kids."

My spine stiffens. "Have you gotten the agreement of your future wife for that astronomical number?"

"I love my siblings. We're so close. Isn't it miserable being an only child?" I never would've guessed that wild-child Antonio Massimino would want to settle down, much less have six kids. But he's older than me, thirty-one, and I suppose guys have their own biological clock. But still, six kids?

"It's miserable being an only child, growing up without a mother and having a crook for a father," I say. "I don't know if I want kids."

His lighthearted expression drops. "Maybe it's an Italian versus American thing. I know American women start later. Maybe you'll come around soon. Thirtyish isn't so young for motherhood." Then he adds as an afterthought, "When you find the right person."

I look out at the water. During undergraduate school, I thought the right guy had come along.

Chase and I met on the first day of a required class—European History. I claimed the empty chair beside him. He was tall and stocky, with rust-red hair, and his voice was the kindest, yet he played the violent sport of rugby. What a surprise to learn that watching the sport's rough contact was enjoyable. We began spending weekends together, studying and taking side trips to enjoy the countryside. On Sundays, we drove to New England estates, where we would race through the house tour and head out to the gardens to take our time strolling around. He was great, or so I thought. You never really know people, though, do you?

After the spring semester ended, I suggested that we go hiking at Mount Tammany, an hour and a half drive from the city. We hiked to a spectacular waterfall, passing a few smaller ones along the way. On our return, I suggested that we scale down some rocks to the base of the waterway and soak our feet.

I tied off the rope, and he started down first, bouncing onto his feet at the bottom.

"Made it," he called up.

"Stand back." As soon as he stood five feet away, I hurriedly pulled up the line and set it aside.

"What the hell, Anna?"

I squatted and stared down at him smiling.

"Stop messing around," he said.

"I think you're the one who's been doing that, Chase. With Blaire?" Blaire was a student in our anthropology class—the popular sorority girl who snubbed artsy types.

"Anna, nothing's happening—"

"Save it. I got texts from three different people who saw you making out with her at a bar in the Village. One of them sent a photo. Plus, Blaire plastered a ton of posts of you and her."

"It was nothing, we were drunk," he said with false bravado. "You and I work."

"Fuck off, Chase. I don't like cheaters." I stood and began walking away, leaving him stranded below—a place from which he couldn't climb out of without a rope. It might take days, even weeks, for someone to find his body.

"Anna, I'm sorry, but this isn't funny."

"No, it isn't," I called to him.

He became completely unhinged. Finally, he cried, "If you're still here and can hear me, I'm sorry. I swear I'll never do it again. I love you, Anna. I was wrong. Made a mistake."

After a few more minutes, I returned to the edge.

"I'm sorry," he said, his face red, his eyes teary. "Please don't leave me here. You've proved your point. And please, forgive me. I don't want to lose you."

I tossed the loose end of the rope to the bottom. "You know what, Chase? The difference between me and you is that if the roles were reversed, I would never beg for you to take me back. We're over."

We drove home in absolute silence. And never spoke again after that day. As far as I know, he never told anyone what had happened.

Antonio reminds me of Chase.

<h1 style="text-align:center">27</h1>

hen day breaks, I change into my sailing gear and head to the docks where I join Antonio and his friends, including Raffaella, who seems cordial as ever. We board a boat. Just as we're about to sail, Paolo Massimino jogs up to us.

"Fratello!" Antonio cries.

Paolo grins broadly. "Saluti a tutti!"

"The hermit comes out of his wine cave and into the light," Antonio says affectionately, pounding his brother's back. "I thought you were too busy to make it."

"Fulvio convinced me to come. Well, ordered me to come, actually. Said I work too hard and need some relaxation. And he wants me to meet girls. So here I am." He shrugs with raised hands. "Why not? The air is good, the company better."

"Will you room with one of us?" I ask. "I have a couch."

"Thanks for the offer, but the owner found me a room, so I'm set. God help me if I had to bunk with Antonio. He snores."

We share a laugh.

I intend to stay out of Antonio's bed as well. I just hope Raffaella doesn't hear about my mistake in Rome. She certainly looks smitten with him again.

The boat shoves off, and I soon have an Italian sangria in hand—a cold drink made with red wine, limoncello, sweet vermouth, and orange juice. Antonio regales us with his art-opening stories. He brags about convincing people to buy artwork that he wouldn't put in his tool shed.

I throw off my beach cover and walk around the boat, Raffaella follows me. She rubs her neck, then turns around and lifts her t-shirt, bare except for a thin bikini top. "Your wonderful, awesome, sinister art is gone. Washed off in the shower. I actually left it on for four days, I loved it so much."

"Raffi, after you saw what I painted on your neck, you—"

"Don't you dare apologize for your art. Everybody loved it. We're still trending on social media. I got thousands of new followers. My profile picture is me with the painted necklace." When we're out of earshot, she says, "Listen, I need some time alone with you. There's something I want to talk to you about."

I get a sinking feeling—she knows about Rome.

Just as I'm about to ask her to tell me now, one of the guys walks up and starts chatting with us. He can't stop talking about soccer—or rather, "il calcio." Finally, we find a way to return to the group. Antonio continues to regale the group with stories—the most recent, our adventure down in his family's wine caves. I look down at my leg. The bruise isn't that bad, but it's noticeable.

Soon, Paolo leaves to join a few guys at the stern. Two more go with him. It's just Antonio, Raffaella, and me now. Seated, Antonio squirms between us and then puts his head in Raffaella's lap and his legs across me. I'm feeling a little happy now that I've had a glass of sangria and don't get uptight about it. But if this guy thinks we're part of his harem, he'll soon find out otherwise. From me anyway.

We near the shore. The waves kick up. Seawater from the side of the boat comes out of nowhere and splashes the three of us.

Antonio springs up and puts on his deck shoes. I pull my bag onto the bench, find my beach cover, and slip it over my head.

We dock at a deserted beach. The group works together to unload supplies and organize a base camp. The men set up an open-air tent and chairs. I help Paolo stake up a net to play volleyball. Then Raffaella, Antonio, and I build a pit to roast a side of pork.

When the work is done, Antonio joins a couple of guys. Raffaella nods toward the water. Just the two of us head down and take a stroll away from the others. Eventually, we stop to let the tide roll over our feet.

She looks around to make sure no one has followed. "I like you, Anna. You're brilliant, and what happened to you as a kid was unfair. A real bad deal. We were such good friends when we were young, we had tons of playdates. Sleepovers. And then you left. I really missed you, and you never reached out. Not even on social media, or—"

"I'm sorry, Raffi. No excuse, but things were tough. I tried to forget about this place. About what happened. Not fair to you, but Italy just seemed like another lifetime ago—a lot of it bad."

She takes my arm. "Never mind. I get it. But listen to me. You can't trust Antonio. He always has some ulterior motive."

"We're just friends."

"So you think. Except he told me about Rome."

I feel like running back to the group and pummeling that guy. "That was—"

She raises a hand. "Whatever. He wants something from you."

"You mean my land? Let him want it. I'm not selling it."

"He'll make you believe you're best friends. Tell you things. Seduce you. Did he tell you he wanted a wife and six kids, like he was confiding in you?"

I'm rattled down to my core. "He used the same line with you."

"No. Yes, but it's different. That happened a long time ago." Her eyes bore into mine. "He'll take your land, he'll take your house, and whatever else he's after."

"No chance of that."

"Aurora's ring." She pauses, and then looks out at the waves and back into my eyes. "He didn't lose it; he stole it from his own grandparents and used it to propose to me."

My jaw falls open.

"I'm embarrassed to say that there was a time when I would've accepted it with total happiness. That's Antonio's power of persuasion—no one in the family is hurt. Aurora's already got a new ring. The insurance company paid. But I've had it. I won't play Antonio's games anymore. I don't know, maybe seeing him with you opened my eyes."

"He's not with me. Please. I'm sorry. It was just a big mistake. I was so high."

"No, no, Anna. Please. I don't care. I get it. He got you high, used you."

I feel like an idiot. "So you have the ring?"

She reaches inside her bathing suit bottoms and gets something from a small inside pocket. She holds up her hand and opens it. It's a diamond ring, three carats, if I'm a good judge.

"What are you going to do with it?"

"I was going to dump it in the sea when we were sailing today, but I didn't have a chance. Have you ever noticed how Antonio watches my every move? Yours too."

What a creep. "Why don't you just give it to Fulvio and Aurora? Alert the insurance people?"

She hesitates, and her eyes fill with tears. "I . . . If I do that, Antonio could go to jail. That would destroy Fulvio and Aurora and Francesca. And Paolo. Especially him. The family knows what he's like. Despite everything, they love him."

"You should give it back, it's not right," I whisper.

"Merde," she says, the first time I've heard her curse. "It's so complicated, Anna."

"You can't keep it. Someone will think *you* stole it. At least talk to Fulvio. You have nothing to fear, you did nothing wrong." Though accepting the ring in the first place was questionable. And if she knew at the time what had happened . . . even worse.

"Oh God, you're right. That's why I have to throw it in the sea."

"And when Antonio asks for it back?" I shake my head. How could she let herself get tangled up in such a mess? "Why did you come if you're not interested in Antonio? Because it sure looks like you're into him, and he clearly thinks you're into him."

"It's difficult—the ring, the family. We've been on and off for years. I really do care about him, but I just can't be with him, not anymore. I don't like who he's become. Truth is, I came for Luca, who's piloting the boat. The guy you met at the art party in Rome. Problem is the two guys are big pals."

Is she really telling the truth about her feelings?

Antonio jogs up to us. Raffaella steps away and slips the diamond ring inside her bathing suit. He doesn't seem to notice.

"Time for water polo, girls," he says.

Raffaella hesitates.

"It's shallow water, Raffi! Have some fun." To me, he says, "Believe it or not, Raffaella doesn't like swimming. We'll be in the shallow part. Feet touching the bottom."

"If she's afraid of the water, she shouldn't go in," I say.

"Anna, don't encourage her to be a spoilsport."

We put our things on chairs.

"My phone is ringing," Raffaella says. "I'll be right behind you. Go!" I never heard the phone ring at all. But Raffaella is soon talking on it.

Antonio comes back and drags Raffaella into the water with the others. We form teams, knocking a beach ball back and forth without letting it drop. The water is only at most waist deep, so even Raffaella looks like she's relaxed. Antonio and I end up on one side with crew members. Paolo, Raffaella, and Luca on the other team.

The ball comes my way. When I don't react fast enough, Antonio bumps into me and returns the ball with a solid whack, and when I start to fall forward, he clings to me and keeps me upright before I go under water. The full weight of his body pressed against me feels strange. Everything feels off. I'm having a hard time with what Raffaella told me.

The current becomes stronger, and I end up closer to the shore. Raffaella tries to get out of the water, but Antonio won't let her. Luca seems oblivious, intent on continuing the game. Someone whacks the ball. It bounces off me and floats toward Raffaella and the open sea. Antonio splashes his brother, and the two get into a water fight.

"Get the ball, Raffi," Antonio calls out.

Gameplay turns into a full-on water-splashing contest. Everyone is laughing and having fun. Then Paolo dunks me. When I surface, I wipe the salt water from my eyes and look around. No sign of the ball or Raffaella. She must've gotten out of the water.

We run to the shore and drop down on chairs.

"Where's Raffaella?" I ask, looking around. "Did she bail on us?"

Others shrug.

Antonio and Luca stand and look down the beach and then out at the water. Paolo joins them.

"She didn't just disappear," I say, my panic rising. I shield my eyes and scan the water.

The group splits up. Antonio, Paolo, and I go straight to the water. Half of the group goes down the beach one way, the others head in the opposite direction. Everyone is calling for Raffaella while frantically searching along the shore and in the water.

"Something . . . Fuck, is that . . . No way." I stare at an object out to sea. "Guys look, out there. Is that her? Fuck, no way she could be way out there." My God, she's completely up to her neck, and the poor girl can't even swim. How long can she last before the sea swallows her whole?

"Dio mio!" Antonio says. "It's Raffi!"

"Oh my god is right," Paolo exclaims. "Stay here, Anna."

I start to follow, but he jerks my arm to a stop. "It's a riptide. For your own safety, stay. Please."

I nod, feeling the pressure on my arm. He's deadly serious.

Both Antonio and Paolo race into the water, high stepping and fighting for purchase to make it through the whitewater surf. They both dive under and surface, swimming hard and fast. I can barely make out what's bobbing up and down.

Then the object disappears.

Has Raffaella sunk below the surface?

The brothers split up.

My heart is pounding so hard that it's a wonder that it doesn't spring from my chest. Every impulse inside of me wants to charge into the water. A hand rests on my shoulder—Luca. I wonder why he's just standing and watching.

"Any sign of her?" he asks.

"No. Wait. Yes. Something is going on out there."

Antonio seems to have found Raffaella. Arms are flailing. My breath catches. What's going on?

Luca pushes into the surf and starts high stepping.

Then Paolo surfaces near Antonio, and the struggling stops. "Luca, they have her," I call out, and he stops to keep watch. Before long, the brothers are on the way back with Raffaella. They've saved her from drowning, and all I can think about is the necklace that I painted around her neck.

Still, Raffaella looks half dead when my two cousins help her from the surf.

28

y late afternoon, Raffaella has recovered from the almost-drowning event. Everyone mothers her until she insists that she's fine and demands that they drop the matter. She's even drinking wine and laughing. I stop worrying, become tipsier because people keep refilling my half-empty glass, but no one seems to care, and no one seems to be all that drunk.

The sun dips lower in the sky. After dinner, Paolo and I take a walk down the beach.

My toe connects with against something hard, and I hop a few steps.

"Anna?"

"Feeling pain reminds me what it's like to be human, and right now I'm very human, because it hurts like hell." I glance down and point. "I tripped over that thing, stuck in the sand."

"It's a conch shell. I love them."

The shell easily pulls loose.

"Bellissimo," he says.

It is beautiful. Holding it to the light magnifies its ribbed and spiny surface. The peachy interior is smooth, and it reminds me of the Fibonacci sequence, the magical pattern so often found in the simplest of nature. "It's so soft, like silk."

"Time and sand. Must be a male shell."

"And you know that because . . . ?"

"Time softens even the hardest man, or so my grandfather likes to say. He also says that a woman can never be softened, and that's why they are stronger than men."

I tease him by rolling my eyes, then hand him the shell and lift my chin toward the sea. We can't keep it; it's against the law. He understands that it's time.

Facing the ocean, he throws the shell, a lot farther than I could've. "He's safe now," he says. "Back to his home."

There's an innocence in Paolo's eyes, as if he's never had a hard surface.

The tide is coming in. A wave crashes hard against the sand. The water rolls over our feet and legs and then slinks away, repeating its endless rotation—the cycle of life, the ever-changing ground beneath our feet, forcing Paolo and me to take a step forward, then back. I think of the sun and the moon, and how their positions in the sky affect the gravitational pull of the water. Is there ever a way anyone can stand in one place and not be pulled by the gravitational forces of life?

"I love my brother," Paolo says. "But he doesn't like to follow rules. People around him get hurt."

It's not my place to tell him about the conversation with Raffaella and about Aurora's ring, as much as I'd like to.

"Antonio stops at nothing to get his way. Do you understand, Anna?"

"I'm not interested in Antonio."

"Think about selling us the vineyard. We've put a lot of work into that land."

"I get that he wants it. I know you do too."

"You don't need the land. Do you ever see yourself making wine?"

"No, but what if my kids, do? If I ever have kids."

I lean forward and kiss his cheek, making him blush. Is he pushing Antonio's agenda? Or warning me off him?

29

omeone taps lightly on the accessway between my room and the one over. "Anna, I know it's early but are you awake yet? It's Raffi. We're neighbors."

Surprised, I let her in.

"Mind if I use your shower?"

"Is yours broken?"

"No, I don't want to wake Antonio." She holds up a hand, wincing. "I know, I know. So stupid, especially after . . . Please don't judge me."

"Not my business." Which is true. And what about Luca?

She showers quickly and takes a seat at the foot of the bed. After twisting her hair into a bun, she slides a sundress over her head and stands to fold the towel, which she then hands to me.

"I'm going boating," she finally says. "I want to get away before Antonio wakes up."

"What did you do with Aurora's ring?"

She gives me a flustered look and starts to leave. "Anna, I told you the truth about him. I'm living proof of the harm he can do."

"Hold it. What happened out there yesterday? Because something happened."

"I stupidly went for the ball."

"Come on, Raffi. You almost drowned. Did Antonio try to hurt you out there? Because it looked like you two were struggling."

Her eyes shoot daggers at me. Then she looks down a moment. "Antonio won't take no for an answer. He wants to set a date. Isn't that obvious? I don't even know why I came on this trip. Point is, I'm alive and well. And I'm leaving."

"Have a good day, Raffi." Unsure of what to think, I head to the shower. When I come out, Antonio pops his head inside my room. Good thing I've got a robe on.

"Paolo wants to meet us in the lobby at nine for breakfast," he announces.

Good. I don't want to be alone with him, even in a crowded café.

At my urging, the brothers agree to hike up to the ruins of an old castle, the Castello del Volterraio. As soon as we finish our meal, Antonio leaves the table. Not as subtly as he thinks, he pulls out his phone and disappears around the first corner he comes to.

"What's he up to?" I ask Paolo.

"Probably trying to avoid paying the check."

Before I get out my wallet, he grabs his and insists on paying.

Antonio reappears. "Raffi is joining us on our hike to the ruins."

"And Luca?" I ask.

Antonio chortles.

When she left my room, she wanted no part of Antonio. What has this man done to my long-ago friend?

"How did you get her to change her mind?" I ask.

"That urbex crap she's into," Antonio says. "She needs new social media posts." He throws up his hands. "Don't even ask me. I'm not into it. Last place I'd ever want to find myself is lying on top of a rusted-out, rickety old operating table that's been left behind in some abandoned hospital. Go check out her social media, you'll see her doing exactly that. Freaks me out. But hey, whatever floats your boat."

I flip open my phone to Raffi's page. God Almighty, my friend is really bizarre. By comparison, I seem almost sane.

30

e park the car at the trailhead below the castle ruins and start up the narrow dirt path to the peak where Castello del Volterraio towers over the region. Once upon a time, the fortress stood as a magnificent symbol of worldly power and influence. Even today, it has an ominous beauty.

With Paolo in the lead, we hike single file. The higher we climb, the more spectacular the scenery becomes. Before long, a panorama opens, drawing our attention from the trail to the view. The drop-off is a little too close for my comfort. But we're safe as long as we stay on the path.

At a lookoff, Paolo suggests that we stop to admire our surroundings and catch our breath. The mountains are set deep inside the island landmass, forming a backdrop for the inlet bay filled with sailboats so distant that they're merely white spots on the water. Green vineyards and forests lie scattered between communities, which fold into the rocky terrain with their rustic-tan and faded-orange structures. It's an artist's dream.

I snap some photos with my phone.

We continue along until we stop at a small building, maybe an ancient sentry post. I take a panoramic photograph and then a short video.

Paolo points out a mountain goat standing on the edge of a rocky cliff. Everyone gathers around and admires the animal's courage. When the goat finally sees us, it tumbles from the edge of the cliff, leaving a cloud of rocks and pebbles behind.

I shriek.

"It's a mountain goat." Antonio laughs. "Do you really think it fell?"

"We'll make this New Yorker a country girl yet," Paolo says.

I catch Raffaella's eye. She remains perfectly composed, even dreamy-eyed. "It's beautiful here," she says. "I adore these structures from antiquity. They remind me that we haven't always been the only ones here."

"This place has been falling to pieces now for a thousand years," Antonio says. "Just like civilization. You think that's romantic?"

"Everything's a joke to you, Toto," she says and then gazes off into the distance.

Toto—I haven't heard anyone call him that, not even his family members. He and Raffaella share experiences and unspoken truths at which I can't even guess.

"The castle was built over an ancient Etruscan structure, renovated in the late thirteenth century," Paolo says. "Resisted an attack by the Turkish, thank goodness, or we would be Turks living in Turkey right now."

Antonio pats his brother's arm. "Paolo's jokes aren't funny. But I love my little brother." Then Antonio grasps one of Raffaella's hands and pulls her along the increasingly steep path, pushing her to go too fast.

"Slow down!" Paulo shouts. "Don't do anything stupid!"

Raffaella breaks free, which stops Antonio, and we catch up with them. Paolo takes the lead, moving at a slower pace—the younger brother is the protective one, it seems. The trail twists as we come closer to the top. Eventually, we reach an uneven stone path with a narrow railing, circle around, climb a walled staircase, and emerge inside the castle ruins. The essential exterior of the castle is largely intact, but the interior walls have eroded a great deal. Like the Colosseum in Rome, the roof is gone, as are the upper rooms.

We stop while Raffaella snaps some shots. Then we pose for a few together. We make funny faces and share the photos. Our laughter lofts upwards, then vanishes into the breeze like bubbles popping from a child's wand. I've often heard that the wind makes people, especially children, giddy and carefree.

"Let's go around to the tower," Antonio says, grabbing Raffaella's hand and urging her along.

"Stop running," Paolo shouts. "We can't enjoy the place racing around like mice on a wheel."

"He's right, you're spoiling the fun, Antonio," I call to them, trailing behind but trying to catch up. "Take it easy, will you?"

We finally reach them when they stop at the edge near a wood platform that crosses over to the remnants of a tower.

"You're crazy, brother," Paolo says. "Can't you see you're scaring Raffaella?"

"Okay, you caught up," Antonio says. "Everything's fine. Right, Raffi?" He tugs her hand for affirmation.

She smiles, doesn't protest. Maybe she likes the thrill of danger.

My head spins when I look over the side—we really are quite high up. Thankfully, steel bars are in place to keep people from falling.

"You've seen the castle, Anna," Antonio says. "Let's head down and go sailing. I could use a few beers."

That's why he's rushing. He really didn't want to come up here.

"We just arrived," Paolo says. "Let her enjoy the place."

When I nod, Antonio sighs impatiently.

Raffaella breaks loose and gazes over the side. She takes more pictures. One of us together. She posts the photo after several attempts to gain cellular service, saying, "Besties." Antonio bombs another.

We admire the view for a while longer as Raffaella posts more pictures. She gets a response from someone, and her mood sours.

"Okay, I'm done here," she says. "Some asshole says this place doesn't count."

"Urbex?" I ask. She shows me the post. "Ever hear of jealousy? That's what's going on with that guy. Block him."

She smiles, gives me a side hug, and we head to the tower. She takes the lead, moving at a reasonable pace. The brothers follow behind me, walking almost side by side. I sense Paolo is trying to keep Antonio in check.

We round a corner in the tower's stairwell. I'm right behind Raffaella, sliding my hand along the wall for balance. God, these steps are uneven, and rather intimidating because the staircase is so steep.

"Hurry the fuck up, Raffi!" Antonio shouts.

She raises her hand and gives him the finger.

A body rams me hard from behind, causing me to stumble. It's Antonio who hit me, and I accidentally careen into Raffaella, who loses her balance, bounces off the wall, trips again, and tumbles down the stairs, shrieking with fright. Her screaming stops when her skull hits the stone landing with a sickening *crack*.

As that horror unfolds before my eyes, I struggle to regain my balance, try to stop myself from falling, but my hand gets caught between the stone wall and rusty railing. I cry out in agony when my hand twists and makes what feels like a hundred-and-eighty-degree turn, and oh my God, there's bone sticking out of my flesh, and is that blood?

De' Medici blood. De' Medici blood . . .

As I struggle not to faint, to free my arm, Antonio stands silently, looking down at Raffaella's motionless body.

What feels like hours later but is probably only seconds, I manage to free my hand. I can't catch my breath, can't speak. I crumple down to a seated position on a step and hold my arm to my stomach. My shirt is now damp, bright red.

That's when I vomit, and not from the pain—I made contact with Raffaella, and she fell down a flight of stairs, and she may be dead.

God, I hope she's alive.

Paolo rushes down the stairs, past Antonio, and toward me.

Suddenly, the pain has stopped, but I'm so woozy . . . I must be in shock. So cold. Shivering, almost convulsing. My mind rolls in an endless loop—I'm going to bleed to death. And Raffaella has fallen down the stairs, just like my mother. Antonio hit me, didn't he, pushed me off balance? Or is this my fault because I painted the necklace on Raffaella?

When Paolo reaches out to touch me, I recoil. The pain starts again, worse than before, shooting up my arm to my shoulder and neck. Excruciating. I start to cry.

"Anna," Paolo says softly, kneeling beside me. "I've had first aid training at university. Let me have a look."

All I can think about is the *curse*. "Raffaella? Oh, God. She okay?"

"We have to take care of *you*, Anna. Just focus on me."

"Tell me, Paolo."

He won't. My eyes cloud over. I can't make out Paolo's face. Is it him? His features look warped, like a cartoon caricature. Am I just having one of those walking nightmares? *Please wake up.*

"Deep breaths," he says.

I try but struggle.

"Anna, show me your hand."

I try to hold up my hand, but it hurts so bad.

Paolo takes my arm. "You've got a bad cut and some broken bones, Anna. A compound fracture. We'll get you to a hospital, and you'll be fine. Just promise me—don't look at your arm."

When I make out the worried expression on his face, I begin sobbing, because I know it's more serious than he's saying. "It's my left hand. I'm left-handed. I can't paint with my right hand."

Antonio is with Raffaella; he's covered in blood. He looks dazed—or maybe not dazed. Maybe just impassive. How could that be?

Oh, God. She's dead. Raffaella's really dead.

"Come here, Antonio!" Paolo says. "Anna needs our help."

Antonio just gapes at us.

Paolo goes down to his brother and shakes him vigorously. "Call emergency services. Anna needs help. Ora!"

Finally, Antonio straightens, walks around the corner, and makes the call.

Paolo tries to help me stand, but my legs wobble hard. I've lost my strength, so he helps me sit back down.

When Antonio returns, Paolo says, "I'm going to carry Anna down. Stay with Raffaella. Call the hospital, ask them to have an orthopedic surgeon standing by. Hand surgeon if possible." Paolo gently lifts my chin. "Hang in there."

"What's happening?"

"Anna, you're bleeding, so we've got to act fast, or it'll be a problem—nerve damage, or worse." His words are elastic, stretching in and out of my grasp.

A flash of clarity. If I don't regain full use of my hand, I'll never paint again. What if it's worse? What if some doctor cuts off my hand? The Medici Falchion has worked its curse on Raffaella and me both in one fell swoop.

Someone whispers to me: *Anna . . . Anna . . . you can't escape your fate.*

"What?" I can't, I *won't* listen to phantoms. I reach for my sanity. That voice isn't real. No, I must be delirious.

"Focus, Anna," Paolo says. "Don't talk."

Was I talking? I can't concentrate, my vision is blurry, and my brain is floating out of my skull.

He strips off his shirt and folds it into a bandage, then tells me to brace my hand and hold it up. I do my best, but when I see the amount of blood, I start to lose consciousness. The last thing I feel is the necklace clenching tighter around my neck.

31

here am I? What's happening?

Right. Paolo is carrying me. We're at the bottom of the trail. My body is numb. Not all of me. My hand and arm are in excruciating pain, the kind of pain that makes you want to scream so loud that you throw up. I do scream.

Lights flash. EMTs hover over me, touching me, working on my arm. Hurts so bad.

I glance down and see Paolo's shirt wrapped around my arm, a makeshift tourniquet to stanch the blood.

Someone begins asking questions. "Next of kin? Emergency contact?"

Oh my God, I have no one. Not in Italy. Not in America.

Paolo tells people dressed in bright yellow jackets that both of my parents are deceased.

I'm placed on a gurney. The loss of physical contact with Paolo jars me into greater awareness. The attendants load me into the vehicle. I hear Paolo talking, to who? To me? Suddenly, he's by my side.

"I'm her cousin, I'll go with her," he says.

Or is that Antonio talking? The brothers sound so much alike.

Horrible thoughts bring me to full awareness: Antonio shoved me into Raffaella. Was he trying to kill me? Or her because he believed she would expose him as a thief? I thought she was panicking out at sea, but maybe she was fighting Antonio off. Then Paolo came and saved her.

Oh God, is Raffaella dead? My mouth is dry, my words are stuck in my throat. An image of my friend lying on the stone-cold ground invades my mind. So much blood, her skull—shattered. Her eyes, bugged out of their sockets; her broken jaw hanging open—a death mask. Those skulls in the catacomb walls . . . Raffaella is like them now. They'll put her in a wall, the ground, or cremate her, turn her body to ash.

"Oh, God," I rasp.

"Don't try to talk, Anna," a man says. I'm not sure, but I think it's Paolo.

A buzzing infiltrates my ears. Fear spikes. I tremble. I have to find the key to the Dungeon Door. Find the necklace and get rid of it. I try to rise up. I have to find it. There's pressure restraining me.

"Calm down," a man says, a familiar voice.

I roll my head toward him. "Antonio?"

"No, Paolo," the voice says.

"Twenty minutes," a woman says.

The rear doors of the ambulance swing shut, and the siren sounds. Is the hospital twenty minutes out? Do I have twenty minutes to live?

The ambulance speeds away; the ground is bumpy, and each bump intensifies the already agonizing pain in my arm. I bite my lower lip hard; I won't cry. Not for myself.

Someone continues to speak to me with kind words, rubs my head. So much swaying and bumping and shifting.

An IV is attached to my arm. Saline and drugs, because the pain is no better but more distant. I'm in and out of it—trying to stay aware.

"Ms. Rossi, can you hear me?" a man asks. "You're in the hospital. You've suffered multiple broken bones in your wrist and hand."

I try to see through my mind's fog. A doctor stands beside me. Paolo is next to him. A nurse undresses me, puts me in a gown. Someone else connects my IV cord and bag to a stand. Warm blankets are placed over me, and I'm tucked in. A moment of comfort for the physical pain, but not for the mental agony.

"You need a transfusion," the doctor says. "You've lost a lot of blood."

The doctor continues talking, but I can't make out the words. Too technical.

I feel calmer. The pain hasn't subsided, but it's further away. Morphine? I nod my head several times.

The nurse places another bag on the stand and starts a transfusion. The red fluid flows down a tube and into my arm.

Everything is happening so fast and yet very slowly.

The ceiling glows red, then swirls and scuds by like fast-moving clouds.

I catch pieces of what the doctor is saying to me or someone else, I don't know. *Helicopter. Rome. Severed radial artery, wrist, hand. Nerve damage and necrosis.* God, my painting future! I feel the tears flow. *Specialist for surgery. Possible nerve damage. Worse, necrosis. She's lucky I got to her in time.*

Lucky? No. Poor Raffaella.

A heavy pressure constricts my chest. Strange thoughts come to mind. How can a simple misstep change a person's life like this? End a person's life? Humans. We're only silver balls in God's pinball game, bouncing against bumpers until we're sent below, never to reappear—except in other people's dreams. Is the goal for Him, or Her, or Them, to accumulate the most points before you go down the gutter? To where—hell?

The nurse has a syringe. "Just something more to relax you and ease the pain, honey."

More time passes. I'm outside. The rooftop. The attendants are wheeling me across the deck.

Someone says, "Rome is 277 kilometers away—as the crow flies."

Crows caw. I roll my head back and forth, looking for them. There they are, on the edge of the roof. Their beaks turn to scowling cartoon faces. They never forget when someone has done them a wrong.

A helicopter engine roars, its rotary blades cutting the air. The wind from its propeller sweeps across me. I'm lifted inside the craft. So loud.

"Don't worry, Ms. Rossi," a man says. "You'll be under the knife within the hour."

"Who are you? What knife?"

"You'll be in surgery within the hour," Paolo says. "We're taking care of you, Anna. I'm right here."

The helicopter takes off. I don't want to lose my future.

Who took my paintings that I put out on the streets of New York? Why do I care about them now? Because I foolishly gave a part of myself away. Flawed or not, those paintings were me. I left that life behind. For what? This?

Tears fill my eyes. Words of comfort are offered.

My chest heaves, and I moan.

Someone adjusts my IV.

A warmth flows through my veins. Reality starts to fade; my eyes feel heavy. No more pain. When I close them, I see black but then the Medici Falchion appears in sharp focus. I'm choking.

32

onotonous beeping, whirring, and clicking of the machines wake me. My eyes flutter open. Where am I? A nurse approaches, tells me I'm in the hospital in Rome, that I'm in recovery. Already?

Sharp, hot pain emanates from my left hand and wrist, then radiates up my arm to my shoulder and neck. I don't look but sense my wrist is wrapped in bandages. Other patients are around, thin curtains separating our beds.

A man stands beside me—a stranger.

"You're awake," he says. He's smiling, looks kindly at me, introduces himself as my recovery nurse. "You're out of surgery, Anna."

"My hand?" I rasp. I can hardly speak. My throat feels like sandpaper.

"The surgeon is a one of the best."

"But . . . my hand?"

He pats my good shoulder. "Your boyfriend is here. But you need your rest."

"Excuse me?"

He turns to speak to another man. "Stay upbeat," the nurse whispers, but I can still hear him. "The surgery was complicated. There's nerve damage, but the surgeon doesn't think she'll lose the hand. We just don't know whether she'll regain full use."

My heart sinks. I'm too weak to demand more answers.

"We're moving her to ICU shortly. Only one visitor at a time. Keep it to you and the family."

What family?

"How long will she be in the hospital?"

"Three days, maybe longer."

I try to speak, but the words come out as a groan. The pain is winning. I'm fading out of consciousness again.

Sometime later, I wake in intensive care. Paolo, who's sitting beside me, places a hand on my uninjured arm.

"It hurts," I say in a hoarse voice.

"We're going to get you some medication."

The nurse enters and excuses Paolo. When he leaves, she says, "Anna, do you know where you are? Who I am?" She reaches for my right hand. Her touch is gentle and warm.

"Hospital. You're the nurse."

"You had an accident."

My eyes widened. "On the mountain. Why did you tell my friend to leave."

"I'm glad you're so alert. I have something to tell you, Anna. Maybe you already know. We have to do these tests for women before surgery, a precaution. You're pregnant."

I gasp, then moan. "That's impossible." I fumble around and place my right hand on my belly, the IV cords getting tangled with the sheets.

The nurse straightens my covers. "I can give you more pain medication, it won't affect the baby."

Another waking nightmare. "I'm really pregnant? I've only had sex once in the last six months, and that was in June." Sure I was late starting my monthly cycle, but that wasn't all that unusual for me.

"We can detect pregnancy as early as six to eight days after conception."

"My partner . . . I don't have a partner. This party, and . . ." My mind is cloudy, my thoughts chaotic. I force myself to think back to that night with Antonio in Rome. Clearly more than two weeks ago. We were so loaded, and no we didn't use protection. I wasn't supposed to be ovulating, then. Did we even think about being careful? So stupid.

"Is this happy news?" the nurse asks. Her face shows concern.

I struggle for an answer. Only days ago, I told Antonio over lunch that I wasn't sure about having a family. And certainly not with him. "You're really sure I'm pregnant?"

"Completely sure."

I'm too stunned to cry. "Please don't tell anybody."

"Of course not. We respect our patients' privacy. This is your news to share."

"And from now on, don't share any of my medical information with anyone. No one, no matter what I said before." I think I gave permission for Paolo to speak with my medical caregivers, although who knows?

"An injury like this is a terrible way to find out you're pregnant," the nurse says. "Do you want the medication?"

Although the throbbing and sharpness persist, I say, "Not yet."

33

ater—how much later I don't know—I'm moved to a private room. I'm in terrible pain and reeling from the shocking news of the pregnancy. All I can do is groan and stare out the window. Someone taps on the door. Paolo. He's so good to me, hasn't left my side since the accident.

"Raise the bed a little, please," I say in a strained voice.

He presses the button on the remote control. When I grimace, he stops. So kind. I reposition my arm, breathing hard.

"Can I get you anything, Anna?"

"No thanks. Did you see what happened on those steps?"

"No, I'm sorry. I hadn't made the turn yet. But let's not think about that."

"What does Antonio say about it?"

"He . . . he says he saw you trip and knock Raffi down."

"What the fuck? He ran into me, Paolo."

"Whatever happened, it was a tragic accident. No one is at fault except those decrepit steps."

"Except the steps had nothing to do with it."

"I didn't see anything until I heard Raffi scream."

Of course Paolo will cover for his brother, but he doesn't know what happened. He just admitted that.

"Raffaella?"

"Let's talk about her later."

"We're adults. She's dead, isn't she?"

"Yes, it's terrible."

My gut wrenches. "Where's your brother?"

Paolo's expression grows tense.

"His whereabouts can't be a secret, Paolo."

"We don't know. He stayed with Raffaella until her body was taken away. Then he just disappeared. It's the grief. He and Raffaella were engaged."

"What did Antonio tell the police?"

He takes a deep breath. "What I told you. That you tripped, knocked her off balance, and she fell down the stairs."

How convenient an excuse, given my sordid history with pushing people down staircases. I'm so filled with rage that if I could get out of this bed, I would find Antonio and pound him until he told the truth. "If he's blaming me, he's a liar."

Paolo says nothing more.

"Thank you for helping me, Paolo. You've been so kind. Now I just want to go home and sleep in my own bed."

Why is Paolo staying by my side? Does he feel guilty? He warned me at the beach that people around Antonio get hurt. Well, his point has certainly been proved.

"My family will look after you," he says. "*Your* family."

He doesn't mention the pregnancy, which I hope means the medical staff hasn't said anything. This is a no-win situation. If I keep the baby, it means a drastic sea change in my life. And I know that I'll be on my own. I'll never be able to count on Antonio being a father, not sure I want that. Why does his family cover for him? Have they always done this? Even Raffaella covered for his theft of Aurora's diamond ring—she slept with him after warning me away—and then paid the ultimate price. If she had stayed with Luca, she would be alive today.

If I hadn't come into her life, she would be alive today.

34

he nurse wakes me later that morning, dresses my bandages, and then offers me a strong painkiller. I decline. I won't take opioids or anything else that might affect me or—and it feels so strange to say this—the baby.

Paolo, Giana, and Francesca enter my room. I didn't expect to see the women, but I'm happy they've come.

"Did Antonio push you, Anna?" Francesca blurts out.

"Mamma, what's the matter with you?" Giana asks.

"It was a horrible accident, like I told you, Mamma," Paolo says. "Both girls tripped."

"Antonio bumped into me hard and knocked me into Raffaella," I say. "That's what made her fall. She didn't trip. Neither did I."

Francesca looks at Paolo. "You saw this?"

"No, Mother."

Francesca's face colors a deep red. She's so angry that she can't speak. But angry at whom? Her son for causing the accident or me for telling the truth?

"Paolo saved my life," I say. "He wrapped my hand and arm with his shirt. I lost a lot of blood. He carried me the entire way down the mountain to the ambulance, which was dangerous for him."

Francesca looks at him and smiles. The color of anger slowly fades from her face.

"Where is Antonio?" I ask.

"He's gone to the Greek Islands," Giana says. "My brother is an asshole. He runs whenever there's trouble."

"Yes, he has run from trouble," I say. I don't add that he's probably afraid he'll be arrested for homicide.

Someone taps on the door. A cop enters my room. Just in time. In the next minutes, I give him my version—the truth version. Now, the family has heard it for the second time.

"We were having fun," Paolo volunteers. "No one was at fault. The steps were hazardous, uneven."

"I need Antonio's phone number," the cop says.

Paolo looks at Francesca who crosses her arms.

"The phone number," the officer says, this time with an edge in his voice.

Paolo, in halting tones, gives him the number.

Antonio's version is that everyone tripped on the uneven stairs. A horrible accident. More lies. How convenient.

❧

Paolo, Francesca, and Giana are gone. The room is dark. So hot. I wipe the sweat from around my neck, rip the IV line from my right arm, and claw at my covers. I can't get them off. Finally, I'm free.

"Where are you going?" a woman scolds. "Get in bed!"

Who the hell does this person thinks she is?

"Anna, listen to me!" It's my mother's voice.

I frantically shake my head. Can't be. It's just a dream.

Something slices through the air, the sound like a blade ripping through sheet metal. The air splits, and a silver swirling tunnel slowly opens.

I stumble a step toward the door; I have to get out of here. But I can go no farther; I'm now bolted to the floor.

"Anna, stop," Mamma says. Her voice tinkles like crystals delicately tapping together. "Stop, little flower."

I see her inside the tunnel, far away. She looks angelic. She's walking towards me faster and faster but getting no closer.

"Pura mentis et corporis maledictum destruit. Aculeum amplectere," she says.

I don't know what those words mean.

My mother now stands at the tunnel's opening. She regards me with sadness—perhaps with resignation. Far in the distance, I hear another voice—Raffaella, she's angry with me. My mother repeats the Latin words.

I race out of the room, down the hallway, and around the corner.

"Anna, stop!" someone cries. "Code gray! Code gray!"

A man runs toward me, intent on harming me.

"Code Gray!"

"Keep the fuck away from me!"

The man stops.

I take slow steps back, then try to get around him. I trip and crumple to the floor, covering my head, sobbing. "No, no, no. Get off me . . . Oh, God, get this thing off."

Someone plunges a needle into my hip. My eyelids droop. But not before I see Francesca standing at the end of the hall.

The following morning, Francesca is sitting on the couch when I come to, staring at me. She has a long scratch on her cheek.

"What happened to you, Francesca?"

"You had a bad dream. It's my fault, I tried to wake you."

"I did that to you?"

"It's nothing. I forgot about your nightmares. That was such a long time ago."

"You know about them?"

She nods. "Your mother and I shared everything."

Of course she knows. Everyone in the family must know. "How old was I when they started?"

"Maybe four, five. They so upset your mother. She blamed herself."

"Why would she?"

Francesca shrugs. "You know how parents are."

I don't. But will I? "That dream . . . It was so real."

"They often are."

I meet her eyes. "So you were here last night? In my room?"

"Yes, to watch over you."

Is it true? If so, is she pretending to help because she wants to protect Antonio? Is she trying to brand *me* as the violent one?

The words from my dream echo through my mind: *Pura mentis et corporis maledictum destruit. Aculeum amplectere.* Pure mind and body destroy the curse. Embrace the sting. It was a dream, sure—one that told me what I have to do.

35

n unbearable week has passed since the accident. Paolo has gone home to tend to his vineyard. Francesca spends her days sitting with me, stays most nights at Giana's place. I see the look in her eyes—warning that she knows about my nightmares, threatening to expose my secrets if I do anything to compromise her son. No—she's just someone who cares; a family member doing everything possible to help me.

Why do I keep doubting them?

Sunday morning, Francesca arrives early and comes alongside the bed.

"Anything wrong?" she asks without even saying hello.

Is my worry that obvious? "You're going to be the grandmother of the child I'm carrying!" I don't care who knows now. All of the family should know. "Antonio is the father."

Her hand flies to her mouth. It takes her some time to gather herself. "You're going to have the baby, then?"

I'm not opposed to choice, regardless of my early upbringing. Should I have this baby? The logical answer is no. What if I have a dream and harm my baby—my baby, not Antonio's.

Emotionally, I feel like I want to keep the child. I don't want to be alone my entire life.

Francesca reaches out for contact and rests her hand on my leg. "We're family. We stand by one another. That's what we do."

Monday, I can finally go home. The doctor is working on my discharge papers. Meanwhile, the nurse takes me down the hall for an afternoon walk. I can manage alone, but the hospital has its rules, especially after I became a "Code Gray" the other night—a combative patient.

Visitors come and go. Some bring flowers; others arrive empty-handed. Children, some clearly apprehensive about being inside a hospital, shyly follow adults to see loved ones. An elderly male patient emerges from around the corner. He's struggling to walk, clinging to a nurse's arm—his IV stand wobbling, the attached cords tangling. Medical equipment clicks and pings from patients' rooms. Someone speaks over the intercom, calling out a code; a television blares from inside another patient's room several doors down. Nurses congregate at their station and prattle on as if sitting at a coffee shop, but then quiet when a few doctors stroll up or the phone rings.

The hospital staff has arranged for me to have physical therapy in the town of Siena, near where I live, in hopes that I'll regain the sensation in my hand and the use of my fingers. The surgeon says that he pinned the bones together, reattached the nerves, and repaired the vascular injuries, but it'll take time to evaluate the full extent of the damage.

I'm also scheduled to see a shrink. Won't be the first time.

My attending doctor writes a prescription for stronger pain meds, but I won't take them. I'm probably having the baby, and I won't risk its health. I may never paint again. But I can build a happy life with my own family. My mother and I were happy—weren't we?

Giana has agreed to drive me home. I'm glad it's her and not Francesca. She's more level-headed, not so emotional. "Before we leave Rome, I want to see something."

"Where do you want to go?"

"The Borghese."

We drive to the center of Rome where the Villa Borghese, the third largest park in the city, is located and find a parking spot near the Borghese Gallery, which houses sculptures by Bernini and Antonio Canova, and paintings by Tiziano, Titian, Raffaello, and Caravaggio. The museum itself is an extraordinary structure built in the architecture of the Classical Italianate. The landscape is equally beautiful, with its formal gardens, fountains, ponds, and sculptures. It's the most enchanting place.

We get out of the car, walk a short way to the museum, and stop at the entrance, only to be told that the museum is closed on Mondays. I'm disappointed until Giana asks the receptionist to contact one of the curators—a friend and colleague in the arts.

Moments later, the receptionist waves us in. Giana certainly does have connections in the art world. I hope I can take advantage of them someday—if I can ever hold a brush again.

We visit the ornate galleries, housing incredible sculptures: *Apollo and Daphne*, *The Rape of Proserpina*, *Portrait of Pauline Bonaparte as Venus Victrix*; and superb paintings: *David with the Head of Goliath*, *The Deposition*, and more. Giana doesn't try to engage me in conversation, just lets me enjoy myself.

In Titian's *Sacred and Profane Love*, painted in 1514, two women sit opposite one another on the lip of what appears to be a sarcophagus. Between them is a baby, who's reaching for something inside the open tomb. One woman is clothed in a white dress with a single lower sleeve colored orange: she holds a clipping of myrtle. She has an orange slipper on her left foot. The other woman is nude, except for an orange cloth draped over one of her arms and a white sheet across her lap. She holds a vessel, likely an incense burner. The women look alike. Both have porcelain skin and long blondish hair. The clothed woman represents the female as a human, the nude her divine soul. They seem to share a secret.

To me, the painting represents motherhood. Some art historians say the two women represent a contrast between a wise, chaste woman and a foolish one given over to lust.

If that were the case and I was one of them, I would be the whore. But my baby, just as depicted in the painting, is pure.

I'm just tall enough to reach the canvas, so I lean forward across a narrow console table just below the picture and lift my left hand. I hesitate but can't help myself. I touch my fingertips to the baby in the painting, slowly tracing the lines of his face and body. Inexplicably, the sensation is like touching real skin—warm human flesh.

Giana laughs. "You're incorrigible, Anna."

I quickly withdraw my hand. The odd feeling in my fingertips lingers a moment and then vanishes.

"If you did that in my gallery, I'd throw you out," she continues. "Except I really don't give a crap about the classics. Unless one is hanging in my place. Come on, we better go before you get caught and I lose credibility as an art dealer. You forget they have cameras in here."

"I hope I have a kind and generous son who loves me. Truly loves me. I've been so disappointed by the men in my life."

"No, shit. That's exactly why I'm not married." She pauses. "You know, you really don't have to keep this baby."

"I know."

She shrugs. "It's your life."

As we leave the exhibit, the fingers on my left hand begin to tingle and burn. I feel moisture when I rub the tips together. I discreetly look at them—my bandage is bloody at the edges. Strange. But so be it. No way am I going back to that hospital.

36

ate afternoon, Giana brings the car to a stop near the entrance to my house. She walks with me up the stairs to the porch, though I tell her that I'm perfectly capable of going inside by myself, that I've adjusted to the pain, which isn't so awful now. It's not like my entire body is out of commission. Before entering the house, I thank her and send her on her way.

A few moments later, Edoardo appears in the foyer. "I've prepared the house for you, Anna."

"Oh, that's so nice. You heard the terrible news? About Raffaella Bianchi?"

"You've injured your hand. Your nightmares have returned. And you're with child." He stops and looks at me more seriously than he ever has. "You're going to need help now."

"The family talks too much."

He gives a noncommittal nod.

"If you want to help me, give me the key I've been asking you for."

"Why are you not happy that the door is locked? Think of it as protection. A security door."

"I have to escape this hell. The only way to do that is to find the Medici Falchion."

"Why would you want to find something that only gives you consternation? If you had such a thing, what good would it do you? Make you fearful?"

"I won't stop looking for it. And I think we both know the answer lies somewhere beyond that door."

"Anna, you can't think like this. It's not good for you or your baby."

"I'm going to find a locksmith to open the door, even if I have to fly them in from the US. And if they can't do it, I'll get a sledgehammer to break it down."

He sighs.

"Just give it to me. I know you have it, or you know where it is."

He shifts his weight. "I can assure you that I do *not* have what you're looking for. I can't imagine why you keep asking for something I can't give you."

"Because you're the keeper of this place. You know where everything is and how everything works."

"Let's get you well and settled in before you do anything else."

"I'm not giving up, injured or not. My legs work fine, and so do my right hand and arm. Something is telling me I put the necklace in the dungeon. It's nowhere else in this house. Believe me, I've looked."

"You were a child when your mother died. Feared darkness, feared being locked in the dungeon. It's a dark, dirty cave. Not a place to casually explore."

I stand my ground. "What better place is there to hide something? A place of fear, darkness."

"Perhaps. Just know that I have your best interests at heart." Then changing the subject, he says, "Francesca and Aurora brought some food over. Would you care to eat first or rest?"

I'm not hungry, but I should eat, so we go into the kitchen. On the counter, a note from Francesca on behalf of the family welcomes me home and again offers to help however they can. *On behalf of the family*—surely they don't intend to include Antonio in their offers. The refrigerator contains enough food for ten people.

I take a seat at the center island; Edoardo stands on the opposite side. "Sit with me, eat something."

"I couldn't eat a single bite."

I try handing him bruschetta on a toasted bread. "Just try it, I insist."

He doesn't budge from his spot, only shakes his head. Even when I suggest that it's not good for a recovering patient to eat alone, he maintains his stance.

A cool chill slides over my arms and neck.

Not hungry before, I'm famished now and gorge myself. Finishing a second serving isn't enough. When I reach for more, Edoardo says, "You'll make yourself sick if you eat too much."

How parental of him. I set my utensils on my plate.

"Shall I stay with you, Anna?"

"Thanks, but not necessary. I'll sleep better without worrying about you worrying about me." The truth is I have a few matters to attend to that I don't want to do while he's around. He probably suspects this—hence the offer to stay. I walk him out.

"Edoardo, we've never exchanged cell phone numbers."

"I don't have one. I don't like what technology has done to our world."

"You're a true Luddite."

He doesn't respond.

"We'll change that. Who can function without a smart phone these days? And what if I need you?"

"There's a landline in the cottage. The phone number is on a piece of paper I left inside the center drawer of the desk, in the study." He gives a half bow and goes on his way.

Daylight is waning. I hate that he has to walk so far at his age. I suppose the exercise keeps him in shape.

As soon as he's gone, I return to the pantry, not to find more to eat, but to climb a back staircase that the staff used in bygone days. Somehow this attic area has escaped my mind.

My jaw drops when I see what's inside. Unlike the other top story, which was completely barren, this one is a treasure trove, although quite dusty and poorly lit.

The roofline is low-pitched, so I watch my head as I enter the area. The floor creaks as I move through the space, but the surface seems solid enough.

All the old memories: a chest; broken chairs; a tall wardrobe; an old globe; and toys, including, most strikingly, a rocking horse with broken legs that was once painted white but is now yellowed with age. The horse's plastic eyes are missing, and wires dangle from the innards. I pulled those eyes out, curious about the glass orbs. My father laughed, but my mother was livid. That toy was expensive.

Inside drawers and cabinets are old schoolbooks, papers and childish drawings and artwork, and clothing for both adults and kids, wrapped in blue preservative plastic bags. The clothes include old coats, vintage dresses, and a few toddler garments.

Losing myself in nostalgia? Not at all. I'm searching for the Medici Falchion.

Pipes from somewhere in the house squeak as though someone has turned on the water. The filament in the overhead light bulb pops, and it goes dark. Star-like flashes of light, phosphenes, streak across my retina. I wait for my eyes to adjust before I take another step.

As I head down the stairs, a thunderous boom rattles the house. Inside the kitchen, I'm greeted by a rush of air flowing in from the living room.

Then a *bang!* I jump and grip the center island.

Another bang.

What is that? Something upstairs pounds or drops to the floor.

I'm lightheaded and have the sensation that the floor has vanished beneath my feet, that I'm falling. I look down. The floor is there. I'm not dreaming, that I'm sure of. Or am I?

I will not be afraid. This is my home.

The wind picks up. It's oddly cool.

"Sii coraggioso, Anna!" I say aloud, telling myself to be brave. Steeling my nerves, I head inside the living room to face the unknown. No one else is here.

The wind flies through the now-open French doors, which swing unhinged and strike hard against the walls. Curtains flutter and flap like an angry giant clapping its hands. One of the doors slams shut as if someone has shoved it to. Sheets of music fly wildly throughout the entire space, flapping like the wings of a hundred birds. Iridescent lights flicker in every direction. Reflections? From what?

A page of sheet music slaps me in the face.

The raised piano lid bangs down, its crash penetrating my ears like a jackhammer. The strings reverberate, a symphony of haunting, off-key notes. Why was the lid even raised?

My breathing becomes shallow. "Sii coraggioso, Anna!"

I go to the French doors, grasp the handles one by one with my good hand, and pull them shut. The sun has disappeared beyond the horizon. But the sky is glowing deep red, dark purple, and burnt brown. Finally, when the doors are secure, all stills. But not upstairs.

I hurry up and follow the noise to my old bedroom, where I find the balcony doors wide open, also swinging in the wind along with the curtains. When I've secured the room, I start toward the other end of the house.

A rattle comes from a room on my left. Not just any room, but my childhood playroom—a place that turned from joyful to dread. Being in that room makes my skin crawl, as if bugs are biting and eating my flesh. Something happened in this room, but what? I don't want to go in there even now. Only once have I dared since my return home, and even then, it was only to hurriedly search through the room.

"Basta!" *You're no longer a child*, I tell myself. Tamping down my fears, as impossible as that seems, I try to go inside, but there's a weight pressing against the door. I push harder. The wood bows and then springs open. Wind sweeps into the room from one of the casement windows. A rocking horse in pristine condition bobs up and down; a doll holding a metal rattle topples over on a shelf. The toy rattle makes jingling sounds as the air blows against it, rolling it back and forth.

Once the lights are on, it's obvious. A pane of glass in the window is broken out. Part of it hangs in the frame, other pieces are scattered across the floor. It looks as if someone or something singled out this pane and hit it with hammer-like force.

My thoughts shift to the pink crystalline pillar inside the Rome catacombs. Once a place of shared peace, it's now broken. And yet, the priest let me inside. Was this his way of telling me that I could be unbroken? The wind dies down, and an eerie calm descends upon the house. Any other time, the abrupt change would've filled me with fear. Not now.

I secure the window and fit a large book inside the broken pane to keep out the weather. Something new catches my eye—a scuffed traveler's trunk on a lower toy shelf. Not the type of trunk usually found in a child's room, and I don't remember seeing this before. Its top is embossed with the de' Medici family coat of arms—the same image depicted in my mother's journal, the basement tapestry, and the knight's chest plate. Inside it's filled with blank sheets of stationery, calligraphy pens, and ink cartridges. At the bottom there's a metallic object—*the key to the Dungeon Door!*

The key is heavy and tarnished, old, unlike any that I've ever seen. It has unusual cuts and bits, designed to guide it into the lock and navigate the wards, allowing it to turn and open the lock.

I flush with electric excitement. I've found what I need to reclaim my life.

Why is the key in this room? Did my mother hide it here or did I secret it away after her fall? Or maybe *someone* led me here. Did Edoardo break the window to lead me to this room? No matter, I have what I want.

Temptation to try the lock tonight is strong, but exhaustion and pain warn me that I'm in need of rest first. I have the key, and that's comfort enough—for the moment.

37

arly the next morning, Francesca and Aurora show up uninvited, but are a welcome sight. Our conversation centers on the pregnancy, the upcoming doctor checkups, and where the baby's room will be—or whether the baby should sleep in my room. Aurora, beside herself with joy, starts talking about names and gender. As a member of an older generation, what does she think about unwed mothers? She seems to accept that my situation is nothing unusual. A modern woman? Or do they have a hidden agenda—to prevent me from terminating the pregnancy? It's not too late, but they shouldn't worry, I've made my intentions clear.

No one speaks of my injured hand, other than to ask if I'm feeling better. No one utters Raffaella's name. Nor Antonio's.

When they leave, I escort them out to the motor court.

Once Aurora is tucked in the car, Francesca nods me to the side. "May I have a private word?"

"Of course."

She takes a deep breath and wrings her hands; she's jittery. "I spoke with Antonio."

Well, this should be interesting. "Okay."

"He says he's not the father."

I chortle so loudly that Aurora looks out at us from the front passenger's seat—and the window is rolled up tight. "Do you believe him?"

Her hands flutter as she nervously primps her hair.

"They have DNA tests in Italy, too, Francesca," I say, trying not to raise my voice. "Trust me, Antonio is the only possibility. I'm hardly following in the footsteps of the Virgin Mary."

She sighs. "I'm sorry. This isn't something new for Antonio. It happened with Raffaella when she was eighteen. He convinced her to abort. He was happy, too happy, but she wasn't."

I gasp in disgust, now having a clearer understanding of Raffaella's words: *It's complicated.* "Reprehensible behavior from a man who claims he wants six children just to get a woman to fuck him."

Francesca recoils at my profanity, but I wanted to shock her. Because she broached this subject probably hoping that Antonio is right, that I'm lying.

"I've had a hard time forgiving him for condoning the murder of his own flesh and blood," she says. "I couldn't bear the loss of another innocent life."

"I'm not eighteen, I'm close to thirty, and I'll make my own decision." Then my anger overcomes good judgment. "Francesca, you deserve to know the truth about your eldest son, if you don't already. Antonio didn't lose Aurora's anniversary gift. He stole it and gave it to Raffaella. She told me the day before she died, showed it to me. She said she was going to dump it into the sea, to protect him, I guess, but

I encouraged her to go to Fulvio. How convenient that Raffi died the very next day."

Francesca's eyes narrow. "I don't believe this, and certainly not what you're implying about Antonio. He loves his grandparents; he has no reason to steal from them or anyone. Nor does he have any reason to hurt someone, and certainly not Raffaella. He loved her." Before I can respond, she turns away, gets into her car, and speeds down the drive.

Believe what you want, Francesca. You're wrong.

Dark clouds pass overhead. How hopeful I was my first day here. I'm not so sure any more. Has my time in Tuscany simply reached its end? Is my true home really back in the States? If that's so, why does it feel like an invisible, unbreakable cord has tethered me to this place?

A crow flying overhead squawks, lands on the villa's roof, and stares down at me. The rest of his friends soon follow. Curious creatures, my ass. More like annoying as hell.

After giving the lot of them the raspberry, I retreat inside. Regardless of whether I remain in Tuscany by *my* choice, I know this for certain: studying with Tringali isn't happening this fall—or ever. My painting days may never happen again. But that's not my present concern. The Dungeon Door beckons.

Standing in front of the massive door, my eyes land on faded letters etched across the top frame. The words are in Latin: *NON SINE MANIBUS IUSTIS*—not without just hands. There's a deeper meaning in those words, I'm sure of it.

I glance at my hands: one injured, and my dominant hand at that. Am I "just" enough to enter this space? Because there's not a chance that this door was arbitrarily placed in this house. Not a door that once belonged on the entrance to a church, a door that kept out evil. Unless I'm mistaken. Unless this door keeps evil locked away inside.

My past experiences inside there as a child were filled with horror and fright. The memories are fragmented now. The trauma has blocked so much. But it's there. If only the fog would lift.

My fifth birthday! A pool party. After, I wanted to stay up late. Big girls do that. An argument. My father grabbed my arm, shook me. He shoved me in. The heavy door slammed. So dark. Then the loud click of the lock. Panic . . . screams. Evil.

Why would anyone torture a five-year-old child like that? What type of person, man, father, would do such a thing? Someone evil.

No wonder the night terrors have returned. I have to face this. Prove to myself that my family, my mother's family has "just hands."

Something strikes me. It wasn't only my father who did this to me.

My anger turns to rage. Time to get this over with. Already, my hand is injured, my future as an artist in jeopardy.

And so it begins.

38

he skeleton key slides into the Dungeon Door's lock. The room resonates with the sound of metal scraping on metal. When the key is fully secure in the slot, I grip the head and slowly twist the barrel. Metal grinds and clinks and clicks as the cuts bypass the wards—the obstructions that prevent a lock from being *unlocked*—and the internal mechanisms are engaged to move the bolts. On full rotation, there's a definitive clunk that signals the lock has disengaged. With that, I withdraw the key and put it safely inside my pocket.

When I push on the door, it won't budge. Taking a firm stance, I grip the handle with my right hand and use all my weight to thrust and shove. The hinges creak, and the door slowly opens toward the inside of the cave. A distinctive earthy aroma fills the air—not just surface-level crawlspace underneath a house but the true sign of a cave.

A flashlight I found in the kitchen utility room illuminates the immediate area. There are several wrought iron torches mounted on the rock walls. Not electric but the kind meant to hold candles. I don't remember any torches ever being lit. I don't remember any of this. Nor do I recall the extent to which this cave has been excavated.

Oh, there's definitely something more going on down here, more than Edoardo let on.

I shine the light all around and down the tunnel, which must be close to eight feet wide and must extend twenty-plus feet straight down before veering off to the right. The height of the ceiling is close to seven feet. Nothing looks dangerous. But I've never been more than a few feet inside—not as a frightened child. From my past caving excursions, I know that my phone won't work underground. That means no GPS. And if this nice carved-out tunnel dead ends somewhere inside, the danger is getting turned around and lost.

I'm itching to see what's beyond the first twenty feet. Tucking the flashlight under my arm for a moment, I feel my pocket just to reassure myself that the key is safe. Then I step down onto the earthen floor with only one foot, testing the base—solid, of course—and slowly start down the center, counting off roughly twenty-two feet. At the turn, I shine the light down the tunnel to my right. The landscape is almost the same—excavated for ease of passage—but the ceiling drops a bit and the width narrows. Ten feet down, the path turns to the left. I look back; the basement door is open. Plenty of light. I'll go just a bit farther.

Ten feet farther, the tunnel cuts to the left. The light from the basement is no more. More torch mounts line the walls. Do I dare continue on, making this turn? My flashlight provides enough light to illuminate the area. I see no harm in continuing.

Another several paces in, the atmosphere turns moist. I touch the wall—damp, though the floor remains dry. Shining the light in front of me, I walk another five steps, keeping close to the wall, but on my next step, my right foot slides out in front of me. When I reach for the wall to secure myself, I drop the flashlight, which slides to the middle of the path.

"Mio Dio!" I rasp. Fortunately, the light remains lit, so I count my blessings that I haven't been cast into utter darkness. Dust fluffs in front of its beam, which means the middle of the tunnel is dry, even though I'm standing in mud.

A cool wave of air passes over me, and I hear a wispy sort of sound.

My stomach feels springy as I inch my way toward the middle of the tunnel and pick up the flashlight. Having the device in my hand floods me with relief.

I shine the beam in the direction that I was heading. Several feet ahead, there's a sheer drop-off. My heart rate accelerates to super-high, so high that my pulse thumps in my ears. What if I'd slipped and couldn't stop? What if I'd failed to notice the drop-off in time?

Anxiety shoots through my veins. I have to get out of here before sick fear takes control of me. I draw in several breaths, think positive thoughts, and then gingerly move back. Once far enough away, I shine the light in front of me. I can't see the bottom of the ravine from where I'm standing, but I sense that it's deep. The tunnel continues beyond the drop off, maybe another fifteen feet, then veers off to the right and out of sight. Most notably, the area on the other side of the gap is excavated and has torches on the walls. But the gap is about seven feet. Impossible to cross. There must've been a bridge here at one time. I shine the light all around, but there's no sign of any extension bridge.

Foolish but driven to learn more, I inch closer to the ravine and shine the light down. The bottom is visible—fifty feet deep—and at the base is a waterway. I lower my center of gravity and move back again.

Edoardo warned me that it's dangerous down here, but if he genuinely cared about me, he would've told me about this. Did he remove the bridge, know that it was missing? Did he want me to die in here, only abstractly warning me of danger because he knew I would defy him?

The faint babble of moving water is obvious now—the wispy sound. I once saw an underground river and even a waterfall in a cave on a trip to Minnesota. So it's not really surprising to find a tributary in here. The region is mountainous, has waterways.

A low rumbling comes from somewhere behind me. Time to go. I retrace my steps, and just before I round the corner to the straightaway out, hinges creak. When I make turn, I discover that the basement lights are off.

Scrambling to get out, I trip on the edge of a rock just feet from the door. Again, my flashlight falls from my hand, this time bouncing, turning off, and plunging me into absolute darkness. I leave my phone in my pocket, not taking a chance that I'll drop it before I get out of the cave. When I try to step up into the basement, I slam into a hard surface. The door is closed—how? I pull it open and step into a dark basement.

Thank God I'm inside the house. I power up my phone's flashlight and shut the Dungeon Door.

Thunder booms and rattles the house.

A thought intrudes—my ex-boyfriend, Chase, and how I made him believe that I was leaving him in that deep ditch without a way out. Is this some karmic payback?

Footsteps sound on the stairs. Someone is in the house. Coming down or going up? Impossible to tell. Visions of being trapped in the basement seize me. Did this person try to lock me in the dungeon? I grab the sword from the knight-in-armor and brave the stairs, but let out an ear-splitting shriek when I come face to face with this other person—Edoardo.

He holds up his hands. "Sorry to have frightened you, Anna. I lost electricity in the cottage. When that happens, the villa loses it, too."

"You could've called. This is exactly why you need a cell phone." Although inside the cave, there's no reception.

"I knocked but you didn't answer. The house was dark. I assumed the generator needed to be switched on."

Is he telling the truth?

"What are you doing walking around here in the dark?" I ask.

"I've lived here so long I'm quite acquainted with where every nook and cranny is in this house. Not to worry."

I huff out some guttural sound. "In the pitch black . . . ?"

"You were always afraid of the dark, as a child. Another reason to remain out of the basement and what lies beyond that door. Please, for your own safety and my peace of mind." He reaches out. "May I replace the sword?"

I hesitate. Did he mean to shut me in by pulling the door to?

More thunder, rattling.

I gasp, shrouded with uncertainty.

"Old houses are full of character and their own oddities," he says in a reassuring tone. "Floors can get a bit off kilter, windows drafty."

"Well, I'm not a fan."

Maybe the Dungeon Door moved on its own accord—unevenness and old hinges the cause, the vibrations from the thunder. He repeats his request for the sword. I reluctantly hand it over.

"It's not a toy," he says.

I try not to laugh. "And I'm no longer a six-year-old. But speaking of safety, why is the blade so sharp? Did you hone it?"

He tips his head to the side. "I'll be sure to dull the blade. Have you cut yourself?"

"I'm fine."

"I don't mean to lecture, Anna."

I give him a little smile, more like a smirk. "How sweet of you." Does he really mean well—or is he just acting like he does? Torn, I want to believe that he'd never harm me. I don't mention that I was inside the cave, don't accuse him of anything. Accusations only make people clam up.

But the fact is that Edoardo knew I would try to go in. Again, I question whether his not telling me about the ravine was intentional. Did he come over to confirm my death? How would he know that I found the key? Unless he meant for me to find it by leaving a broken window in my old playroom to lure me inside. He knew I'd go in, unable to ignore the sounds coming from inside that room, the wind rattling things about.

I start up the stairs.

"I've already tried flipping the circuit breaker in the utility closet," he says. "The one just off the kitchen. Since the lights didn't come on, I thought I might turn on the backup generator. The controls are down here."

Not rounding the bend in the staircase, I stop and look back. "Where exactly?"

"The cedar closet down the hall."

I shine the flashlight down on him; the beam glints off the sword. A shiver courses throughout my body. What if he means to charge up the stairs and slash me? I reach deep inside and urge calm. If he meant to kill me, I'd already be dead.

"You mean the closet with the figure of my mother? Is that the one you're talking about?"

He nods. "I'll just go switch on the generator on right after I put this up." He raises the sword. "It'll turn off automatically when the main electricity returns."

"Oh, and Edoardo, there's one more thing. Bring that wax figure upstairs and put it in the foyer closet, please. I'm sending it to a museum."

He gives me a dubious look but says, "Of course, my pleasure."

"Well, I'm off to bed," I say, intending to make sure I lock myself in. "Watch your step, and I assume you can see yourself out?"

"And Anna, if I may, you might want to wash the mud off your shoes. I'll clean the floors."

Damn it. He knows.

39

leep ends when someone bangs angrily on the front door. Dragging myself from bed, I pull back the curtains. It's Antonio Massimino. Let him wait. If he wants to leave, fine with me.

I take my time dressing and then go to the door. He's still there.

"Are you stalking me after disappearing for weeks after the accident? Or did you just think you would hang out on my porch and pound the knocker like some lunatic?"

He barges inside. Too shocked at his behavior to tell him to get out, I can only watch as he paces the length of the foyer and stops. We go into the kitchen.

With my phone open and my finger poised to press the emergency button, I head around the island to put space between us. "Why are you here?"

His face is contorted; he stands with arms tightly folded.

"Do I need to be concerned about my safety, Antonio? Because you look as if you might try to push me. Again."

He rakes his hands through his hair. "It was an accident. A horrible, fucked-up accident."

"Did you tell the cops you rammed into me first?"

He doesn't answer. What a liar. We stand staring at each other—a total faceoff.

"Your mother told me what you said. Maybe she wasn't being forthright with me either. Do I need to get the police report to find out what you really told the cops?"

"What does it matter what I told the police? The whole thing was an accident. Which is what the authorities found."

"If it was only an accident, then that makes you an asshole for disappearing. Not to mention the other shit I've learned about you."

"So let me understand you, Anna. You're pregnant, you claim it's mine, and you want to have it?"

"I don't 'claim' anything. I'm pregnant. *You're the father.* Or in our case, the sperm donor. As far as the future goes, it's my body, and it's my decision."

He pounds his fist on the counter. "Bullshit."

"Calm the hell down. You're a guest in *my* house." He paces more. "Now, putting aside my own beliefs, you come from a devout Catholic family, Antonio. You're here. What do you want? Let me guess. You want me to abort this baby."

"You understand perfectly."

"Go fuck yourself."

"You know what you are, Anna?"

"No name calling, Antonio. Especially from a blood-sucking asshole like you."

He grits his jaw and rasps, "Get rid of it."

"You made your choice, I'll make mine."

"*You* pushed Raffi," he blurts out. "That's what I told the police."

"Oh, nice. So you lied to the cops. Let me tell you something you're well aware of, asshole. You pushed me into Raffi. My only question is which one of us you wanted to kill. Or was it both of us? It's not too late for me to talk to the cops and tell them you stole your own grandmother's diamond ring. And that you had a motive for getting rid of both me and Raffi."

He flinches.

"Yeah, Raffi told me what you did, Antonio. If you don't know already. But I think you do, so stop the innocent act."

"The cops won't believe you. Not with your history. Everyone thinks you're a crazy murderer."

"Oh, I think the insurance investigators will believe me even if the cops don't."

His face reddens, and he clenches both fists. Anger and hatred can make an attractive person look downright ugly. "Why would you want to have a baby without a father? I won't have anything to do with the kid."

"Great, we agree, Mr. *I Want Six Kids*. I'll have my lawyer draw up papers to where you relinquish your parental rights to the child. So that you can live happily ever after and go on fucking up other women's lives. I'll email you the papers. It'll be more efficient than another one of your visits. Faster too."

Another hard fist meets the counter. "You're ruining my life."

"Stop being overly dramatic. I thought you would be happy about this." Then it hits me. "I get it now—if you give up parental rights, you'll piss off your mother and grandparents. Big, tough, Antonio afraid of Mamma and Nonna."

"You'll pay for this, Anna."

I walk over and stand no more than a foot from him. "Don't threaten me again, Antonio. Because if you do, you will be facing harassment charges."

He rips at his hair.

"Get out. Don't make me say it again."

His cheeks flush crimson. When he doesn't move, I hold up my phone, which shows the emergency number to summon the cops. All I need to do is touch my finger to the call button.

"You're a fucking bitch," he says before storming out.

"Don't come back, or you will be arrested for trespassing."

When he's down the front steps, he looks over his shoulder and trips over his own feet, but luckily for him, he catches himself before his face smacks the rocks.

I can't stop myself from laughing.

He picks himself up, brushes off his ripped pants, and then gives me the Italian salute: the screw-you or up-yours gesture by bending one arm while using the other hand to slap the inside of his elbow. He climbs onto his motorcycle, fires up the engine, and takes off at full speed, raising his rump and pointing at it as if mooning me or telling me to kiss his ass.

What a jerk. But I don't take his hostility as a joke, or just anger. He was threatening me. Would he truly hurt me? Probably not after what's occurred, I hope.

A short while later, an approaching vehicle crunches along the drive. My first thought is that Antonio has returned, but this isn't the sound of a motorbike. Francesca stands on the stoop, her face wet with tears. We walk to the living room and sit.

"Antonio told me what he said to you, and I told him he's no longer welcome in my home. He's no son of mine." Her body shrinks further into itself. "I'm so ashamed of him. Embarrassed for the family."

"He threatened me, Francesca. Do I need to be worried? Because I told him if he comes back, I'll have him arrested."

"Antonio loses his temper, he shouts, calls names, but he's not violent. I know what you say happened on those stairs, but my son isn't like that, especially with women. He's angry now, yes, but eventually, he'll settle down, and I'm sure he'll be sorry for acting like this."

I'm not so sure.

"Fulvio will see to it that Antonio doesn't trouble you again. I promise. Now that my husband is gone, my father is the only one who can control him. I tried to find Papà before Antonio got here, but he was off in the vineyards."

"Can you do something for me, Anna?"

"Go ahead."

"Please don't mention the ring to my parents. It would destroy them. Giana and I will handle it."

"Okay. I get it. Can you do something for me, Francesca?"

"Anything."

"Make sure Antonio signs and returns the legal papers my lawyer will be sending him."

Francesca's face contorts. "What kind of papers?"

"I'm asking that he give up his parental rights."

"And . . . what about the rest of the family?"

"I don't want to cut off the rest of you. I think it's important for the child to have a loving grandmother and great-grandparents. But if it comes to Antonio refusing to sign or us going to court, that leaves me no choice. I'll sell this place to someone who isn't a family member and move to States. Non-negotiable."

She goes pale. "There's something more I want to say. I'm not sure how you feel about this, but Raffaella's funeral is tomorrow morning."

I think about the pictures she posted of us on social media. How she smiled but didn't look into the camera. No, she was looking at Antonio. There was something more in her expression, subtle but there—apprehension, fear. Did she believe Antonio would harm her? Did she have a premonition of her impending death? How odd that she leaned into the urbex, because her life was robbed from her in such a place.

"Anna?"

"Oh, I'm sorry. The funeral hasn't happened already?"

"The autopsy delayed everything. When someone young dies in an accident, I'm told the authorities always perform one. Especially when the person dies a violent death. The police tend to suspect a crime has been committed. Or they want to rule it out. They concluded her death was an accident. It was an accident, right, Anna?"

40

n this gloomy morning, I drive myself, with some difficulty, to Raffaella's funeral. I shift gears with my right hand while holding the steering wheel with my left arm. I don't know that I belong at the service, but I was present when this tragedy occurred. And Raffaella and I were once such good friends and about to be again.

There's a large turnout. Many of the mourners sniffle. Others wear sunglasses to conceal their tears. The ushers give me hard looks. Do they know who I am? Do people blame me for Raffaella's death because of the lies that Antonio has told them? Or do they recognize me—that notorious girl who committed matricide?

I'll leave right after the service so I don't attract the attention of others.

At the rear of the church, I slide onto a pew. The Peruzzi family sits up front, just behind the Bianchi family and their close relatives. I notice the broad shoulders of Paolo and Antonio, who flank Giana. Antonio has a lot of nerve showing up. He caused this.

I can't get Raffaella's fall out of my mind. The sickening crack of her skull when it split. All that blood. How suddenly her life ended. She was so young with so much unfinished business—just like Mamma.

The casket is open. Even from the rear of the church, I see her dead body. No sign of the broken skull. She looks beautiful, at peace. A slight, pleasant smile on her face. Ironic. She died in such a horrible way. Even in death, we find ways to fool the living. Those who prepare the dead for burial are artists too.

The service ends after an hour. I sit with head bowed as the coffin passes by. Someone scoffs as they approach my row.

A woman stops at the end of my pew—Raffaella's mother. I haven't seen her since I was a child. She looks the same, just more wrinkles. Dark circles surround her red-rimmed eyes, and she points an accusatory finger at me. "Anna Rossi—I want to talk to you after the graveside service."

I gape at her in astonishment as she walks away. There's another emotion descending upon me—guilt. Why do I feel guilty?

Aurora, Fulvio, Francesca, Giana, and Paolo pass by without a word, but Antonio stops and says, "What are you doing here? You have no right."

"I'm here to pay my respects to an old friend. Besides, your mother suggested that I come. The real question is why did you come after you killed Raffi? After the way you treated her."

He takes a menacing half-step forward, but Francesca reappears and gives him a sharp shake of the head. He leaves with his mother, but not before sending me another switchblade glare.

As I make my way into the aisle, Paolo returns and offers me his arm, which I accept. I want to go home, but there's no getting out of this. And I'm curious about what Raffaella's mother has to say. If she accuses me of causing her daughter's death, I'll tell her what really happened. No matter who's present, who can hear me.

The mourners walk in procession to the gravesite, where I stand at Paolo's side. Guests surround us. There's no bolting now, not a chance.

Antonio frowns at me, then focuses on the casket. It's open again, which isn't typical. But Raffaella's mother requested it. No one here would dare deny a grieving mother one last look. Not even the priest. I feel sick.

The priest utters additional prayers, talks to the family. When he finishes, Raffaella's family members step forward and, one by one, lay calla lilies inside the coffin and on her body. Someone behind us starts wailing and sobbing.

Paolo slips his arm through mine. Antonio scowls. The cemetery workers close the casket lid, then lower Raffaella into the ground. The family members each throw a handful of dirt into the grave. The rest of the mourners take more flowers and toss them in. When it's time for the Peruzzi family to pay their last respects, the elders go first, then Francesca, then Giana, and finally Antonio, who snatches a handful of calla lilies from a box, steps forward and, with a huffing sigh, throws the flowers in. At that moment, the ground beside the grave gives way, and he slips, landing face down on top of the casket.

There's a collective gasp, and some of the mourners scream in horror and disbelief. Then stunned silence. Raffaella's mother storms over, grabs a fistful of dirt, hurls it at Antonio, and shouts, "How dare you!"

He rolls over, looking like a naughty child who's just been reprimanded, then gets up and propels himself out of the grave. Fulvio steps forward, grabs Antonio by the sleeve, and slaps his head as if he were an unruly schoolboy growing up in the 1950s.

Raffaella's mother faces me. I fear that I'll be attacked next. But she says, "It's a wonder you're not dead, too. Count your blessings." She turns back to Antonio and says, "I never want to see your face again." She takes Aurora's hand. "My darling daughter called me the day she died. She told me she was going to return the anniversary ring to you as soon as she could. She thought of tossing it into the water to save Antonio, but Anna talked her out of it, convinced her to do the right thing."

"I don't understand," Aurora says.

"The diamond ring for your anniversary. Your grandson took it and gave it to Raffi, proposed. Wouldn't take it back when she refused. She left it in the hotel safe that morning."

Aurora's cheeks go ashen, and I really think this time Fulvio will punch Antonio in the face.

Then, to my shock Raffaella's mother turns to me. "If you think this is the end. It's not. You'll never escape that curse. Raffaella suffered for it. I know you didn't intend it, but you brought evil here when you returned. You shouldn't have painted the necklace on my daughter. God help you."

My legs buckle, and the only reason I don't fall is because Paolo steadies me. There's a buzzing sound in the distance. A black swarm is heading our way, spiraling like a cyclone. My skin crawls.

No one else seems to notice. If I say something, everyone will think I'm crazy.

"Anna?" Paolo asks.

I look at him, desperately struggling to regain my equilibrium.

Raffaella's father ferries his wife away.

Aurora is staring at Antonio with a level of disappointment that I've never seen in another human being, the tension between the two louder than any words could possibly be. She breaks eye contact when Fulvio takes her arm and leads her away. Francesca and Giana follow them, the daughter putting a comforting arm around her mother's shoulders. The rest of the guests quickly disperse, not a word exchanged. The cemetery workers stand with feet on shovels, staring at me, like ghouls ready to claim my body next.

"I have to get out of here," I say to Paolo as I look at the approaching swarm.

He follows my line of sight, confused.

I hurry to my car.

"Anna, wait!"

As soon as I get inside, the black swarm flies toward me.

The insects attack the car and bang against the windows. I start the engine and race to get out of the parking lot, leaving the swarm behind.

I stop at the exit and look back. The bugs have flown to Raffaella's grave, where they circle. The undertakers are gone, nowhere to be seen. How can that be?

Only Paolo stands, gaping at me, untouched by those devil bugs that now circle him.

Then they disappear into thin air.

41

ack in my studio later that day, I turn on a fan and open the windows. Screens are now in place, thanks to Edoardo. He hasn't been around much lately, not since our meeting in the basement.

A morbid but irresistible urge compels me on to paint a portrait of Raffaella in death. After mixing acrylics and trying to paint with my right hand, it's no use. The brush and paint seem to have minds of their own. I walk up to the tower, which is open on four sides. Rolling hills, majestic mountains speckle the background. Vineyards, villages, fields of sunflowers stretch for miles. No matter how much I try, I can't get Raffaella out of my mind. Can't get her mother's warning out of my mind.

My phone chirps with a reminder. Damn—I'm late for my first OB appointment; I have physical therapy, as well, but later today. With the funeral, I should've rescheduled everything, but I completely forgot. If I hurry, I can still make it.

By the time I go to bed that night, exhaustion has consumed me. The OB appointment went well; the PT was painful and grueling. But it was good to get out of the house and actually see people who seem to care, who seem to lead normal lives—if there is such a thing as a normal life.

Downstairs, something crashes to the floor. I go to the balcony overlook and peer into the living room. The French doors are open again, and crows are flying inside.

Not waiting a minute more, I traverse the front staircase, making my way through the foyer and into the living room. There, I wave my arms and shout for the birds to get out.

The crows caw. They're laughing at me.

Snatching a pillow from a couch, I swing and swat at them to leave. Eventually, they fly outside. I secure the doors and pick up a lamp that has fallen off a table—the loud crash.

Metal clanks against the stairs leading down to the basement. Someone or something is coming up. Sounds like that knight in armor. Can't be. But the movement of armor is distinct, certain. I have to close off the basement, quick, now.

As soon as I reach the hallway, a woman says, "Annnaaaa." The word is elongated, its sound ghostly, haunting.

It's Raffaella.

Oh, Dio! She blames me.

I'm hyperventilating, can't stop, and soon fold down to the floor and place my arm over my head. *Go away!*

Another female voice calls to me, not Raffaella, not my mother. "It's time."

"Time for what?" I shriek. "Who are you?"

No answer.

I'm not safe. I rise up, unsure where to go. There's no place to hide in this house. I race out to the veranda and into the pitch-dark night, shouting for the person speaking to me to go away. I turn full circle. The voice follows me. I hurry down to the pool and squat down behind a chaise lounge.

"Annnaaaa, it's me."

My breathing is ragged now. Who?

"Anna, it's cold out here."

"No, no, no, no, no," I say, not recognizing my own voice. "I can't feel my hand. Where's my hand?"

"Come down here, it'll be fun," the woman says.

"I can't, no, I don't want to." I tell myself I'm dreaming, but it's so real.

Someone blows in my face.

"No!" I scream.

"I promise, everything is just fine," she says.

"You always say that, you always do. You're a liar. It never is." I claw at my neck. "Get it off me."

"Only you can take it off."

My nightgown gets tangled in my limbs. The bandages on my left hand are unraveling, flowing into my gown. Except, the doctor removed the bandages days ago.

No wait, this isn't my nightgown. I'm wearing the Medici wedding dress! The bottom is ripped to shreds, and so are the arms.

"Mother!" I scream.

"I'll get you."

As I run, the pavement rips at my feet. I'm falling, falling, sinking under the water.

Then clarity. I'm in the deep end of the pool. I try to swim to the side and climb out, but I'm sinking, fading out of consciousness. Then I feel it. The Medici Falchion is around my neck, choking me.

Someone grabs me from behind. They mean to drown me. I fight back, kicking and punching. With each second, the necklace gets tighter. The wedding gown tangles more. I struggle until I'm so tired that I give up. My body rises to the surface. Something, someone drags me to the shallow end.

I gasp for breath as I'm lifted out of the pool and set on a chaise lounge. My body shivers violently. Oddly enough, I don't feel cold.

"Anna, wake up."

I lift my head. Edoardo.

"Please, answer me!" he says, panic engraved across his face.

I try to speak but only cough.

"Nod your head if you're awake and can recognize me."

I do as he asks.

"Is your hand all right?"

"What are you doing out here?" I manage to force out.

"I saw the lights on in the house. It's late."

He's right. Every light in the house must be on. I must've done that. My teeth chatter wildly. I'm now cold. So very cold.

"Come on, let's get inside."

"Oh, God. The baby."

"I'm sure the baby is quite well. Tucked inside Mamma, nice and warm. But we need to get *you* tucked inside too." He slowly walks me upstairs to my room.

"Shall I call someone to come help you?" he asks after my mind clears a bit.

"No, I can manage."

"I'll wait just outside the door until you tell me that you're settled."

Once the wedding dress is off, I find dry towels and wrap one around my body and another around my head. Then I dress in a warm nightgown. There's no point in arguing with Edoardo when he tells me that he'll remain downstairs until the morning to make sure that I rest through the night. The clock reads just after three a.m. I slip underneath my bedcovers.

That was a nightmare, right?

I break down in tears, fighting back my sobs so Edoardo won't hear me.

42

hen I wake the following morning, sharp pains spike from my clavicle up to my jawline. I touch my skin. The burning makes me groan. Struggling out of the bed, I labor over to the mirror. There's broken skin on the sides of my neck and weird abrasions that are already beginning to scab over. The dream—blurred fragments come to me. I thought I had the necklace on.

I shower, disinfect the wounds, and head downstairs to be greeted by Edoardo, who's prepared breakfast—my favorite, pancakes with fresh bananas and cinnamon. Oh, right. He said he would stay and watch over me.

He saved my life last night, and that should speak mountains. And yet my doubts about him linger. Have I truly lost my ability to trust anyone? Probably happened a long time ago.

"The scratches on my neck, Edoardo. How?"

"You had another nightmare. You ran into a bramble bush."

Bramble bush? No, I don't think so. "I haven't had any nightmares like this since I became a teenager. Now they're back."

"About your future plans, if I may say." He pauses and waits for my permission.

"Go on."

"If you intend to stay on in this house, it's not safe for you to be here alone. You could've died twice in this house already. In the cave earlier and then again in the middle of the night when you went racing around during your dream."

I suddenly feel hot, sweaty. "Why didn't you warn me about that ravine?"

"I warned you that the basement is dangerous, not to go in there. I foolishly thought you would trust me and heed my words. The point is your sleepwalking and nightmares are dangerous. To you and to others."

I wince. Everything he says makes sense. "Did you break the window in my old playroom? Plant the Dungeon Door key in the room?"

"No. Neither. You need to make immediate plans, Anna."

"I don't want to talk about this now."

"I understand this is upsetting for you, that you feel as though I'm lecturing you, but I fear that I'm the only one looking out for you. You've also got the baby to think about. If you get hurt, there's a chance the baby will, too."

"I would never hurt my baby."

"I don't think Francesca Massimino would agree."

This is a surprise. Francesca has been nothing but supportive. Or was.

"You had an episode at the hospital. You attacked Francesca in the middle of the night and scratched her face. And now, you've harmed yourself."

I look into his eyes, which convey a deeper worry, one that hasn't surfaced before. "What are you saying, Edoardo?"

"There's no guarantee that you'll win a lawsuit over custody of the child. Francesca and her parents will maintain that you're unstable. They'll bring up not only your current behavior, but also the events surrounding your mother's death, and the emotional trauma you suffered after she died. Then there's Raffaella. No matter that her death wasn't your fault. That's not how the Massiminos will portray it. Haven't. You could lose everything. Including your freedom, if they convince a court to hospitalize you. Francesca's family has influence."

"You think they'll really try to take my baby away? Slander me to do it?"

"Would it be slander or the truth, Anna? The walking nightmares. The violence."

I have no reply to this.

"You must tread lightly. That family is tight-knit. Often avaricious and quite ruthless, no matter how friendly they seem on the surface. What do you really know about Fulvio?"

"That he's a kindly old man who runs a winery."

"Fulvio Peruzzi eased out his now-deceased older brother to take over his family's wine label. And he didn't do it ethically. You're carrying Francesca's first grandchild. That's important to her and her parents. So, yes, they would try, especially if they think you're defying their wishes. Money certainly won't stand in their way. They're able to pay quite a penny on legal fees without feeling any pain."

"I'll go to America. Before the baby's born."

"If they go into court on an emergency plea and say you're mentally incompetent, you won't have the luxury of time on your side. I told you; they have friends in the police and the courts. You might not be able to leave."

I narrow my eyes. Who do these people think they are?

"As I said," he continues, "you might even be confined to a hospital for so-called psychological reasons."

I slowly shake my head.

"Anna, you shouldn't have threatened Francesca with your leaving the country. You revealed your hand."

My stomach drops.

"For your own good, I'm being blunt with you—there's no telling what the authorities will do. Do you understand?"

A stab of anxiety hits. "Wait. How do you know about that? My attacking Francesca? My possibly going back to the States?"

"Employees' ears are never far from their bosses' lips. The powerful don't hesitate to speak secrets in earshot of those whom they consider to be beneath them."

I try not to let my anxiety over this news turn into panic. I get up from my chair. "I have to apologize to her now."

"Not now. They can't see the scratches on your neck."

I sit again. "I can call."

"Continue with your therapist and hire a nurse, if only to make a record that you will make a fit mother. And don't do anything rash."

I think for some long moments. What he says makes sense. A man like Fulvio Peruzzi doesn't achieve what he's accomplished by being a friendly old man. And his grandson Antonio is hardly a model of integrity.

Is Edoardo helping me because he's my great-uncle and genuinely cares? I'm still perplexed about the caves. "Have you ever looked at my artwork?"

From his momentary glance down, I know that he has. Of course—he put the screens in the windows.

"Now that my hand is injured and I'm not sure I'll be able to paint again, I don't want to forget that I once had talent. At least a little bit. There's a painting that I especially want to hang. The one with the woman and the two older men. I drove past those guys sitting on the porch drinking wine the day I arrived. Made me angry, really, until I thought of the woman getting after them with the broom."

"Humorous. Emotionally moving, in an odd way. You should know that not all elderly Italian men treat women that way." He pauses and gives me a grandfatherly smile, a break in his formal demeanor. "You've always been supremely talented, even as a child. Blessed with a vivid, artistic imagination. You're young, and your career is not over. I would be happy to have the painting framed for you. Where would you like it hung?"

"In the living room. I think I'll call it *The Triumphant Brush*. Those men gave her the brush off, but she'll triumph by outliving them. Probably the last painting I'll finish."

"You learned to paint with your left hand as a child. You'll learn to use your right hand as an adult. It doesn't matter if you never paint the same way again. You will create new art, even make history. Your mother always knew that, and so do I."

I smile. "You really are a great friend. Also, delusional. No offense. And look who's talking?"

"Just promise me, Anna, that you won't give up on your art."

I shrug agreeably. Whether he's pacifying me or not, I'm glad he's in my corner.

"You always seem to be here when I need you most."

"I'm never far, and it's my job to keep watch, to monitor things."

Maybe it doesn't matter if he always knows when to show up. Or maybe I'm just lucky. "There's something I would like to ask you. It's personal."

He seems to know what it is. "If you don't mind, Anna, could we take this conversation up at a later time? I'm afraid I'm exhausted after not sleeping a wink last night. Not that I sleep a great deal these days anyway."

"Oh, I'm so sorry. Of course. I never meant for you to stay awake the entire night."

"Sometimes these things can't be helped. Call it the necessary consequences of age." He promises to return this evening, but I tell him not to worry.

When he's gone, I go to the foyer coat closet. Inside is the figure of my mother in her wedding dress. A dress that's dry and in pristine condition. Which proves that I was only dreaming.

43

patchwork of autumn colors dab the October land-scape. The grapevines are turning vivid shades of red and orange and gold. Before long, truffle hunters—the tartufai—will begin scouring the forests, looking for hazel and poplar and beech trees, hoping to find the highly valued white truffles. The changing season reminds me that my life is changing as well. I've still got to furnish a baby's room. But isn't decorating too soon considered bad luck? Or just practical, which is my way of thinking. The baby-furniture shop in Sienna has rows of possibilities. It's easy to get absorbed in all the choices, so hard to decide. Francesca Massimino appears at my side.

"Hi there," I say, surprised that she's appeared.

"No, I am not stalking you, Anna," she replies, as if reading my thoughts. "I wanted to check out what they're doing these days for baby cribs. Every single one has poor construction, as my father would point out. Don't worry, we have plenty from earlier generations you can choose from. Excellent construction. And much prettier."

This is *my* baby. *I'll* pick out my own furniture. But heeding Edoardo's advice not to antagonize her, I gush, "That's so nice of you, Francesca," hoping that I'm not overdoing it. "But I'm redecorating the entire house, because it's a bit like an old museum, as you know. Since I'm staying in Tuscany, I want to freshen things up and go a bit more contemporary—especially with the baby's room."

"I understand," she says, although I can see from the narrowing of her eyes that she's wounded. "I'm happy to help you in any way possible. Aurora is making you a few things too."

"That's so nice. I haven't made any decisions yet, so I would love to see your furniture," I say to ease the tension, and this pleases her.

"When do you see the OB? Aurora and I would really enjoy taking you to the appointments."

"Where is Antonio these days?"

"Rome with his sister, I believe."

"Please get him to sign those legal papers."

"And the doctor appointments?"

I smile. "I'll check my calendar."

"Mother, it's time to go," Paolo says, joining us. "Anna, so nice to see you. You're out baby shopping already? If you like, you can have my old stuff. Completely retro. I don't know why my mother keeps it."

"Anna wants to go contemporary," Francesca says.

"Let's go, Mother. You need to rest." He gives me a surreptitious wink, points to his chest, and mouths the word "stress."

"Are you feeling sick, Francesca?" I ask, and I'm genuinely concerned. While I can't figure her out, her motives might be pure. *Might be.*

"It's nothing. Change of life issues."

When she turns to go, I signal to Paolo that I'll call him.

After browsing a bit more and not buying anything, I return home and pack a few items for an outing. I ring Paolo, but he doesn't answer, so I leave a message asking him to join me for a picnic and head out alone toward the front olive groves east of the property. Those damn crows follow me and perch nearby. I find a secluded spot among the trees, spread out my blanket, and set down my book, some cheese, bread, olives, and water.

I lie back and take it all in—the cobalt sky and a few cotton-ball clouds peeking through the branches; the hum of the bees, the song of the birds, and the rustle of leaves in the gentle breeze. Olive-tree warblers flit through the grove, singing their happy little ditties. A bird of prey cries in the distance. Then a Montagu's harrier soars past, drifting with air currents that take him not much higher than the tree line. A collared flycatcher, its feathers also a stark contrast in black and white, alights on the branch above me and begins singing his slow, strained whistles. Another bird returns his song. I close my eyes, listening.

Something scurries over my legs. A field mouse?

I open my eyes to find dark clouds moving in fast. How long was I asleep? A loud crack of thunder tells me too long. A gust of wind sweeps through the trees. I quickly pack up. As soon as I stand, the rain pelts down like a fire hydrant on full blast and soaks me from head to toe. I hurry along. The wind intensifies, and the rain slaps my face hard, which feels like a deluge of tiny shards of glass. I shield my forehead with a hand, but it isn't enough, so I keep my head down.

I careen into the gnarly trunk of an olive tree.

More cracks of thunder. A flash of lightning strikes so close that I feel its heat. Somewhere above comes tearing and cracking, and the sound of leaves and branches and twigs rustling. I look up against the hard smacking rain. Directly above me, a large branch is about to split in two. I drop everything, cover my head, and run. The enormous limb falls to the ground, landing with a loud thud and splashing water on me before I can get away.

"Anna," someone calls out—a man's voice.

"Over here!" I cry out.

A beam of light swings in my direction. A flashlight? "Stay where you are." It's Paolo. After some long moments, he finds me.

"I'm happy to see you, Paolo. I'm lost on my own property, believe it or not."

He takes my hand, and we hurry to the villa, which is about a quarter of a mile away. Inside the foyer, water pours off of us.

"What in the world were you doing out there in weather like this?"

"It wasn't like that when I started out. That storm just came out of nowhere. I left you a message about a picnic, but I didn't think you'd make it."

His cheeks flush light pink. "When I realized the time, I came to apologize, and to check in on you. I just worry about you alone in this big old house."

Electrical sounds resonate throughout the house, then appliances click off, and the lights go out.

I groan. "This makes twice in a week. There's a generator downstairs in the basement in a storage closet, but I'm not exactly sure where. I thought it was supposed to turn on when the lights went out. It's never worked."

"Do you have candles?"

I tell him there are decorative candles and matches in the bathroom of my mother's old bedroom. He powers up his phone's flashlight, and I follow him upstairs and grab a few towels while he lights candles.

"You can't stay in those wet clothes, dude, or you'll catch your death. But I'm not so sure you'd look all that great in a dress either. How do you feel about flannel pajamas?"

He laughs. "I'm always ready for a slumber party."

"I'm not opposed."

We get dressed and go down to the living room. I'm surprised that Edoardo hasn't made another appearance.

Paolo slicks his damp hair back with his fingers; it's short and well-groomed, not long and wild like Antonio's. He grins, then asks, "How are you? After what happened at the funeral, and all that nonsense with Antonio." He shakes his head. "And your hand? Is it healing? And the pregnancy? Are you feeling all right?"

"That's a lot of questions."

"Sorry, I'm just concerned."

I smile, so happy to have a friend in him. "I'm trying really hard to put aside everything that's happened between your brother and me. He's not entirely to blame that I'm pregnant. It's my doing as well. But I can't lie, it's been crazy. Has Antonio always been such a hotheaded?"

Paolo chuckles and rolls his eyes. Of course he has. We sit in silence. There's something he wants to say. But he's his usual reticent self.

"Just say it, Paolo."

"Antonio won't sign the papers giving up parental rights because he's afraid once you have what you want, you'll go to the police and tell them that he pushed you and Raffaella. That'll only reopen the investigation; it'll make something out of nothing. Nobody wants that. He's gone to Rome to live with Giana. Fulvio won't let him come home. But he's family, so it'll probably blow over in time. It always does. Even something this bad. Even after the theft of my grandmother's diamond ring." He laughs bitterly. "Charming Antonio is always forgiven. And . . ."

Paolo is still holding back. I stare at him.

"I'll just say it. If you deny my mother and grandparents access to the baby because of Antonio, it won't sit well with them."

"You mean they'll take me to court."

He slowly nods. "Yes, that . . . And . . ."

"You don't have to say more."

"You have the advantage, Anna. Use it. What's the point in fighting? None of us are responsible for my brother's behavior. Granted, what he did to you, to everyone, was terrible. Off the charts even for him. I didn't see what happened with Raffaella, but I heard everything. You got hurt. It'll come down to your word against Antonio's if you take it there."

I don't respond.

"The family isn't mad at you for what happened, Anna. That's on Antonio. But lines shift when things get messy."

Edoardo was so right about that family.

"Can we have peace?" he asks. "It would mean a lot to me. I don't want to lose you . . . your friendship. Let my family be involved in raising the child. They just want to help you, to share in the joy. Giana has no children, and look at Antonio's behavior, and I may never find . . . Or you could leave, sell everything, and go to New York . . . before it gets messy. But I think my family would try to stop you."

Edoardo had clearly learned what might happen. Twice now I've been warned.

I wonder if Paolo came on his own or whether Fulvio sent him. And is this reference that his family will try to stop me from leaving a veiled threat or a sincere warning? It doesn't matter, they're extending the olive branch, and I won't automatically withdraw my hand.

But do I trust them? Not until those papers are signed.

I can use the situation to my advantage. I hope. "I won't run away. And tell them they can come with me to the OB appointment. I'm just at four months, so it's time for a baby-scan. I'm sure that will make the women happy."

He smiles so broadly that I want to hug him, although I also don't want to give him the wrong idea. I realize that he's smitten with me, that he wants to be more than friends.

44

uesday, I head to Siena for my obstetrics appointment. It's so good to get out, to drive along the country roads and take in the view, especially the expansive fields of sunflowers. When I arrive at the medical complex, I'm beside myself with excitement, but I'm also anxious about the baby's health—*and* about seeing the family.

Inside the waiting room, to my surprise, I find that almost the entire family has shown up: Fulvio, Aurora, Francesca, Giana, and Paolo. Not Antonio, fortunately—not that I expected him. And a good thing, because I would've ordered them out. Everyone hugs me and smiles. The whole scene feels like a happily-ever-after ending.

But aren't fairy tales only horror stories dressed up to look pretty?

A nurse asks me to come inside the examining room by myself first. After the initial questions, a physical exam, and some preliminary tests, she calls for everyone else. There's barely enough space for the family to squeeze in.

The technician runs the wand over my bare abdomen. Nothing. Nothing. More nothing.

"Is there something wrong with the baby?" I ask, my breathing accelerating, and the churning butterflies moving from my abdomen to my chest.

The technician lifts a palm, ordering me to keep quiet. My God, why?

"Tell me what's going on," I demand, hearing my voice crack.

Finally, the technician locates the tiny fetus and gives a thumbs up. The heartbeat is strong and clear and steady.

"Listen to that," Fulvio says. "That's a little salsiccia." He meets my eyes and grins. "A bambino!" He puts his hand to his jaw. "Oh, I spoiled it."

I smile. "No worries. All I want is a healthy child, girl or boy."

Paolo nudges his grandfather. "What makes you think it's a boy, Nonno?"

Fulvio taps the instrument measuring the rate of the heartbeat—126. "If it's a low number, it's a boy. But that's because boys are calm and steady. Like me. Girls are always too excitable and emotional." He winks at the technician. "What says the expert?"

"No matter what the science, I'm always surprised," the man says.

"How did you know this?" Paolo asks his grandfather.

Fulvio makes a show of looking offended. "I can read, I can even search the Google. You think all I do is dig in the dirt day and night?"

There's laughter.

Everyone's face is glowing. Maybe this one-big-happy-family thing can really work.

The technician rolls the wand over my stomach again. He frowns slightly and looks at me. "I'm going to ask the doctor to come in."

"Is there a problem?" I ask, and the elders repeat the question.

"I'll be right back," the technician says.

Not butterflies this time but rather swooping swallows, gliding and flapping throughout all of my innards.

We wait in tense silence. The doctor and the technician file into the room; the doctor does a double take when she sees so many of us. She takes the wand, views the screen, and rolls the device across my belly. After several rounds, she says, "Anna, you're carrying twins."

"Mamma mia!" echoes through the room.

My jaw drops in a combination of surprise and joy. "Are you sure? You didn't mention anything during my last visit."

"It's not always definitive early on. But now, your hCG levels are sky-high, and the ultrasound confirms it," the doctor says.

I'm so overwhelmed that all I can do is laugh and giggle nonstop for the next minute, from happiness or mere shock I'm not sure which. The family joins in the laughter and even applauds.

"You still think the babies are due in March?" I ask.

"Officially March, but twins usually come a bit earlier."

Then the laughter stops. An invisible gloom descends—all coming from my extended family. Francesca and Aurora look worried.

"You can't possibly manage two infants," Francesca says. "You'll need our help. It's better if the babies come home to live with us."

The air catches in my throat, and I force myself not to choke. My happiness, which turned to momentary shock, now transforms into indignation. "Thank you, but no way can I just pick up and leave my house. I wouldn't be comfortable." That's putting it mildly.

Francesca crosses her arms and steps closer to her parents. "One baby is challenging enough. You need mine and Mamma's help. At least in the beginning." She pauses, then seems to add as an afterthought, "Of course, you'll come live with us too."

So much for Francesca moving in with me to help at *my* place. How foolish of her to suggest her new plan. How overreaching. As if I would consider allowing her to take possession of my babies and let me hang around as some sidekick. Not in a million years would I move in with them.

"I'll manage on my own," I say. "I'm physically capable, and if I do need help, I won't hesitate to call on you. I'll hire a full-time nanny so I don't take advantage of you." I'm doing my best to keep my cool, but I'm sure my face reveals my shock and upset. I don't want a war with these people, but if it comes to that, they'll get a war.

Francesca frowns.

"You'll have a nice cat to skin," the doctor says—an Italian saying that means I have a challenging task ahead. "Take what help you can get," she continues, winking at me. Did the Peruzzis get to her in advance? They're local; I'm the American interloper.

I look over at Fulvio and Aurora, who say nothing. The situation is clear: the Peruzzis want to take the babies from me. How could I have fallen for Paolo's sweet talk?

ays pass, and Antonio hasn't signed off on the papers relinquishing his paternal rights to the twins. I can't stay in Italy, can't live a life where I always doubt my relatives—and where I live in fear of their capacity for violence, or at least Antonio's savage nature. I'm worried, though. The real estate agent hasn't even listed the property.

Have the Peruzzis somehow gotten to her?

My obsession with the Medici Falchion continues to mount. Thankfully, the nightmares have stopped. Is it hormonal?

My phone rings—Paolo.

"Just the friendly voice I needed to hear," I say. "I wanted to talk to you about something. A favor."

"Good timing then. Would you like to go with me to the fall festival in Greve today. Do you know it? It's a small town built around Piazza Matteotti. You don't have to drink wine; there's also food and activities and nice artisan shops."

"How lovely. Yes, I accept." I enjoy his company, true. But selfishly, I hope to get more intel on what his mother and grandparents are thinking.

A half-hour later, we're on our way to Greve. He tells me about the families who produce wine in the region and amuses me with gossip about the vintners. He revels in his own plans to produce a Super Tuscan with the new grapes he's growing on my land, a style first produced by Sassicaia.

When I ask, he explains that the Marchese Marito Incisa della Rochetta was the first to begin venturing beyond the protocols that required winemakers in the area to produce only an official Chianti. With the help of enologist Giacomo Tachis, the Marchese planted Bordeaux varietals at the estate in Bolgheri and blended Cabernet Sauvignon and Cabernet Franc, which were then aged in oak. For two decades, the new wine was only consumed on the property. Once the drink began to find its way into the outside world, it was labeled "table wine," but eventually, because of its high quality, earned the label Super Tuscan. The development was coined the "wine Renaissance" of Italy.

"You're really passionate about making your new wine. What about Antonio? Will he continue to be involved? I don't want to make unpleasant conversation, but you should know that I won't renew the lease if his name is on it. Only in your name."

"That's a problem."

"I thought Fulvio kicked him out. Grandson or not, does the family want to do business with a person who ripped them off and committed insurance fraud?"

Paolo exhales hard. "It's complicated. My grandfather wants the men in the family to run the business as we have for generations, and Antonio is the oldest, so . . ." He shrugs helplessly.

"Antonio must've shed more of his fake tears."

"It seems that my prodigal brother will return to the fold."

"You're okay with that, Paolo? You do the work. You're the winemaker."

He tightens his jaw. "I'm stuck with him because he's my brother, even though I can't trust him. What he did to his own grandparents was completely nauseating. We almost got into a physical fight when I told him he should get the hell out of Tuscany, move to Rome, and work for Giana full-time."

How I wish he had.

"That's what he's good at, conning rich and thick-headed art buyers. But as I said, it's not my call." He exhales hard. "Why is our family so messed up?"

"Let's not talk about this. It's unpleasant. Just promise me that you and I will always stay friends."

He squeezes my shoulder. "Always."

We enjoy the festival and head toward an outdoor play about to start. From left field, a familiar voice calls out, "Fratello!"

A shiver creeps up my spine.

Antonio walks up to us, carrying a glass of wine. The brothers embrace, odd given that Paolo just claimed he wished Antonio would go away.

"I wasn't expecting to see you here," Paolo says.

"I got in from Rome today," Antonio replies, slurring his words. "Home to work our vineyards. I wouldn't abandon you just before the harvest."

"Fulvio knows about this?" Paolo asks.

"Who cares what the old man knows?" Antonio looks in my direction and scowls. "You two seem awfully chummy. Don't go chasing my leftover breadcrumbs, Paolo. You can do better than that bitch."

"You're drunk, Antonio."

"And you're obsessed with some crazy person who murdered her own mother and pushed Raffaella down the stairs. Anna's murder weapon of choice."

Paolo shoves Antonio, whose wine spills.

A wave of fear and disgust overtakes me. "Let's go, Paolo."

Antonio chortles and throws his wine glass toward a metal receptacle that's a little too close to me. He misses, and the glass falls to the ground, wine splattering on the sidewalk. Thankfully, the thing is made of plastic.

Others frown and move quickly away.

Antonio advances on his brother, who sidesteps and shoves him back. The older brother stumbles.

Paolo is about to pounce on the prone, drunk Antonio, and part of me wants it to happen, but I shout, "Stop it."

Paolo hesitates, then takes my arm and leads me away.

Antonio struggles to his feet, shouts, "You bitch, Anna!" and makes as if he's going to follow us.

A cop appears. Paolo pulls me around the corner and down a cobblestone road, where we dash into a curio shop. I decide that now isn't the time to ask for a favor.

"What an idiot," Paolo says. "He's really losing it."

I couldn't agree more.

After Paolo and I leave the festival, we don't discuss the encounter with Antonio. He says he needs to make a quick stop at the vineyards and parks at their house. He leads me to the utility building where Fulvio and Aurora are standing beside a large wine cask that's cut in half.

"Finally," Fulvio says. "I thought you might've fallen into someone else's barrel." He pats the cask. "Come look, Anna."

Paolo and I peek inside. The bottom third is filled with grapes.

Fulvio grins. "You know what they say—never keep a grape waiting. It's time to christen the harvest with our Anna's feet."

"My Nonno wants to make the feet wine," Paolo says. "Let's get in."

We kick off our shoes. Paolo jumps in while I knot the hem of my dress on both sides so it won't get wet. With a boost from Fulvio, I make it in. We squish the fruit between our toes. It tickles so much that I start giggling.

The elders begin clapping and singing a traditional harvest song.

Paolo grasps my hands, and we dance around, sloshing, slipping, and practically falling until we do. I'm making a fool of myself, but I don't care. This is the most fun I've had in a long time.

This family is doing everything possible to charm me into staying in Italy *and* bringing my twins to live at their house. Of course, I don't breathe a word of my plans to leave.

The sound of an approaching motorcycle sours the mood.

Paolo, soaked in purplish-red juice, jumps out and strips his shirt off, lifting me out just as his older brother parks his bike.

"What the hell is this?" Antonio asks.

"The first harvest—The Feet of Our Anna," Fulvio says.

Paolo flicks his hands, and grape juice flings onto his brother.

Antonio barks, "This woman is not our friend. She's reneged on the deal to sell us the property. You forget, we need that land to grow *our* grapes, to keep *our* vineyard going." He glares at Paolo. "Embarrassing, taking my sloppy seconds."

"Where's your famous charm when you need it?" Paolo asks.

"It's my place to say whose feet touch my grapes," Antonio says, then pushes his brother. Paolo shoves him back.

"We have a guest, Antonio," their grandfather says sternly. "And you have obviously been drinking—and riding that motorcycle intoxicated. Stupido! Get inside until you can behave like a civilized human being."

When the shoving continues, Fulvio walks over and wallops Antonio on the backside with a rope. I look away. At one time, I might've laughed at the incongruity, but nothing involving Antonio and this type of violence is funny.

"Throw it out," Antonio says, banging another fist on the barrel. "Or I will."

Fulvio holds up the rope. "Guardati, idiota! Just who do you think you are? This is *my* winery. You're only here by my good graces. Don't challenge me, boy."

Antonio steps away and raises his hands, surrendering. The way he looks at me, however, signals that this war is far from over.

Bring it on, I think.

46

arly the next day, it's back to the Peruzzis to ask that favor of Paolo. After spending yesterday with him, I trust him—at least, enough to get him to help me. As soon as the car slides into park, Antonio comes into view. He's just inside the cellar—*la cantina di vinificazione*—directing workers. We ignore each other. Fulvio is visible deep in the crushing room—*a area di pigiatura*—where grapes are processed, crushed, de-stemmed, and then transformed from fresh fruit to juice. The area is filled with sorting tables, presses, crushers, and large fermentation tanks. The heavenly smell of crushed grapes greets me as soon as I step outside the car. Fulvio, all business, doesn't stop what he's doing, only points me in the general direction of Paolo, who's across the street at his vineyard. I hike over and start down a dirt row, admiring the grapes. When I spot Paolo, I call out to him, and he waves me over.

We talk about when the fruit will be ready for harvesting. That this step is an art just as much as blending the grapes and making the wine.

Today, he's out in the fields running tests on the fruit. He explains all the factors they check from the sugar levels to pH levels, acidity, tannins, phenolic maturity, and even the taste and aroma. Any day now, they'll take the grapes.

"I have a favor to ask, Paolo."

"Anything, Anna."

"I want to explore the caves under my property, and I was wondering if you'd go with me."

"Why would you want to do that?"

"Don't you think it'd be fun?" It's only a small lie. "I've done some caving in the States. Tons of people are into it."

"That's a terrible idea."

"How so?"

"For one, it's too dangerous. Especially for you. Did you forget that your hand is healing and that you're pregnant? My whole life, my grandfather has warned us how hazardous caves are around here, has ordered us to stay out. Our own wine cellar is the only cave I'll go in. Even that one is easy to get lost in and can be dangerous. You witnessed that yourself when those barrels came loose. God only knows what's in yours. Certainly not cellars. No, not a good idea."

"It could be fun. We won't know until we try."

He gives an emphatic shake of the head. "I'm sorry, but that's not for me. I don't like being closed in. Life for me is outside in the vineyards, that's what I love, and that's what I call fun. I don't even like going into our caves alone, and those have been reinforced."

"You said you would do anything for me."

He searches my face. "For you, yes, I would try to do this, but only if we could go in with someone else who's an expert. And anyway, we're preparing for the harvest. If I'm out of Fulvio's sight for more than an hour, he's all over me. Let's wait until after the work is done and arrange for an expert guide."

"You're stalling. You won't ever go in, will you?"

"Let's speak to Fulvio and see what he thinks."

I grab his sleeve. "No, please don't. I'm sure he'll only get upset. I'm too controversial with your family as it is. I'm sorry, it was insensitive for me to ask this now during harvest. Just forget that I mentioned it. Since I can't paint, I'm looking for things to do."

I don't say that I've already ventured inside. That there's a treacherous ravine that I can't cross over without a bridge, which I don't have. And I certainly don't want to mention that I really want to go inside because I hope to find the Medici Falchion there. He'll think I've totally lost it. Maybe I have. Except for the fact that the tunnels in my caves have been excavated too and there are sconces on the walls. Maybe not electric like his, but candles would work fine.

"If you need any help with stomping grapes, you know where I am," I say.

He looks embarrassed—as if he feels like a coward. "Anna, whatever you do, don't go in those caves alone."

I shrug.

"I mean it. I'm worried about you."

I prop a hand on my hip and give him a look.

"Promise me you won't go in. Please."

"Thank you, Paolo. I love you too."

The drive to the nearest camping store that carries most of what I need isn't that far, just in Siena. I get the remaining items after visiting two more stores, including a lumberyard. Later that morning a delivery person carries to the basement the wide wooden planks that I need to cross the gap.

"Hey, a favor," I say to the delivery person. "Could you put those planks inside the cave?"

"Not part of my job, ma'am."

Not an unexpected response, so I reach in my pocket and take out a lot of cash—enough for him to agree. I light the way with the powerful flashlight that I just bought, and he lugs the first plank inside.

"It's spooky in here," he says.

"No, it's fine. Now stop where you are."

He complies.

I shine the light over the ravine. "It's really deep, so be careful. And be careful of any wet ground."

He sets the plank down and gingerly tiptoes to the chasm—this large man moves so daintily.

"Oh, no. This is crazy." He tries to return the cash.

Instead, I pull out another wad of banknotes. He hesitates but takes the money. After he lays the planks, another stack of euros convinces him to take a case of long-burning candles across the ravine and place them there, so I won't have to carry them across myself.

"What's in this cave?" he asks.

"That's what I hope to find out. Always looking for adventure."

"You're not going in there alone, are you?"

"No way," I lie. "I've got some expert caving friends coming in from America in a few days. One is an archaeologist. I'm just getting ready." I warn him not to speak about the cave to anyone, that I don't want a bunch of nosey strangers coming onto the property

and bothering my guests. I tip him more money. He looks at the
cash and agrees.

After lunch, I dress in pants and a jacket with plenty of pockets, put on
a helmet with a flashlight, fill my pockets full of tools, and clip other
items onto my belt. The act of preparation has completely changed my
mindset. My fears have vanished. I know what I'm dealing with, know
to take every step slow.

To be sure that the door doesn't close this time, I push a crate in front
of it to hold it open. It might seem crazy to take this risk, but I do have
some caving experience, and my injuries are mostly healed. My left hand
isn't fully functional, there's numbness in my fingers and full use hasn't
returned. But I can still use most of the extremity. It all comes down to
one thing, and that one thing is keeping me here in Tuscany—finding
the Medici Falchion. This can't wait much longer, because I leave soon
for America. I don't need to sell the estate to vacate the premises. I could
rent out the villa instead.

I turn my headset on and place long-burning candles inside the old
wrought iron sconces, lighting each wick before I proceed. I arrange
a few lanterns near the drop-off and test the strength of the planks.
Steady. I hammer an anchor into the rock wall and tie a rope to its hook.
The rope should provide added security when I cross over—*should*
provide.

Making sure not to look down, I walk slowly across the boards,
hanging onto the rope. There's only a slight bow by the time I reach the
middle. The underground stream flowing below gurgles and babbles,

reminding me of the depth—and the grave hazard. But I push those thoughts aside.

Once across, I breathe a sigh of relief. After hammering another hook into the wall, I attach the rope. Now it's situated on both sides. I light another sconce and walk to the bend in the path, which goes right. Advancing down the path, I light more torches and frequently look back to confirm that the candles have remained lit.

The pathway continues on without any openings to go in a different direction. So far, one way in and one way out. Twenty minutes elapse. Strange feelings begin to surface and I pick up my pace, as if an invisible magnetic force is pulling me forward. Soon I'll need to turn back, but I'm not quite ready to call it quits today. If I'd started out earlier, I could've gone farther. But there's always tomorrow. An hour has passed, much of which was taken up with placing and lighting candles, but I will not go forward relying only on my headlamp and handheld flashlight. There's something to be said about the value of good-old-fashioned fire.

Then I come across the most unimaginable sight.

47

he tunnel leads into a massive cavern of incredible beauty. Stalactites glimmer and sparkle when my light reflects off their surfaces. These spectacular dangling rock icicles hang downward from the cave's ceiling. I know from my rudimentary caving experience that the stalactites were formed by rainwater seeping through limestone and leaving calcite deposits on the cave's roof. On the floor are stalagmites—the pillars that grow from the floor upwards, and which are also formed from the dripping calcite deposits. Where a stalactite is found, its mate, the stalagmite, is usually right underneath it.

The floor—the *cave fill*—is composed of a mixture of sand, clay, and gravel. And that base is ten feet lower than my current position. The immediate area around me is still on the same level as the tunnel and has a ten-foot-wide lip at this far edge of the cavern. A wrought iron railing blocks off the room so that people remain back and above the cave fill. I shine my flashlight on the railing and see that the pathway continues along the edge of the cavern, maybe fifty plus feet. Of course, the cavern's interior expands as you enter it. But I'm not about to do that today, and I see nothing but nature from here. But how gorgeous this is, a hidden treasure trove. And to think, I own this, because I own the subterranean rights as well as the land above. My caving friends in the States have seen many such marvels, but I've never seen a collection like this.

Yawning, I realize that I can't go much farther. Maybe this is where the path ends, and I've seen everything there is to see. If so, that's very disappointing, because I've detected no likely hiding places for a necklace. I don't see an easy way in or out, so it's unlikely that I would've ventured down into the cavern as a young girl. Before I leave, I want to know if the pathway across the cavern continues on. If it ends, I'll head back, knowing that at least I've tried. If I come across more tunnel, I'll return when I have more strength.

What I see on the other side thrills me. There is more tunnel. Yes, I'm tired, but my adrenaline kicks in with this new discovery, so why not venture forward just a little farther?

I travel twenty feet down the path, round a corner, and come face-to-face with a Gothic iron gate.

"Caspita!"

Beyond the gate is another cavernous space, this one not as large as the first cavern, but big enough. I shine my light—a crypt. There must be a hundred tombs in there. My hand quavers as I move the flashlight this way and that. The entire burial chamber, including the tombs, is finished with light-colored stone. Many of the tombs are inserted into the walls with only their ends visible. Others are stacked sideways and six levels high. Some are placed inside large cavities and have small statues or decorative items on each end.

The entire crypt is pristine, as if someone has maintained the area. It's so clear who that person is—Edoardo. Why would he keep this from me? There's an inscription engraved at the top of the gate: the Latin script: *NON SINE MANIBUS IUSTIS*—not without just hands. The gate won't open. I look for a lock, but there isn't one. Then it hits me—at the catacombs in Rome, the priest manipulated the stones to unlock the gate. Maybe this is a puzzle lock too.

I slide my hand along the wall and come across a large, loose rock, which I tug on until it starts to pull away. I let it fall to the ground. Ten smaller rocks are visible now. I think about the doodles in the journal—altogether a combination of ten circles and squares—and the order in which they were drawn. All I have to do is push or pull on a square or a circle.

So I start by pushing on the circles, pulling on squares. That doesn't work, so I reverse the process. The locking mechanism clanks open. With my uninjured right hand, I yank on a bar until the gate slides open.

To the far right of the crypt are several stone benches and a pulpit. The area resembles the chapel in the Rome catacombs. On the north side of the room there is a second iron gate, also constructed in a Gothic style. I go to it and grip one of the bars to test its strength. Solid. Beyond this second gate is another manufactured tunnel that looks walkable as well.

The words in the journal come to me. She visited a place to be near her own mother. Of course. This is my family's crypt. And no one, not my father, not Fulvio, not Edoardo, thought to tell me about it. Why?

I approach the tombs and begin looking at the names of the dead inscribed in the stone. Bourbons, de' Medicis, Peruzzis, and surnames that I don't recognize. My eyes fill with tears of sorrow, but also of anger.

Why the big secret?

Fulvio and Aurora must know about this crypt. If Paolo or Antonio knew, one of them would surely have mentioned as much, especially when the topic of caves came up, and especially when the brothers took me into their cellar. The other gate can lead only one place—to the Peruzzis. My entire family on the de' Medici side is down here. My great grandparents, Filippo, Maria; my grandparents, Marco, and here's Silva. The section where the Bourbons are buried has dates extending as far back as 1735, 1847. Are these even real?

The lettering and markings on the vaults were clearly made by chiseling the stone, a traditional art form still practiced by the scalpellini here in Tuscany. I know this from having spent hours studying art in museums. My mother wrote in her journal that we're related to the Bourbons. That may be true, but not all Bourbons are of royal blood. People make things up. Names are common. As to the Medici? Am I descended from someone important? It wouldn't matter; Giovanni di Bicci de' Medici's lineage is extinct. So they say.

I can put this madness to rest by asking experts to come and evaluate the crypt. Get archaeologists and anthropologists and art historians to examine the tombs and the remains and accurately date everything. Do some DNA testing as well. How amazing that would be, to discover a real piece of history tucked away down here? No matter, I won't let my imagination get carried away.

My eyes fall on an elaborate tomb that sits sideways in the wall. Sculpted angels stand on each end. I take a closer look. The inscription reads *Vittoria de' Medici Rossi*. I'm stunned.

Why is there an empty tomb with my mother's name on it? She was cremated, her ashes spread across the grounds. Or so my father told me. There was no funeral, and he wouldn't let me attend the memorial service that he arranged before we left the country. I was in the hospital after my "breakdown," and the doctors said that attending wouldn't be good for my mental health.

Maybe my mother *wasn't* cremated, and her bones are in the tomb. Or maybe her ashes are in there. Edoardo must know. Of course he does. He's the keeper of this crypt.

I slide my hand across the lettering on her tomb. Strangely, I don't cry. There's a sense of comfort being so close to her tomb, whether she's in it or not.

When I look away, a ghostly image flutters ten feet away—a specter, its features fuzzy, ill-defined.

My throat constricts. I close my eyes.

I look again; my mother is still there. I'm frozen in place, can't draw my eyes away. The features crystallize, and she stands in front of me.

"Oh, mio Dio!" I gasp and look away.

It's only the light playing tricks. This happens in caves, or so my experienced caving friends have said. When inexperienced people first go in, they don't realize that the darkness or the tight spaces can cause the mind to play tricks—create hallucinations, visual and aural. Humans aren't used to true darkness and silence. Sometimes phantom images result from the artificial light reflecting off colorful minerals in the rocks. These occurrences aren't mystical but rather physical or psychological. Not hocus pocus, not supernatural.

I face her again. The apparition of my mother is so vivid.

I stumble back. She fades in and out. Tricks of the mind, just tricks.

When I block the light from my headset, the room dims, and the image disappears. I uncover the light. The image returns. I exhale. It's only a reflection, maybe intentionally placed in the crypt as an ancient device used to ward off intruders. But it seems so real, so spirit-like—and why would a trick created centuries ago resemble my mother?

I relax, glad that I didn't scream. Loud noises can have fatal consequences underground. There's no sky to buffer sound vibrations, often no open spaces, and cave ceilings can be fragile.

Time to head back. But before I turn to go, another elaborate tomb pulls me near. The inscription reads *Anna Maria de' Medici Rossi, 1995–*.

Why is there a tomb with *my* name on it, and why did no one tell me about this?

My breathing accelerates. I need to sit before I pass out, so I retreat to a bench. Am I overreacting? Many families arrange for their future burials, especially in crypts. Did my mother arrange for this soon after I was born? She must have, because my father wouldn't have done something like this. He never wanted to return to Italy, didn't want me to, and wouldn't have spent money on something that didn't benefit him. Did he even know about the crypt?

My chest heaves. If my mother had my tomb prepared, it was only a gesture of love—which doesn't make it any less creepy.

As I'm adjusting my headgear, I glance across the room—there!

48

y headlamp shines on a pulpit made of solid marble and stacked stone, drawing my attention to a corner where a single brick sits slightly askew. The stone is visibly worn at its edges. Not enough that it stands out to the unobserving eye, but enough for someone like me who has an eye trained for even the smallest of details. I tug on the brick, which pulls free. I crouch down and direct the light inside a small cavity.

A wooden case! A jewelry box!

My heart leaps. The thin, not-so-light case weighs several pounds. Tucking it under my arm, I carry it to a bench and set it down. Atop of the box, rendered in metalwork, is the de' Medici coat of arms—the same design that I've seen on the tapestry, the knight, the small trunk—and my mother's journal. The wood is in immaculate condition considering its age, which must be a couple of hundred years old.

My mother hid the necklace in this sacred place where no one would think to look for it unless they read her journal.

I swing a leg over to straddle the bench, brace myself, and slowly open the lid. A royal-blue velvet fabric covers whatever is underneath. I lift the cloth and find nothing other than more velvet lining the box. Empty.

"Che delusion."

There are definite impressions in the velvet—impressions of the Medici Falchion. I think back to that fateful night. As a young girl—if I had known about this place, which I have no memory of in the slightest at this moment—I wouldn't have had time to return the necklace to this pulpit. Not that night, anyway, and after the accident, I was hospitalized and then whisked off to America. And how would I have crossed the ravine? Unless a permanent bridge used to be there. If I took the necklace, I hid it somewhere inside the house. But where?

The cornerstone of the pulpit fits snuggly back into place. No chance I'm leaving this box behind. Something else occurs to me. Morbid, yes. Perhaps the "twins" from the Rome party aren't the only ones fascinated by the macabre.

The cover of my mother's tomb is only an inch thick, but must weigh two hundred pounds. I insert a small crowbar that I'd strapped to my lower leg underneath the lid. Using my body weight and all my strength, I push and shove until the cover slides an inch. Bracing my legs, I give it everything I have. After multiple tries, I'm able to move the top just under a foot, wide enough to reveal what is or isn't inside. The tomb is not empty. Skeletal remains rest in my mother's sarcophagus. I jump back and cross myself; though I'm not that religious, I'll take whatever grace God will throw my way.

Whose bones lie in my mother's grave?

Is this the product of more lies? Some sick karmic joke?

Upon further examination, it's clear that the deceased's skull was fractured—depression fractures, as if a fist made its way through the bone to the inner tissues. The head has detached from the neck. The weight of time could account for the head-neck separation, but not for the large cranial perforation, and not for all these fractures. The rest of the body reveals more injury: the left radius and ulna and left femur are completely severed—displaced fractures, jagged separations.

How dispassionate I feel—why?

Because I can't accept that these bones were once my mother? But I know in my heart this is her. That here lies the remains of Vittori de' Medici Rossi. That I killed her, murdered her, and now disturb her in rest—who am I? A thief who comes here to Tuscany, my mother's home, to steal from her again—this time, her family's priceless heirloom?

The deed is done, the disruption complete. I lift the head to study the skull. Is this the once-beautiful face of my vibrant mother who could bring down a house with her voice alone? The bone structure is hers—I'm sure of that.

The reality makes me lightheaded. But I dig deep to regain my center.

I return my mother's skull to her tomb. Dust fluffs into the air. Or is it fibers from the gauzy, once-white, silky dress that's now threadbare and clinging to her bones?

My mother was *not* cremated. Her remains were just too gruesome for a child to see, that I have to believe, because otherwise it's a cruel punishment to deny a child the rightful presence at her mother's funeral.

What other lies have people told me? Who are they to be my deciders? And what rituals have they performed deep in this underground crypt?

My flashlight reveals nothing more than my mother's bones inside her tomb. No sign of the Medici Falchion.

The lid slides back in place. "Rest, Mamma. Don't be angry with me. Just give me some answers."

I sit on a bench for a long moment of contemplation, letting the quiet consume me. I feel no evil lurking, only a peace. The truth, a truth that can save my babies and me, is near.

Like a white cloud, a veil of warmth hugs my being. Maybe I didn't hide the necklace because maybe I'm not my mother's killer. If that's so, could the necklace be hidden in another tomb? Would Edoardo have hidden it somewhere in this crypt? Opening every one of the lids would take days, maybe weeks. Time to leave this place and regroup.

I glide my hand across the cool stone of the tombs as I head out. Then I feel a pain in my palm—an edge on one of the lids is sharp. A cursory examination reveals that the chamber belongs to my great-grandfather. The flashlight illuminates the rough spots, the sharp edges on the lid and sarcophagus. The chipped edges on the lid show no signs of significant age—its color value is much too light. None of the others have this type of damage. The marks look repetitive and are present at only one end of the lid.

Using the crowbar, I move yet another lid. Inside there's not a thread of clothing, only dust, because every stitch of fabric has been eaten away by time. Just bones. But across those bones, atop the middle of my great-grandfather's sternum plate, lies none other than the Medici Falchion!

No, it can't be. I can't take my eyes off the necklace. Though covered in dust, the blood red of the rubies and the shimmering diamonds glint against the light of my headlamp.

Finally, the truth—I didn't hide the Medici Falchion, because I never took it.

With my fears—even in my dreams—there's no way I would've come down to this crypt. I've never been here—nothing would ever let me forget this place. And I certainly didn't stash the necklace in my great-grandfather's tomb. At twelve, I didn't have the strength to move the lid.

Filled with a mixture of triumph and serenity, I remove the necklace, dangle it in front of me, and closely examine the jewels, their facets, the settings.

"Magnifica!"

Myriad emotions hit me at once. I want to scream, to cry, to rip the necklace to pieces, and worse, to place it around my neck and parade down the streets of Siena and Florence and Rome, all of Italy, just to prove there's no curse.

How has this inanimate object caused such hysteria?

The necklace fits precisely into its case, melting into the grooves. With the tomb sealed off, I make my way out of the crypt, careful not to leave any trace that someone was here. One fact is now overwhelmingly clear—someone, and it wasn't me, hid the Medici Falchion, and they were here more recently than not. Someone who has a lot to lose if their identity is discovered.

49

hen I arrive at the ravine, the makeshift bridge is gone. The boards have fallen into the deep crevice. All of them.

I stagger to the wall and steady myself. There's no possible way to cross seven feet over a fifty-foot drop.

Someone *does* mean me harm. Or maybe the necklace *is* cursed.

Am I jumping to conclusions?

Maybe a sudden release of moisture pulled the boards down. The walls are cool to the touch. Damp. But no more than when I slipped in the mud or crossed over. Nor does the ceiling show signs of a sudden downpour. The boards were firmly in place. Someone must've shoved them down.

Edoardo. He kept the caves his secret, tried to keep me out. Was he the one who took the necklace? Who else besides my father had the opportunity to steal it?

If I don't get out of here, I'll die. Is it possible to cling to the rope and cross safely?

Oh no! The rope is missing!

Inside a crevice in the ravine, about twenty feet below, the rope dangles. The metal anchors are still attached. Portions of the wall where the spikes were inserted have crumbled. Rocks lay scattered along the tunnel floor directly below.

My stomach drops. This was no accident.

Someone wants to lock me inside this cave and leave me to die. My conversation with Paolo about going in together—he must've realized that I would whether he accompanied me or not. He must've mentioned my plan to others. To Antonio? Fulvio? Field workers? But how would anyone know when I planned to go in? They couldn't have.

What about Francesca? She had access to the house. Did I miss an exterior door, a way that her key would let her inside? Is there a secret way in? The villa is large with lots of access points—windows, doors.

Who else knows that I might be here? The cleaning staff that Edoardo brought through before I returned home from the hospital? Groundskeepers? What about that delivery person? He was overly curious.

My phone has no signal—as expected and feared. No way to call emergency services. A cry for help might be my only resort, but raised voices have no place inside caves. Too risky. And who would come? The perpetrator of the crime?

What have I overlooked?

The Medici Falchion will find a new home in the waterway below if someone doesn't come to let me out. Because I know that's what this is really about—possessing the necklace, an object people believe has powers, good or bad.

If Edoardo is really on my side, he'll eventually come to the house and discover the open door. But when?

Panic threatens. Sobs rest at the tip of my tongue. But none of that will help. I have to do something, must be proactive, because doing nothing except feeling sorry for myself means certain death. So I retrace my steps and head to the only other conceivable escape route—the second gate inside my family's crypt. Locked, and I can't find a way to open it.

The battery in my flashlight has become low on power. If it dies, I'll likely die with it.

There has to be another way out. Back inside the massive cavern, I'm greeted by blue light streaming down from the ceiling. The sight steals my breath away.

This light is like that in the famous Blue Grotto in Capri. Only, this illumination comes from glowworms, tiny organisms that spin web-like, fibrous strings that hang from a ceiling. When the worms release droppings, the substance rolls down and clings to the fibers, giving each of the strings the appearance of a beaded-glass necklace. Harmless. An incredible bioluminescent phenomenon.

The stalactites across the ceiling reflect so much of this light that the entire cavern is swimming in a blue aura. An alien world. One of heavenly wonder. You don't need a flashlight or headset to see.

At the far end of the cavern and beyond, there's a stream that wasn't visible earlier. Its water reflects the glowworm's light, an indication that the worms are widespread throughout the cave. The presence of running water is a good sign, because that means rainwater is entering this cave somewhere from the outside world. That also explains why the air inside remains fresh and odorless, and why there doesn't seem to be any dangerous mold. The runnel at the bottom of the ravine must connect with this waterway. The earth around it was likely solid at one time but has since given way, explaining the gap.

I need to get over to the waterway and see where it leads. Is it possible? Now that the entire space is lit, a rough surface beyond the railing is visible. It extends around the perimeter of the entire cavern. Placing the jewel case on the other side of the rail, I climb over, retrieve the box, and make my way along the rough edge of the cavern wall. This area hasn't been developed like that of the tunnel. When I reach the stream, the ground alongside it is smoother, worn by the flow of water rising and falling.

The elevation rises as I move along the damp bank. The flow goes in the opposite direction from where I'm heading, which indicates that I'm moving toward the source of the tributary. Another opening appears just ahead of me, a cavernous space, though not nearly as large as the great cavern. The acrid odor of bat droppings assaults my nostrils, a smell similar to that of a dirty rabbit cage.

"Speranza!"

If bats fly inside to roost, then they fly out at night to feed.

The pipistrelli filled their cavern with squeaky chatter. The closer I come to the roost, the louder their chirps and clicks. I've been in caves where I've seen a few, but never an entire colony. With no sudden movement, no noise, I finally get close enough to peer inside.

Thousands upon thousands of bats hang from the ceiling. And hundreds fly around. The rank odor makes me gag. I want to throw up but fight against it. Dim light spills through a large-enough opening across the cavern, and that beautiful sight leads to the outside world.

There's no time to delay, so I slowly make my way through the bat's sanctuary without disturbing them much. A miracle. Out on a narrow ledge, I'm greeted by fresh air. My sense of empowerment rises. Dusk is descending, with sunlight rapidly falling below the horizon.

Who cares what time it is? The fresh air tells me I'm alive and well. The bad news is that I'm high on a rocky hill, and the flashlight has lost power.

The squeaking intensifies, which means it's feeding time.

My phone still has no reception. I can't be here when the bats swarm, so I begin my descent. But not soon enough. A low rumbling fills the air. Then loud fluttering, as if a massive fan has switched on—but that's no fan, those are wings.

From the opening of the cave, hundreds of the creatures are now flying outside. With no way to outrun them, I crouch down and cover my head with my jacket. The screech of thousands and thousands of bats now fills the air. When the vast majority have left the cave, I rise on stiff legs, give myself a moment to recover, and take my first step home.

Keeping my eyes focused and not looking down the mountain, I continue until I finally reach bottom. Night has fallen. I walk in the direction where the sun set.

Along the way, I find myself revisiting the night my mother died—up until I arrived in Tuscany, a blank. But that's no longer true. Facts are emerging, fragments are returning—blurry to be sure, but ever more intelligible. I've gone through life believing that I'm a bad person, have gone through shrink after shrink to help me overcome the guilt and depression. Electroshock treatment causes retrograde amnesia, and memories don't always return. Yet I'm now carrying the Medici Falchion.

Who hid the necklace in my grandfather's tomb? Who moved the sarcophagus lid? Did Edoardo do this? To keep me safe? Or did he kill my mother for the jewel, angry that he was denied his inheritance? Is he the one who left me to die? Or is the person I'm looking for one of the Peruzzis?

As my late father taught me, you can't trust anyone.

50

ungry and exhausted when I arrive at the villa, I kick off my filthy shoes and go inside. Without bothering to shower first, I text Paolo and ask how he's doing. He sends me a sad face emoji and says that Francesca woke up with intense chest pains and that he took her to the hospital. He's still with her at the ER.

If this is true, he couldn't have pulled the planks.

Once the necklace is secured in the safe and the combination changed, I head down to the basement. The Dungeon Door is still open. Of course it is. The culprit would've gone out of their way to make sure everything was left exactly the same—to make it look like I foolishly ventured inside the caves, didn't properly secure the boards, and got stranded on the other side. Maybe even fell into the ravine.

After a shower, I make the mistake of lying down for a few minutes and falling asleep. A pounding on the front door awakens me. It's a messenger service delivering a large manila folder. Has Antonio finally signed off on the papers? No, the papers are only the final documents closing my mother's estate and my new trust documents.

A cursory look through the papers gives me a pleasant surprise. Pleasant shock, actually. The financial manager kept my father away from most of the assets. The monetary value of the trust has tripled. Or did I misjudge my father? Did he sincerely care about me and my future?

My thoughts turn to the wall-length painting of my mother from *Madame Butterfly*, the painting with those cut-out eyes. My father disapproved of many of my mother's activities. Risqué parties? Orgies? Recreational drugs? He might've been a crook, but he drew lines.

Correspondence about the proposed sale of land to the Peruzzis is here. My father never agreed to a deal. On the contrary, he rejected their proposal. The family lied about that. Every last one of them.

The truth seeps out more and more.

A notarized copy of the deed is enclosed. No encumbrances. I asked the lawyer to search the title to be certain. It's mine free and clear.

Too bad my father never mentioned this proposal to me. Was it the first of many of the Peruzzis' failed attempts to grab what was not theirs?

Time to speak with my great-uncle Edoardo. He has motive to kill me, and how convenient I've made it for him—my death the result of my own stupidity.

Edoardo shows up. Perfect timing. He doesn't look surprised to see me.

"You went down in the caves," he says.

"How would you know that?"

"Because I can read your face, Anna."

"Oh really?"

"You shouldn't have done that. Why can't you trust me?"

"Trust you? Why, Edoardo? Because you're my great uncle? Another long-lost relative I left behind when my father spirited me off to America?"

His stern expression breaks, the change barely perceptible. But there is a change. A hint of warmth softens the lines in his face. "Where did you hear such a thing?"

"My mother's journal. And you're listed in it as Aurora's and Marco's brother, sired by my great-grandfather Filippo."

He clasps his hands together and looks away for a long moment, his shoulders slumping. "Their bastard *half*-brother. It's not spoken about. No one in the family except your mother recognized me as a true member of the family."

"Not Aurora?"

He gives a bony-shouldered half-shrug. "She speaks kindly. But Fulvio controls her, and he isn't a friend."

"So that's why you have a different last name."

"My father—your great-grandfather Filippo—had an affair with my mother, who was Sicilian. She used to work for the family as a cook. She never married after. It was a huge scandal. I was the result of their supposedly sinful behavior, born months before your grandfather, Marco. So I suppose that makes me your great-uncle."

"Why didn't you tell me?"

"There was a lot of tension surrounding the situation. My father never openly acknowledged me. But he left me a life estate on this property—and the cottage."

"So my grandfather Marco rightfully inherited the property under the law, including the necklace. But only because he was the legitimate son. Yet my mother wrote your name in her journal as her uncle."

"I was very fond of your mother. I never had children. When your grandfather died, I was something of a father figure to your mother, much to the family's displeasure. And later, I got to spend time with you until your own father took you to America."

"It's awful how they treated you. This family . . ."

He shrugs, resigned. "The only thing that mattered to me was being close to your mother—and you. So, you see, now that you're back, I'm perfectly content. Or will be once I know you're out of danger."

"And you don't blame me for taking my mother away from you?"

He straightens, his eyes full of conviction. "You were asleep. It was an accident. You did nothing wrong."

Maybe it's overfatigue or tension or just my innate bluntness, but I say, "It's a sweet, heartrending story, Edoardo, but why should I believe you? Especially when you, maybe more than anyone, have a motive to harm the family and steal the necklace? I almost died in the cave today."

My accusation doesn't seem to perturb him in the slightest. "You should believe me because I'm telling you the truth. You know that in your heart. That's what you should trust."

"Did you put the Dungeon Door key inside the old trunk and stuff it away in the playroom?"

"I did not."

"That playroom. I have terrible memories of it. Why?"

"You and your mother spent a lot of time in there. It was your special place. You would sing and dance and laugh. Then you suddenly became fearful of the room. I don't know why. It happened at the same time the nightmares began. You said a witch lived in the room. That she was mean to you. You'd fight tooth and nail if someone tried to take you in there."

All of this feels familiar. "What else was I scared of?"

"You became deathly afraid of bugs and spiders and imaginary things."

"What happened the night my mother died?"

He blinks hard and inhales deeply. "After your mother left for the opera that night with Francesca and Giuseppe Tringali, I went to my cottage."

"Tringali?"

"He drove them to the opera and back here, which he often did."

"And Francesca? She rode with them?"

"The women were inseparable."

So two more people were nearby the night my mother died.

"I went home after they left. Leo phoned me late that night and told me there had been an accident and that Vittoria was dead. He said he didn't hear her come in from the opera. That he woke when he heard arguing, then he discovered the body. He sounded distraught, didn't know what to do. I arrived within minutes and saw her . . ." Edoardo's rheumy eyes begin to glisten.

"And you saw me?"

"At the top of the stairs, looking down at your mother's body. You were hysterical, inconsolable."

"My father just let me stand there?"

"I suppose he did until I arrived. Then he went up to you and started shaking you to wake you up. You were in the throes of the nightmare, but you woke as soon as you heard my voice, telling your father not to shake you. You snapped out of it, and your father told you that you were having a dream and hurried you to bed. Wasn't a dream, Anna." Edoardo starts to say something more, but before he can, his eyes well up. But he stops himself from shedding any tears.

"And the necklace?"

"Gone."

"What dress was she wearing that night?"

He reflects, looks confused. "A gown."

"What color?"

"I don't exactly recall. She would only wear red or blue."

"Did she and Francesca disagree a lot?"

"They grew up together, cousins close in age. They were like sisters, and sisters have their quarrels."

"Does Francesca think the necklace should've gone to her?"

"You'll have to ask her that."

"What about Fulvio and Aurora?"

"They don't want anything to do with it. Neither should you, Anna."

"Why didn't you tell me any of this?"

"Because I assumed you would know your family history."

51

he bright, new sunny day is the perfect time to lie by the pool. The warmth of the sun lulls me to sleep. Strange whispers come to me while I dream. A psychic jolt wakes me. No one is around. It's not a nightmare that's woken me. It's an idea.

Back inside at the scene of my crime, I stand looking up the staircase and imagine where my mother must've stood that night. Everyone says I shoved her down the stairs. Why is it so hard for me to accept this? Is it because my mind is full of cobwebs? Because I can't recall the act of murdering her? I might not have hidden the necklace, but that doesn't conclusively prove that I didn't kill my mother. It occurred to me out by the pool that if I reenacted the night, maybe it would all come back. Then maybe I could stop torturing myself and move on. I drag the mannequin out of the coat closet and up the stairs.

The wedding attire is wrong. Edoardo mentioned that she wore a red or blue gown that night. Taking the private stairwell, I go down to her parlor and sort through the evening wear and costumes. A red dress looks right. Or does it? Why would my mother have worn red with that ruby necklace? She would never wear red on red. Not a fashion diva like her. Anything like that would distract from the necklace. My hand slides across the fabric of a blue gown, the first one that I'd admired so much. If she died in this one, it's been well cleaned. Because it's free of any blood stains. Whether the dress she wore that night has been disposed of or not, the color blue feels right.

Passing through the art studio and into the bedroom, I'm greeted by my mother's wedding portrait. Seeing her image gives me courage.

Without too much effort, I dress the mannequin in the gown. But there's an item missing—the Medici Falchion. I take it from the safe and place the necklace around her . . . around *its* neck and secure the delicate clasp. Once the figure is positioned by the staircase, I go to my old room, get in bed, and pull the covers up. For the first time in my life, I try to conjure a lucid dream.

Time passes. I breathe deeply until and the pull of sleep nips at me . . .

My palms sweat. My breath quickens. I summon fear to serve me. I summon the witch, my playroom, the pain. I'm locked in the darkness of the dungeon. The tornado of devil bugs approaches. The skull falls out of the catacomb wall, a harbinger. The villa's French doors fly open, the piano lid crashes down, sheet music flies wildly. A suicidal crow smacks into the window, leaving feathers and innards stuck to the glass. Raffaella is falling. My arm wrenches in the staircase railing; it tears off at the shoulder. Blood. Everywhere.

The Medici Falchion chokes me.

The witch comes for me. I cry out for help, throw off the covers, race across my room, and rush into the hallway. I have to get away.

Mother is finally home. There's a fierce storm outside. But I hear her magnificent voice, singing when she's speaks. I want to run to her. She'll protect me. But her voice is harsh? What has upset her? The witch!

Breathless, I scream at the witch and then run to Mamma. I have to help her. She screams my name. There's so much noise, banging and banging. I reach her as she's tumbling down the stairs, and then a crack when her head hits the hard marble floor. She lies at the bottom of the stairs.

Motion draws my attention, someone runs through the front entranceway, a faceless woman wearing a red dress.

Mamma is dead. She's not moving. Blood. So much blood. Medici blood.

I force myself to look at her neck. Bare.

Wide awake now, no longer in bed but downstairs in the foyer, I slump down to the floor and place my head between my knees. I didn't push my mother down the stairs. I'm not a killer.

I pick up the mannequin—incredibly, it isn't damaged. How it fell down the stairs, I'm not sure. But it went down just as my mother did that night and showed me the truth.

Here's what I now know—not everything, but enough. My mother attended the opera that night. My father didn't go. I was upset that she wouldn't take me along, but she said that the show went on too late for someone my age. She and I fussed, and I said some things that I shouldn't have. She left with Tringali and Francesca. Which means that my mother's cousin must be the woman I saw running away that night, although I never saw her face. All I saw was the red dress.

Tringali must've seen my mother wearing the necklace that night. Why didn't he tell me that? I'll talk to him first. But before that, I need to figure out which opera they attended so he can't evade my questions. He, my family, they're all liars.

Back in the parlor, I sort through my mother's papers. One drawer is filled with useless photographs. But another has pamphlets, newspaper clippings, and magazines. I find an opera news magazine dated just after my mother's death. How very strange to find a magazine in my mother's things that was published after her death. Did Eduardo place it here? Francesca? The cover features the opera *Turandot* that was performed on the night of her demise. An article with photographs has one of my mother, Tringali, Francesca, and Francesca's husband, Claudio, posing for the camera. Others, not the subject of the photograph, stand in the background, all dressed in fancy attire, as well. My mother wears a blue dress. But Francesca wears red.

52

umping in the car, I drive to Tringali's latest digs. In the past weeks, he's relocated to Montepulciano, a beautiful hilltop village. He isn't home. But the landlord directs me to a wine tavern, where the artist, reeking of alcohol, sits. His longish, thinning, gray hair is greasy, and he looks as if he hasn't slept in days.

When he sees me, he staggers to his feet and calls me over. "Mio caro, Anna! I heard something happened to your hand. The arteries severed and nerve damage. Why didn't you tell me yourself? You should have."

"Nice to see you, too, Giuseppe. We need to talk." Without asking, I sit down in the chair opposite to him.

I tell him briefly about my injury, that there's hope for a full recovery. He asks the details, but I won't kowtow to this arrogant man, famous artist or not. He's obviously a drunk, and what a cliché.

I set the magazine on the table. Inside is the picture of my mother and the others at the *Turandot* opera.

"When we met the first time, you didn't tell me that you went to the opera with my mother the night she died. And that she wore the Medici Falchion. Why not?"

Without answering, Tringali calls for more wine. The server brings two glasses, but I pass. It's none of Tringali's business that I'm pregnant. Even if I wasn't, I wouldn't drink with this man, an obvious liar and charlatan. This man may very well be my mother's murderer. As the server starts to take the second glass of wine away, Tringali takes a big sip from his own and says, "Leave it."

The waiter gives a curt nod and hands the glass to Tringali.

"What the hell happened the night my mother died? And before you go on, I know that, despite what people say, I didn't push her down those stairs. Did you?"

He rakes a hand through his hair, gives me a befuddled look, and turns to a page in the magazine. "*Turandot*. A difficult opera." He takes another long drink and then raises his empty glass to the server. "Carra took this photograph."

So Carra attended the opera, too. She didn't mention this at the party, although she should have, since we were talking about the necklace's curse and how it passed her over. Another person who keeps secrets.

Tringali taps the photo, his expression wistful now. "I hired a car to make a grand impression. Francesca and Vittoria rode with me. Vittoria always drew a crowd. She was a wonderful singer. A wonderful woman. I would've taken her away from the drab domestic life she mistakenly chose, but she stayed with your father because of you, Anna."

He's so inebriated, I wonder how much of this account he'll fabricate. And as usual, he's the hero of any story he tells.

Pulling the page closer, he studies the photo at length. His expressions change from wistful to angry to downright sad. "We sat in a private box. The one always reserved for Vittoria."

"Who else was there?"

He points to the people in the picture. "Vittoria and me, of course. Also, Claudio and Francesca and their children. Carra sat in our box. And the poor girl, Raffaella, who you saw die, and also her parents." He names two other families that I've never heard of. Then he leans forward. "Some people are saying you pushed Raffaella the way you pushed your mother. I don't believe it, of course. But did you?"

My instinct is to slap this asshole for his callousness, his crassness, but I need him to keep talking, so I hold my temper. "Why didn't my father go to the opera?"

Tringali lets out a derisive laugh. "He hated the opera, hated your mother's artistic friends, hated anything tasteful. An American—did you know he liked country music? You must've. It's so odd that he and Vittoria ever got together. Well, we hated him because he was a brute."

I sigh hard, exasperated.

Tringali narrows one eye and continues, "When we arrived at the opera house, Vittoria signed some autographs. We drank some champagne and found our box. Then the quarreling started. Francesca was so envious of Vittoria, though they were supposed to be best friends. Jealous of Vittoria's looks, her voice, her fame."

"What did they argue about?"

"Francesca was always making little digs, supposedly only friendly banter, but not really. You know what they say about jokes being half true? I happen to think that every truth is a half joke, but . . . She raved about the female lead's exceptional voice, implying that the younger woman was more talented. Kept needling your mother with such comments. You know Francesca. She's like that, no?"

No, I want to say. *You're like that, Tringali.*

He slurps his wine. "At the close of intermission, I noticed that Vittoria wasn't wearing the necklace. She panicked and started looking for it. I went to the box to search, Francesca was there, squatting behind Vittoria's chair. She held the Medici Falchion to her neck, then looked up and saw me. She smiled, said she'd found it, and asked how it looked on her."

Francesca.

"Vittoria came in and was relieved to see that her cousin had the necklace. The two stepped behind the curtain, Francesca fastened the jewel on Vittoria. Francesca whispered something in her cousin's ear. I could see that Vittoria didn't appreciate the remark. I'm guessing something about the curse. Your mother never believed in the curse—"

"At lunch you told me she believed it was a powerful amulet."

He stammers a moment and then says, "That's not the same thing as a cursed object."

This man will say anything.

"Francesca did, or she said as much on more than a few occasions. Which didn't stop her from coveting the thing. After the opera, we drove home."

"Why would Francesca want the necklace if she thought it was cursed?"

"An accursed talisman can bring its possessor great power." He takes a sip of wine, swallows, then takes another and begins rambling. "I will never forget that night as long as I live. No matter how much alcohol I drink. I took the women home. Claudio and the kids left right after the performance. Francesca stayed behind with us. Vittoria always liked to go backstage to congratulate the performers. Francesca loved being part of all that pomp and circumstance. Gets to be drab, you know? One of the performers asked if she could try on the necklace, tried to touch it. Francesca slapped her hand, shocking all. The woman wasn't the only one who was enamored with the jewel. Many were. Drawn to it, like a powerful magnet."

I want to spit. "Francesca acts like she's afraid of the necklace, doesn't want it."

"Who knows what Francesca wants. She says this, does that."

Hypocrite.

"Who got dropped off first?" I ask.

"Francesca, then Vittoria. I offered to walk her inside the villa, but she refused because Rossi was jealous of me. He knew I was in love with his wife and that she was in love with me. I didn't want to get into a physical confrontation with your father. I don't like hurting people. So, I parked outside the front entryway, and the caretaker escorted her in."

My father, once a New Jersey street kid, would not lose a fight with Tringali. But that's not what's so disturbing. "Did Edoardo let her in?"

"Who remembers the name of the help?" A loud moan. "I've always felt responsible for causing your parents to quarrel that night. Rossi knew I was encouraging Vittoria to leave him, that it was only a matter of time before she would be with me. He was always so possessive of her, even though he was such a philanderer himself."

"How do you know they quarreled?"

"I lingered. I could see their silhouettes in the window. Your father. He was a real player. No offense."

Tringali is a walking offense. "Can we stick to the events of that night?"

He raises up his hands, which judder, and I'm certain it's not because of our discussion. How can this man hold a paintbrush?

"Why didn't you tell me the truth to begin with?"

"Who tells his prospective student, the daughter of the woman I adored, that I was in love with her mother and her mother was in love with me?"

No, that isn't it. Tringali would withhold the truth if he had inappropriate designs on me and didn't want to scare me off. Disgusting.

"My own father told me my mother died by my hands. The rest of the family has made it clear they believe that too. Everyone agrees, so it seems. Why do people believe this?"

Tringali exhales. "You were . . . different; emotionally fragile. You had a vivid, artistic imagination. Vittoria used to bring you along on our Sunday strolls through the museums. Your father wouldn't take you. Right from the start, I could tell you were an artist in the making. I encouraged you to study painting when you were a mere child. The person who first sent you on your way, who revealed your calling. Don't you remember those days?"

"No. None of them. My mother was my inspiration. Now, please answer my question."

My rebuke doesn't seem to faze him. "Let me tell you about yourself."

This ought to be good.

"Don't look so skeptical. Because now I'm going to tell you something precious. Something your mother told me about how she saw you, Anna. These were her words: *My dearest Anna, she's like a magnificent tree with its trunk and leaves visible and beautiful, swaying in the wind. But hidden deep below that beauty also lurks a root system that's unreachable.* Isn't that beautiful? Of course it is. Your mother was a poet. The point is, you are your mother's child. You were born to be an artist. It's not so much what we see on the canvas, those visible leaves, your beauty, sure that's important, but it's what lies below that gives you and your art meaning. Or it will. The deep roots that are unreachable, the depth of your soul, the suffering."

I don't quite know how to respond to this. Is he full of crap? "My mother really said this?"

"Ask Francesca or Carra. Though I felt like Vittoria's and my conversations were meant only for us." His head droops, and suddenly he appears miserable.

"Honestly, I don't know whether to believe you. You drink too much, you're drunk, and you like to talk gibberish."

He sits more erect and places a hand on his chest. "I swear on my life. It's true."

"Based on what you say, why would anyone think I killed my mother? Even during a nightmare?"

"Because you argued with her that night. You wanted to go to the opera, and she didn't take you. You knew Raffaella was going, and she was your age. Vittoria told everyone how upset the quarrel made her, that you'd never been so angry. That you told her you wished she was dead."

⁂

On the ride back to the villa, I let the convertible top down to feel the wind, to get lost in its murmurs, so I don't think so hard. But my mind won't shut off.

I bang the steering wheel. Tringali is a self-centered, lying asshole who likes to hear himself talk.

Maybe *he* was after my mother's property. Not just the necklace. He admitted to being with her the night she died, to dropping her off at the house. If Edoardo is telling the truth about his own whereabouts, Tringali could've walked her inside. If Tringali is telling the truth, Edoardo saw her in. Who's lying? One thing is certain, Tringali is a drunk, and I could easily see that he's convinced himself of another reality.

Was Francesca really dropped off first? Why was she even riding with Tringali and my mother in the first place, and not with her own family? Was she my mother's hanger-on, so enamored of show business? Tringali said my mother and Francesca argued that night. If that's the case, more reason why Francesca wouldn't have ridden home with them.

Unless Francesca had designs on the necklace.

If anything Tringali said is true, then Francesca had the perfect alibi to sneak back to the villa without suspicion and commit the crime. She could use Tringali's presence at the house to proclaim her innocence and cast doubt on him.

Maybe the explanation is simpler. Maybe the two women returned to the villa together. They started arguing again, and the fight escalated. My mother fell, accidentally or by design. Francesca saw that mother was dead, so she snatched the necklace to make it look like a robber was in the house. If it was an accident, maybe Francesca hid the necklace to protect everyone from the curse. If not that and she doesn't fear a curse, then she's biding her time until she can freely possess the jewel. That's a time when her elderly parents are deceased, and I'm out of the picture.

My head spins: Francesca, her family, Edoardo, Tringali, Carra. Everyone has a different version of the facts, a clash of conflicting realities. I use my phone to listen to music and get lost in song—one thing I had in common with my father was our love of country music.

53

he following afternoon, I show up unannounced at the Peruzzis'. The family is gathered on the veranda. Fulvio, Aurora, Francesca, and the three kids, Giana, Antonio, and Paolo, are present.

A smiling Fulvio rises from the head of the table and opens his arms. "Benvenuta, Anna! You're just in time. Come join us." He gives a pointed look at his oldest grandson. "Antonio, go get some sparkling water for our guest."

There's that word again—guest.

Antonio frowns but does as he's told.

Paolo gives me his seat across from Francesca and moves to another one beside her. Everyone wears cheerful smiles. Oh, yes, here we are, right where it began—dining al fresco. Except everything has changed.

Aurora places a warm hand on mine. "So good to see you, caro. Don't be such a stranger."

I place a hand over hers. "I'm so sorry. Some days I feel nauseous—the twins. The doctor said to expect this. I did come by the other day to say hello to Paolo, I should've come inside too. Forgive me."

When Antonio returns, sees his grandmother speaking so affectionately to me, he almost drops my glass of water. We don't look at each other.

"Antonio, have you signed those papers for Anna yet?" Giana asks.

"Shut the hell up, sorella," Antonio says.

"You have no manners," she replies, glaring at him. "Or good sense. You never learn your lesson. You should be more like Paolo."

Fulvio raises his hands. "Great. We've settled the matter that Antonio has no manners. Antonio, pay attention."

"So how are you, Francesca?" I ask. "Your heart?"

She places a hand on her chest. "I thought so, but it was a panic attack. My son took such great care of me." So Paolo was telling the truth about Francesca being in the hospital.

Paolo is smiling; Antonio looks away.

"Tell us what you've been up to, Anna," Francesca says.

"Going to doctor appointments. Eating for three. Oh, and I discovered my mother's old journal in her desk. I thought Paolo might've mentioned it."

"Why would I?" he asks.

"I thought I told you," I say, to which he looks confused.

"I didn't know she kept a journal, but I'm not surprised," Aurora says. "You mother was old-fashioned. In a good way. Also very smart."

"Like the women in the family. Smart."

Antonio scoffs.

"She used to scribble her thoughts in it," Francesca says. "She had a knack for poetry. Is that what's in there, Anna? Poetry and your mother's deepest secrets?"

"That and much more," I say. "Even our family's history: dates, marriages, births. We're all in there, including your side of the family, of course."

"How nice for you to find something so personal from your late mother," Aurora says. "I hope it gives you comfort."

"It even mentions the Medici Falchion," I add. "She talks in detail about the curse, and how it has affected our family over the generations. How it's so often torn us apart." This is an exaggeration, but important for these people to hear.

Everyone's expressions grow stern. Aurora crosses herself.

"It seems that the Medici Falchion once belonged to Marie Antoinette," I say. "If you believe in that junk. Do you believe it, Aunt Aurora?"

"The necklace doesn't have a good history, whatever the truth is," she replies.

"Just forget about it," Francesca says. "It's lost, and you're better off without it."

"I'm sure you're right," I say. "Maybe I'm obsessing about the necklace as a way to preserve my mother's memory. My parents are both dead. I don't even have a grave close by to visit like you do."

Aurora presses her lips together. Will she admit the truth about the crypt?

I clap a hand to my forehead. "I didn't mean to be rude, Francesca, and everyone. I know you lost Claudio not so long ago. A father, husband, son-in-law. But at least *you* have the comfort of going to the cemetery and visiting his grave. Or is he buried overlooking your vineyard? Such a peaceful spot. I wouldn't mind being buried in such a beautiful place. What a difference it makes knowing where loved ones are put to rest. I wish my mother had been buried on the grounds." I pretend to be overwrought, even wring my hands until I start feeling pain in my damaged fingers.

"Our father is buried in Milan, with his parents and grandparents," Antonio says tersely. "Who would bury anyone near their home? That's creepy, overly morbid."

Paolo and Giana nod.

"But you are a creepy person, Anna," Antonio adds.

"Antonio," Fulvio scolds.

"More rudeness, Antonio?" Giana asks.

"Having a vivid imagination is what makes me an artist," I say. And I'm glad Antonio took my bait—the Peruzzi grandchildren clearly don't know about the family crypt.

"Enough," Francesca says.

"Oh, no, *I'm* the one who's being rude," I say. "It's just so . . . I have some questions about our family history and the necklace."

Aurora shakes her head, but Fulvio says, "Ask your questions, Anna. But only today. Never again." His frown conveys the fierce man masked under his usual avuncular exterior.

"That's very fair," I say. "Thank you. So, my mother wore a ruby-and-diamond necklace in her wedding portrait. Not just her. The same necklace is painted around the necks of the other women in the family, in their wedding portraits. The Medici Falchion, of course. Those paintings hang in my living room, in case you've forgotten." I make myself visibly shudder. "What a weird name for such a beautiful jewel—the

Medici sword. Why a sword with a cutting edge? Is it some symbol of our family's thirst for blood? Or some reverse meaning that's directed at the women who've worn the necklace?" Again I shiver.

The tension on Francesca's face is palpable. She's definitely disturbed by this conversation.

Aurora nods. "Yes. Gruesome. And something no one should wish for. But there's no explanation for the necklace's name."

"All this about a curse is bullshit," Giana says. "It's embarrassing that anyone in my family would believe this crap. Even you, Nonna."

"Hush, Giana!" Aurora says.

That was the first time I've heard Aurora speak harshly to anyone. In response, Giana bows her head to her grandmother and apologizes.

"I haven't asked my real questions yet," I say, in an intentionally meek voice while looking at Fulvio. "You sure it's okay?"

He nods.

"The necklace went missing the night my mother died. I think it's somewhere inside my caves. I can access them from my basement. People think I'm to blame for her death, that I'm a thief, but I know that's not what happened." Aurora starts to say something, but I hold up a hand. "And even if I'm wrong about that, and I took the necklace, who knows what I did with it that night or in the days after? You see, I found more than her journal. Inside of it, I found a special key—the one that accesses the caves under my house. I thought the key was lost, because I searched the whole house . . . But then I found the journal, and there it was."

"You think someone would put a valuable necklace down in a cave along with spiders and bats and dirt?" Antonio asks. "Who in their right mind would do that? And where would they put it? Inside rocks?"

Fulvio and Aurora exchange a look. I'm even more certain they haven't told their grandchildren—or at least this one grandchild—about the crypt.

"Maybe you think there's buried treasure down there," Antonio continues, his lips curled in a sneer that once again makes him look ugly. "Or maybe the lost ark? That's it, the necklace is in the lost ark. We know you have a vivid imagination, Anna. So do your shrinks."

"Excuse me?" I say harshly.

He doesn't stop. "Everyone believes you pushed your dear mamma down the stairs because you wanted her necklace. You always talked about it when you were a kid. Of course you deny it now. Every killer denies their crime. But here you are again, back in Tuscany, obsessing about the stupid thing. God knows what else you're after."

"Jesus, shut up, Antonio," Giana says. "Anna never talked about the thing."

"No more," Fulvio says, staring at Antonio.

This family—they show disdain for the once "disowned" Antonio, yet he sits at the table, mouthing off. Forgiveness doesn't justify apathy toward a wrongdoer's bad actions.

"There are no treasures in the caves," Fulvio continues, focusing his attention on me. "No one should be down there. It's dangerous, not some playground."

"Don't go in, Anna," Aurora says. "I beg you."

"Thank you, Aunt Aurora, but you don't have to worry about me. I'm not afraid. I've been inside caves before with my friends."

Antonio scoffs. "Where, at Disneyworld?"

All this time, Paolo has looked at me with concerned eyes. But is he worried about me or about what his family thinks?

"Anna, you should be afraid," Fulvio says. "You could get hurt. Worse. And you're carrying two children."

Then Paolo surprises me. "Maybe this is crazy, but what if there really are family heirlooms down there? What if the necklace *is* there? Now I'm curious. What's the harm in looking?"

"Not a pregnant woman alone!" Fulvio bellows.

"Please don't worry about me," I repeat, unintimidated because he's neither my boss nor my grandfather. "I've actually gone into the cave already, but not too far. It doesn't look that bad. It's been excavated. I just need a bridge to cross a ravine, so I had some planks delivered. The gap is only seven or eight feet wide. A big nothing. I'm going in again tomorrow. If I find anything interesting, or it gets too difficult, experts from Rome will go with me."

Fulvio huffs. "Don't be ridiculous. There's nothing down there but bugs, bats, and dirt. Just like Antonio, with his nasty mouth, has said."

"You never know what you'll discover in the most unlikely places," I say, glancing at Francesca.

"You're nothing but a selfish bit—" Antonio stops talking when Fulvio half-rises from his seat.

It looks like Aurora is going to slap her grandson, but Fulvio touches her shoulder.

"Oh, don't tell me now that you're dying to be a daddy, Antonio," I say.

"People can change their minds," he says.

"Except not you," Giana says. "You're disgusting. The way you treat women."

Aurora fidgets with her silverware. "If Anna goes into the cave, Paolo should go with her and make sure she's safe. Or let Fulvio and Paolo go."

"Of course, I'll go," Paolo says.

"No, I forbid this," Fulvio roars, slamming a fist on the table. "No cave is safe, not even our wine caves."

I look at Paolo, wait for him to defy his grandfather, to insist that he'll go with me, but he stays silent.

Everyone falls silent.

"I want to share something with you because we're family," I say, suddenly tearful. "I've been having crazy dreams lately, but they're not really dreams. They're more like memories, and I think . . . I think I know who killed my mother."

"You did," Antonio says.

"No, my father. He was jealous of other men, especially of Giuseppe Tringali, and he wanted control of my mother's property. Everyone knows that. He must've taken the necklace and hid it inside the caves. When the authorities came to question him more, he took me, and we ran. Happened late one night. We barely had time to pack. He didn't have the necklace with him when we got to the States. I'm sure of that."

"Far-fetched," Antonio says.

"Why couldn't it have been the father?" Giana asks. "Just as plausible as any other theory."

"Exactly," I say in a tremulous voice. "And then he said I was crazy, put me in the hospital, and let me take the blame." Tears stream down my cheeks. "When I find the Medici Falchion, I'm putting it in a museum or I'm going to destroy it. I asked a priest what to do with a cursed object. He said to destroy it. Sounds like the safest thing to do. So I think Aurora is right; Paolo you should go in with me."

Fulvio glowers, one arm by his side, the opposite hand curled in a fist and resting on the table. Paolo, caught between his grandfather and me, won't look at anyone. Antonio slugs his wine down, pushes his plate away, and goes inside.

I stand and smile bravely. "We have to do this."

54

efore leaving the family, I sidle up to Francesca and
ask for a private moment.

"Is this about the caves?" she asks as we walk to
my car.

"It's about the night my mother died."

She bristles, but at least she doesn't pirouette and storm away.

"I had a talk yesterday with Giuseppe Tringali about that night. He
told me that you rode with him and Mamma to the opera and back
home. Even though Claudio and the family went with you to the opera.
Why did you ride with Mamma and Tringali if you were there with
your husband and kids?"

Her shoulders droop. "Your mother asked me to ride along because
Tringali was always very handsy with her. She didn't want to be alone
with him. He's a predator. You should stay away from him too."

From what I learned from Tringali, this rings true. But do Francesca's words? "You knew this about him, knew I was going to study
with him, and yet you're only telling me this now?"

She starts to speak, but nothing comes out.

"It's okay, I can take care of disgusting, dirty old men. Who got dropped off first, you or my mother?"

She frowns. "Where is this going?"

"Is there a problem with telling a grieving daughter about her mother's last minutes on earth? Don't you think I deserve to know? The person whose life was thrown into turmoil more than any one of you?"

She looks away.

"No matter how close everyone felt to Mamma, I suffered most, Francesca. For years, up until a short while ago, I thought I was to blame for her death."

Her rigid exterior breaks. "I met your mother at her house an hour before Tringali picked us up. We did our makeup and touched up our hair. After the show, he drove us to your mother's house. I got in my car and drove home. The only person who went inside the house was Vittoria. At this point, with so many questions, you surely know more than I do about what happened after."

"So Tringali didn't pick you up at your house?"

"No, I just told you. I drove to your mother's house first."

"Was Edoardo there when you got back after the opera?"

"He might've been inside, he was the caretaker, but I never saw him. He could've been anywhere."

So Tringali or Francesca or Edoardo are lying—or one or all of them have poor memories.

I take a half-step toward Francesca and reach for her arm. "Please, tell me this. Do you think I'm to blame? That I pushed her while sleepwalking?"

She shuts her eyes for a moment, and then looks at me sympatheti-cally. A concerned surrogate aunt or a superb actor? "I don't know what happened, Anna. I wasn't there. I know this—you loved your mother. She adored you."

"And that night?"

"You two argued. Anna, I'm worried about your obsession with the necklace, and now with figuring out the circumstances surrounding your mother's death, you will suffer harm, and I don't mean only physical. You're still so fragile, not as tough as you pretend to be. Best to go on with your life and raise your new family. Make a happy life."

"If I didn't push her, then what do you think happened? And please don't tell me you weren't there. I know that already."

She lets out a long sigh. "What is that old saying, when you hear hoofbeats behind you, think of horses, not zebras? Accidents happen, so it's highly likely Vittoria just tripped and fell. We drank quite a bit of champagne that night." Francesca's chest heaves once, and she seems to suppress a sob. "This is hard to talk about. She was like my sister."

She clearly wants me to stop. Not happening. "My father said my mother wasn't wearing the necklace when he found her body."

"I'm sorry, I wish I had your answers." She folds her arms, hugging herself. "A few months before that night, your mother saw a lawyer about divorcing your father. I don't know if he knew. She was young enough to return to the stage, and her audience missed her. I was her biggest fan, other than you, and I wanted to see her perform again. I used to tease her, but only to encourage her to go back to the stage. Eventually, she contacted her agent. She planned to resume her career as soon as the divorce papers were served and your father was out of the house."

"Tringali said you and Vittoria argued that night. That you tried on the necklace."

Francesca huffs in disgust. "He's a drunk and a liar. You can't believe anything he says. In his younger years, he had some charm and good looks—his flaws overlooked. Not anymore."

I think of her own son, Antonio, but stay mum.

"Vittoria and I didn't argue that night." In a lowered voice, she says, "Anna, your father was experiencing financial troubles. He wanted your mother's money; she wouldn't give him anything."

"Tringali claims to have been in love with Mamma. And she in love with him."

"The only person ever involved in Tringali's love affairs is himself. He's a narcissist. If he told Vittoria he loved her, he was after something."

If everything goes according to plan, by tomorrow I'll know the truth.

That evening, I make a few phone calls and turn in early. I need a good night's sleep.

I don't get one.

55

arly in the morning while it's still dark, an owl hoots outside my bedroom window, waking me. Sleep soon comes again. Then a rush of adrenaline surges through my veins. My eyes flash open, but I don't move an inch, only shift my focus toward my bedroom door. Dim light spills inside the room—the door is now open.

The floor squeaks. A shadow of someone moving stealthily inside the room.

My heart bangs against my chest; a hard pulse hammers in my ears. The urge to pant is strong. My father's words come to me: *To win a game against a stronger opponent, you have to strike first.* And what better way to strike first than to ambush your enemy?

Feigning changing position in my sleep, I move my arm in the direction of my phone on the nightstand.

The person creeps closer. No time to dial the police even if I can grab the phone. Instead, I reach for the lamp, clumsily knocking into it and a picture frame. The lamp crashes to the floor, the ceramic base shattering.

"Don't move!" The intruder is a woman. "And stay away from the phone!" The cold, angry voice of the person I expected to come not tonight, but tomorrow—Francesca.

Vittoria de' Medici Rossi's murderer has struck first.

The lights flick on, momentarily blinding me.

"Get up," Francesca says. "Very slow."

When my vision returns, I don't see Francesca. No, I see her daughter, Giana! The voices of mother and daughter sound so similar, and I thought . . .

She holds a gun, which she points at my heart. "Where's the necklace, puttana?"

"I thought you didn't care about it."

"The necklace should've passed down through the female line to Aurora, then to my mother, and me. But oh, no. My stupid grandmother and idiot mother don't want it. And you know what? I'm next in line, which makes the necklace mine. Now move. We're taking a little trip downstairs to your safe."

Clearly, she's already tried the safe, but the combination has been changed.

"I don't have the necklace."

"Don't play games with me. You think I believed your lies that you were going down to find the necklace tomorrow?"

Giana's appearance has shaken me to the core. To survive, I have to get control of myself. "You pushed the boards over!"

"Shut up."

"People call me crazy, but you're the one who's insane. So why should I help you? You're only going to kill me. Just like you killed my mother. You were the one I saw running from the house that night. You and Francesca *both* wore red to the opera." The photograph in the magazine proved that. Francesca faced the camera, but there were others in the photograph, another who wore a red dress, her back to the camera. It's now obvious that the second woman was Giana. How had I overlooked her?

"She deserved it," Giana says. "The ostentatious bitch. Always demeaning my poor, talentless mother."

"You're forgetting about my babies. Your nieces or nephews."

"You think I'm worried about your babies? You should've listened to Antonio and gotten rid of them. Now move, or I'll make sure you and those bastards inside you don't ever move again."

I rise, looking for a chance to fight back, but Giana is smart, cautious. She doesn't let me get close to her or to anything I might use as a weapon.

Once we reach the study, I squat in front of the safe. My hand trembles as my fingers struggle to rotate the dial to the correct numbers. Then the shackle releases and the lock opens.

"Look inside for yourself," I say when the door swings to. "I don't have the necklace. Just like I told you at your house. I was telling the truth."

With the gun trained on me, she looks inside. No necklace is in there, only the Dungeon Door key. She snatches it.

And in that moment, when her attention is redirected, I run the short distance and jump on her.

The gun slides from her hand and across the floor. We topple down to the floorboards, knocking over a glass vase as we fall. I level a punch to her nose, hoping to smash it in. No good. She headbutts me and knees me in the stomach, leaving me breathless. I curl into myself, grasping my stomach—oh my God, my babies!

She scoops up the gun, gets to her feet, and kicks me hard in the kidneys. With a foot, she shoves me with great force. My body rolls over and on top of the broken glass, the shards digging into my flesh like a thousand needles.

"I'll show you where the necklace is," I shout. "You deserve to have it. You'll be the next one to suffer its curse."

Giana chortles. "Get moving."

56

truggling for breath, willing myself not to break down, I force myself to stand and glance at the clock on the desk. Four o'clock. Too early.

Both sides of my nightgown are damp—blood. Fortunately, from cut glass and not related to the pregnancy. I wipe my hand off on a dry portion of my gown and head down to the basement, doing my best to ignore the pain in my stomach and back. Not easy.

My breath is ragged. My legs tremble like jelly.

Keep your composure. Fight.

We reach the basement. My caving gear is sitting on the table in the middle of the room, just where I left it. Giana picks up a flashlight. I look at the crossed swords mounted on the wall. Impossible to reach. To get to the knight's sword means I'd have to go through Giana and her gun aimed dead center at my chest—an easy shot.

"Don't try anything again," she says. "Next time I'll shoot."

Why doesn't she just pull the trigger? Because she intends to leave me in the cave to die, doesn't dare leave evidence that will prove my death wasn't some accident. When she has what she wants, does she mean to shove me into the ravine, where I'll fall so deep that no one will find me or where the stream at its base will carry my body down current? If I'm ever found, the authorities will believe that I recklessly tried to cross over and then plunged to my death.

The family certainly has warned me enough not to go in. Her perfect cover.

"I need a flashlight," I say.

"No chance of that happening. You'll have to use your keen artistic eyesight." She shoves the key inside the lock without taking her eyes off of me, or the gun.

Who is this woman? Not just a fraudulent art dealer, not just a liar. She's *the witch.* "You were my babysitter. It was you who terrorized me when I was so young. Hurt me, put bugs on me, the kind that stung."

"I should've put a thousand fire ants on you, left you in that room with a thousand of those devil bugs. You were a spoiled, little brat, then, just as you are now."

"Devil bugs. Your name for those awful bugs. Not mine."

She laughs.

"You threatened me. Said you would throw me in the dungeon if I told. I never did, but you locked me inside anyway. To torture me. Why?"

"I told you. Vittoria stole the necklace from me. And now *you* are trying to do the same."

"I don't even want the necklace. Have it, it's yours."

"Your bitch mother is to blame for this."

"You're family, Giana. Everyone trusted you. My night terrors started because of you. You were the one I hid from, yelled at during the nightmares."

"Shut up."

We enter the cave, go down to the bend in the path, and turn right. She waves me to the left and toward the ravine. A bridge is now in place. So one does exist. We cross over and when I hesitate, she gives me a not-so-gentle shove.

Stumbling forward, I fall hard to my hands and knees and let out a loud groan. "Two seconds," I say. I take some time to get to my feet and brush myself off.

She gestures with her weapon for me to stand against the wall, as if I'm facing a firing squad, then goes to the bridge, takes ahold of the end, and heaves. The bridge falls into the ravine, smacking and banging hard against the rocky sides, toppling all the way down to the bottom. The sickening vibrations rise in volume. Then a tremendous splash.

I quake, overcome with fear.

"Down the tunnel," she says.

When we reach the crypt, the gate is already open. She shoves me inside. The north entrance is open too. Giana knows how to unlock both access points. The tunnel on the other side of the room must lead to the Peruzzis' wine caves. Just as I suspected. After all, generations of Peruzzis are buried down here too.

So how did she get inside my house?

If she went through the caves, that means she has another key to the Dungeon Door. But that seems unlikely, since she used mine. She must've somehow entered my house first. Through a window, a door. What does it matter?

I have a more troubling thought. Maybe she's working with Edoardo. Maybe he let her in or left a door open.

Filippo de' Medici's tomb is open. Giana didn't even have the decency to close it after she ransacked it, looking for the necklace where *she* had stashed it. When I peek over my shoulder, my mother's image flashes onto a wall. I gasp, pointing to the aberration.

"Stai zitto," she says. "I mean it. Not another word. I'm not falling for parlor tricks. Where is it?"

When I don't answer, she points the gun at my chest and cocks the trigger. "Tell me, or I shoot your hand—the good one."

She means it; I see the determination and evil in her eyes. What pleasure and joy she would take in seeing me in excruciating pain.

"In the pulpit," I rasp.

"Open it. I'm sure you know how."

Reluctantly, I remove the stone to reveal the cavity, and slowly step away in the direction of the north gate, which leads to the Peruzzis' property.

She peers inside, and a look of malevolent joy spreads across her face. She opens the wooden box, retrieves the Medici Falchion, and holds it up, making grotesque, almost animalistic sounds of pleasure while admiring the necklace.

After we crossed the bridge earlier, she shoved me hard, but not hard enough to make me go down. I did that all on my own. My fervent hope is that she failed to notice that I stashed a few rocks in my undergarments when I writhed on the ground, feigning injury.

With everything I've got, I hurl a sharp stone at her, striking her square in the face. She screams, grasps her head, and falls to her knees, losing her grip on the necklace, its jewel case, and more importantly, her gun. I want to go for the weapon, but it's too close to her.

As I start to make my way out, I throw more rocks, with most hitting Giana and inflicting more damage.

She's bleeding from the face and scalp, and with any luck enough to have impaired her vision.

I yank the north gate closed and engage the lock. Now there's only one way to get out of the crypt, and I intend to use that gate alone to lock her inside. I once again silently thank the priest in Rome who taught me about old gates and ancient locks.

I scoop up the necklace and case, then level a hard foot to Giana's kidney, which causes her to fold down to the ground and roll onto her side. I kick her flashlight out of reach and stomp on it until glass breaks and metal crunches.

I have to find the way to the south gate in total darkness, a huge risk because she's still alive. But I won't finish her off. Unlike what too many people think, what too many have brazenly said to my face, I'm no killer.

I locate the south gate, slam it shut, and continue down the tunnel to the cavern, using the wall as a guide. Then a miracle. The glowworms are alive and well, shining their brilliant blue magical light—bright enough to light the way.

Footsteps beat down the tunnel behind me. Impossible. But a beam of light shines through. Giana must've had a second flashlight. But the gate. How did she open it? Did I fail to engage the lock? Did I miss a way to open the gates from inside the crypt?

Once over the iron railing, I head down the narrow edge that circles the cavern, going as fast as I can toward the stream. I can't let her see me. Tucked behind an outcrop of the rock, twenty feet from the railing, I squat down and hold my breath, hoping she'll just head down the tunnel toward my house.

"Come out," she shouts. "You can't get away, you stupid bitch. There's no place to go."

A crackling sound comes from the cave ceiling. Dust rains down. The fool doesn't know enough not to raise her voice. I learned that lesson from my caving friends long before I ever set foot inside a cave. I learned it a second time when I started to speak above a whisper, and an archaeologist named Marit swatted me on the arm.

"You can't hide from me," she snarls in a tone that is the human equivalent to the growl of a rabid wolf. "Come out," she shouts. More dust. "Or I'll make sure you and your babies hurt when I kill you."

I try not to breathe, to not make a sound.

Giana goes quiet, maybe realizing that she was stupid to holler. The particles stop falling, the dust settles. A long minute passes, too soon to make a break for the stream.

Stones crunch. *Oh, caro Dio!* She's getting close. I should've run.

She laughs manically. "Poor Cousin and her precious bambinos." She cocks the trigger on her gun; I see her now. She's very close but hasn't seen me yet. "The necklace, Anna."

My heart beats so hard that it feels as if it'll explode.

Something about her mocking tone draws me back to my first year of high school. What a thought to have now. I had a best friend—Justine. We did everything together. Then she outgrew me, because I was weird, artsy, and she started hanging out with the popular kids. Except that the boy Mark whom she liked, a popular jock, showed too much interest in me. She won him over by having sex with him. She had no clue he was using her and talking behind her back, slut-shaming her. When she found out what was going on, she didn't accuse the guy, she blamed me, because he claimed that *I* was the one who spread the rumor across social media.

"Justine fucked Mark," I shouted. "He says she's a cheap lay."

The boys laughed. No, everyone did.

She and her new friends cornered me in the gym showers and cut my hair to pieces. Ripped it every which way possible. Never had I been angrier in my life, hated feeling helpless. I had a lot of explaining to do when I saw the head-of-school later that day.

"My hair got caught in the magnetic mixer in chemistry lab," I said. "I tried to even it up—in a pixie cut. Looks good, don't you think?"

"We need to call your mother."

I let out a loud, snarky laugh. "Good luck with that."

The head-of-school turned bright red. "I'm sorry, Anna, I forgot in the heat of the moment . . ." Maybe she never alerted my father because of her embarrassment.

I got even with those girls. Prom night. I waited four long years until we were seniors. I was supposed to go with my friend Spencer, who was gay and hadn't come out—until that group of mean kids outed him at school. He was just as fed up as I was. We found their secret stash of vodka and spiked it with laxatives. We didn't go to the dance. Just took pictures at the entrance and then snuck off campus. With our fake IDs, we went to a gay bar a few towns over and hung out with his friends. One of the best nights of my life. The next day, we heard about our success.

I've never given up a fight after that, and I won't do so now. Those kids who tortured me in school were just juvenile Giana Massiminos. Fuck them and fuck her.

No time to be the victim, no time to wait. In the throes of my glacial anger, I hold out the necklace, dangling it in front of me. She sees the movement, sees me, then lunges forward and goes for the jewel.

In one fluid motion, I rise and body slam her hard. Her arms fly up, and as she fights to regain her balance, she staggers back, grappling for purchase. But there's only air. I shove her again, even harder, and she falls ten feet down to the cavern floor. Dust balloons around her.

Still conscious, she hacks and coughs and struggles to stand.

I hurry toward the stream.

There's a loud screeching in the distance. Within seconds, the cavern begins filling with pipistrelli—their squeaking beautiful and awe inspiring.

Giana screams. She shoots once, then twice. The bats leave as quickly as they came.

But the vibrations created by the gunfire are ominous—and perhaps deadly. The ceiling gives a foreboding creak and then another and another. It crackles like a thousand pieces of ice are breaking atop a frozen lake—the byproduct of her attempt to kill my precious night-fliers.

If I don't get out now, I'll be buried under tons of rock—if this madwoman doesn't shoot me first.

The ceiling begins to rain down rock and stones and pebbles and clouds of toxic dust. Behind me, a massive stalactite breaks loose and crashes to the floor. An explosion of dust fills the entire cavern.

57

hen the ceiling's collapse seems to halt, all goes quiet, except for the dull drip and sibilant crackle of rocky debris still falling. The great cavern has gone dark, except for a precious few glowworms lighting my way to the stream. I use the wall as a guide, trusting that the light of the surviving worms won't completely vanish.

Then a click—a gun misfiring.

How is it that Giana's fall to the cave floor didn't kill her? How has she survived the cave-in? All that falling rock and debris?

I press forward.

Another fruitless click.

"Don't shoot, the whole place will cave in," I say a little too loudly. But better that than more gunfire.

Giana lies on the cavern floor, barely visible now, but in a different spot from where she was before. She must've risen but collapsed.

The stream is close, so very close. The glow from the worms reflects off its water.

Gunfire rings out.

I cover my head but don't stop.

More stalactites splinter, and pieces of rock begin to fall—at first like a light rain, then a deadly hailstorm. The domino effect begins. Rock bombards the cavern floor. Dust fills the air.

No way will Giana survive this. Will I?

I pull my gown over my nose and mouth and move faster.

The cavern goes pitch dark. The glowworm light is extinguished; the creatures have either died—I hope not—or the dust has obscured their light.

I use the cavern wall as a guide, but there are so many hazards. No choice, so I go slowly. If I don't get out soon, I'll suffocate or be pummeled by rock.

I cough and gag, barely able to suck in a breath.

Then I run into a rockface, smashing my nose and cheek. I feel around, retrace my steps, and lift a foot to go forward, but there's no ground to place it on. I'm near the ledge that drops to the cave floor. I lower myself and crawl, using the edge as my guide. I'm getting light-headed from inadequate oxygen.

Then the sound of flowing water. A few feet more, there's the stream and the tunnel alongside its banks. I crawl deeper inside, staying close to the edge of the water. The air has less debris. Then a glorious sight. The light of glowworms gleams farther down the stream, their glow reflecting against the water. As I move closer toward their light, the air begins to clear more and more.

I reach the pipistrelli cave; its smell, though rank, is truly welcome. Bats flutter, chirp, and titter. Faint light spills inside from the opening to the outside world.

A bat flies at me. Then another. My heart skips a beat, but I don't dare scream. I wave my arms, and thankfully, the pipistrelli keep their distance.

When I make it to the mouth of the cave, a whoosh of fresh air slaps me in the face. I can finally breathe. A full moon lights up the sky. I go slowly, slipping on rocks and moist vegetation. My God, I'm alive.

A third of the way down, I stop to rest on a grassy knoll. Its blades are slick and damp. I'm so thirsty I could lick them, but don't. Fatigue hits me hard. Daylight will come soon. I lie back, place the case behind my head, and close my eyes. I just need a few moments to rest.

The ground crackles. My stomach drops. Somehow, Giana still lives.

58

iana is covered in debris and dark red stains of blood. Her face and hair are littered with dirt and dust. Her eyes are wild.

How many bullets did she fire? No matter. I'm certain there's one left with my name on it.

"Give it to me!" she growls. She has no gun, but a knife—exceptionally long and deadly sharp. Its blade glints in the moonlight. "Don't try anything stupid. And don't even think about throwing the necklace over. You'll be dead, and I'll find it anyway."

Too tired to fight, I take the case from behind me and retrieve the necklace.

She tells me to drop it, to get up, and back away. Something inside me snaps. She's going to murder my babies and me. I'm not giving it to her.

What kind of fool would do that?

If she wants the necklace, she's going to have to take it from me. Even if that means I have to fight to the death.

Adrenaline floods my body; a rush of energy that I've never felt before. I stuff the necklace in my pocket, grip rocks on the ground, and jump to my feet as if weightless. I bombard her with fists full of dirt and stones. Sometimes ordinary minerals from the soil are more valuable than rubies and diamonds.

She lunges at me, swiping the knife at my neck.

I dodge her thrust. She tries again, stumbling close to the edge.

I back up, the rocks sliding underfoot. When I slip on wet grass, she advances and swings the weapon, but again misses. She shoves me with her free arm. My foot goes off the edge. I land on one knee. She holds the knife above me. I twist hard and throw my body weight to the ground, landing on my back. When she comes at me, I kick her legs as hard as I can.

Slumped over, she stumbles.

I scramble to my feet and start down the mountain, trailblazing my way on this narrow ledge. A fall from the edge means certain death.

I hurry along, tripping and righting myself. She's right behind me, mirroring my steps. I feel the air as the blade swishes past the back of my neck. How long can I keep this up?

I hear the thunk on the back of my head before I feel the pain. Turnabout—she's now throwing rocks and stones at me. Out of breath, I'm dizzy. The cliff's edge is more inviting than the knife's blade. Another rock to my skull. I can't stop myself from going down. I land on my knees and right hand.

Giana stops, laughs her hideous laugh. "Anna's Blood. Isn't that what you wrote in my brothers' wine cellar? There's no sweeter taste than a weakling's blood. You sniveling, whiney cagna."

A blend of buzzing and humming wafts through the air. The serenade of the devil bugs. Have they come to claim me in death? They were there for Raffaella at her funeral.

Giana stops and looks around. She must hear them too.

"They're coming for us," I say. "They'll kill us both, eat our flesh and bones."

Enraged, she flies at me with her knife. I roll and manage to avoid the blade. My right hand catches her blouse and rips her shirt. She has a birthmark above her right breast.

I'm thrust back to the moment I looked through the cut-out eyes in the closet and to that scene I saw in my mind. I thought that the woman, the one performing the sexual favor, had a tattoo on her chest. It wasn't that, it was a birthmark, the same birthmark I see on Giana now.

It wasn't my mother having those parties. It was Giana and her friends. While babysitting me. Revolting.

I'm empowered and fight harder, but the weakness in my left hand limits me. I lash out, but I need to grab her wrist to steer the knife away from my neck. I go for her hand with both of mine.

She pulls away, and then, thrusting her knees into my armpits, she pins my shoulders to the ground. I try to kick her with my legs. I thrash but can't get momentum. She's on top of me, forcing my head over the ledge, the broad-bladed dagger suspended above my throat.

The buzzing and humming intensifies.

"Face the sting of the falchion, bitch," she snarls, poised to behead me.

Time slows.

She thrusts. My eyes remain locked on hers—I don't know why, but I'm not frightened anymore. Maybe this is what happens just as you're about to face the inevitable end of your days. Will my babies feel the pain? I pray not.

I think of my father and release my anger toward him. I don't want to die with hate in my heart. Did I misjudge him?—he didn't cheat me out of my trust fund. I pray he forgives me.

I think of my mother. It's like I can hear her singing "In questa reggia" from *Turandot*. The powerful aria sung by the titular ice princess. It's a song bemoaning her pain, the trauma her ancestors have suffered, how it's affected her ability to love. The princess cuts off her feelings; she cuts off the heads of her male suitors. All in her mind to avenge the rape and murder of her family over the centuries.

I refuse to live a second more in pain. If I die, I'm at peace.

A weight in my pocket—the Medici Falchion—reminds me of my courage. I jar my good arm free, retrieve the necklace, and swing it at Giana's left eye. Blood spills; she jerks back, gritting her teeth. Before she can strike again, the devil bugs descend. I don't feel their sting, don't feel my flesh being ripped apart. Neither do I feel the rip of Giana's blade.

The tornado of insects surrounds Giana. Her knife disappears.

My mother vanishes, but still I hear her singing anew. A beautiful aria, "Casta Diva" from Bellini's *Norma*—a prayer for peace to the goddess of the moon.

White light fills my vision, I see nothing. My mother's magical voice fades.

59

aylight appears on the horizon. My eyes flutter open. I pinch my arm, feel the wonderful pain. I'm alive. How? I'm on the mountainside. How did I survive?

The devil bugs. They killed Giana. Devoured her so quickly she had no time to scream or cry. I search the ground. No skeletal remains. I peer over the cliff's edge. No sign of a body. Not even bones.

Did I imagine everything? Another nightmare?

I look at my arms and legs—scratches, cuts. I lift my gown—bruises on my chest. Thankfully nothing on my abdomen. I place a hand on my belly; I pray my babies are alive and well.

A weight tugs in my pocket—the Medici Falchion.

More crunching sounds, not from the caves but coming from below. My stomach tightens. Who else must I face? Giana again?

From around the corner, Edoardo appears. Does *he* mean me harm?

"I thought I would never find you," he says. "A thousand apologies. Are you ready to go home?"

Stupefied, I nod.

Before he can extend a hand, I rise.

"You'll never believe what happened, Edoardo."

"Save your energy until we get home, then we'll have a nice, long chat."

Our plan was simple, or so Edoardo and I thought it would be. I set the stage with my visit to the Peruzzi family that Sunday afternoon. The evidence pointed to Francesca as my mother's killer, especially because she wore a red dress the night of the opera. I told the entire family what I was going to do—go into the caves and search for family heirlooms. I made sure they knew that if I found the necklace, I would destroy it.

I thought it was Francesca who had stashed the Medici Falchion inside Filippo's tomb. I couldn't be sure what she would do when she heard my plan to go into the caves, but there was a good chance that if she murdered my mother and stole the necklace, she would try to retrieve it before I found the crypt. If she knew sixteen years ago that my mother hid the jewel in the pulpit, she would've just taken it. There would've been no reason to kill her.

But I was wrong about Francesca, though correct that the perpetrator would show up. The culprit was Giana, not Francesca.

Edoardo was the only wildcard. I had to trust him. I knew I could trust Paolo, but he also refused to defy his grandfather's wishes. For decades, Edoardo could've found the necklace and run off with it, had he really wanted to. Instead, he always supported my side of the family, even kept the villa ready for my homecoming.

He hated my plan, but he eventually agreed to help because he knew I would go ahead without him. So he kept watch at the Peruzzis', waiting for someone to enter their caves and make their way to the crypt. He was supposed to call the police as soon as he saw Francesca go in, but he never saw a soul. When daylight broke, he returned to the villa to tell me that no one had shown up. But I wasn't there.

We were wrong to assume that the wrongdoer would go in through the caves. Instead, Giana went straight to my villa and entered through one of the windows, which wasn't as secure as it should've been. We know this because she, too, didn't fully secure the window once inside.

I even questioned whether Edoardo had set me up, not overlooking the possibility that he and Francesca might be working together. But that proved false.

Home again, I change my clothes, put the necklace in my pocket, and stash the case in a drawer. Until I'm certain that no one is still after it, I won't let the Medici Falchion out of my reach. Only then do I call the authorities. If the police get ahold of the necklace, there's no telling when I'll see it again—if ever. I don't trust anyone, not even law enforcement, especially them—a lesson learned from my father. That's what he would've advised. He might've been a crook, but he was also street smart.

I've done nothing wrong, but the Italian cops might search the house and even the safe. There's no Fourth Amendment in this country, although I probably have some rights. I'm just not willing to take a chance.

While waiting for the authorities to show up, Edoardo, with shaky hands, makes me a cup of herbal tea. He claims that he knows how to brew it best, tells me it will calm my nerves. The tea is good, but it doesn't settle me.

I sit at the kitchen island. "Giana is dead. She tried to kill me."

Edoardo folds his hands. "I found her body in the grotto."

I keep silent. If I tell him that she survived that cave-in, that she pursued me, that the devil bugs consumed her, leaving no trace of her behind, he'll think that I've had another mental breakdown. I'm no longer sure what happened. I only know what I saw. "So my beautiful cavern is gone?"

"Most of it is intact. Leave it be and time will restore its full beauty."

Then something else hits me that doesn't make sense. "Wait, Edoardo. How did you cross over the ravine? Giana threw the bridge down."

"She threw *her* bridge over. Not mine. As soon as I realized you weren't home, I went to the cavern. I feared the worst, that things had gone a muddle." He says he saw the body, and when I ask how, he explains, "Giana died when a stalactite impaled her."

I cringe. "Where exactly?"

He looks at me as if I don't want to know, but says, "Through the neck. You mustn't think about that. You keep your mind focused on your life and the babies. It's over now." He bows—actually bows like we're in the early twentieth century and I really am some kind of aristocrat.

"You're so formal, Edoardo," I say, smiling. "You do know you're not the butler or the gardener, you're my great-uncle. And another thing, we're living in the twenty-first century."

He returns a smile. "I am all those things. But you can rest assured, I'm perfectly content. I've done my job. You and your babies are safe, Anna."

I break down in tears. "Am I dreaming? Is any of this real? Are you real?"

"I can assure you that you're not dreaming. Everything about your life is real now. Speaking of reality, you should go to the hospital. I can see that you've been injured. And you must speak with your—the baby doctor."

"Of course," I say. "There is one thing I want to ask you."

He nods.

"Why was I led to believe that my mother was cremated?"

"A horrible lie, arranged so that your father would have no reason to step foot on this property, claiming that he was taking you to your mother's place of repose. He couldn't be trusted. That was clear when he took the jewels in her parlor before he left."

"Go rest, Edoardo, you look so pale. I'll call for you when the authorities arrive."

He tries to resist, but finally retreats to the room off the pantry, an old servant's room. I phone the Peruzzis. Fulvio answers. A relief. I tell him that something horrible has happened and ask him to come over, alone.

Half an hour later, a car heads down the drive. Fulvio or the authorities? If the cops, they sure have taken their sweet time.

Without a knock, the front door bursts open. Police? Fulvio? No—Paolo.

60

aolo storms inside the foyer, pointing a gun at me. The look of hatred in his eyes far exceeds any look that Antonio has thrown my way. How the younger brother deceived me, played me for a fool.

I slip a hand in the back pocket of my jeans and hit the emergency button that rings the police. They should've been here by now. Where are they? What's taking them so long? Then, making sure that I show no fear, I walk toward Paolo with calm and determination.

"Where's Giana?" he shouts in my face.

"Dead."

"You murdered my sister."

"No, she brought it on herself. Or more accurately, the Medici Falchion killed her—its curse."

"Cagna!"

"You call me a bitch? Just look at yourself. Giana's poor baby brother all alone. He can't think for himself. Can you, Paolo? You're lost."

He shoves me.

I fight to stand upright but don't lose my smirk. We circle each other.

"You were in on this with Giana," I say, as the pieces fall into place. "Right from the start. You sweet-talking asshole. Fooling the world with your nice guy crap. You shoved Antonio into me on the staircase at the castle, thinking I would fall. But it didn't work out that way, did it? You murdered Raffi."

Paolo chortles. "I wouldn't trust my stupid brother to open a wine bottle with a screw cap. The fucking, dumb peacock. Yeah, I pushed him, shoved him as you say."

"Asshole. So big brother did his part, said nothing to the authorities. Always protecting his weak little brother. I'm sure you somehow blamed Antonio, accused him of stopping too fast—the reason you bumped into him. Poor Raffi, robbed of her life."

"Should've been you."

I retrace the moment. "But you took your mother to the hospital."

"Antonio did, not me."

Right—Francesca talked about "her son." I wrongly assumed Paolo had taken her.

He swipes at me. I dodge him and continue circling.

Where's Edoardo?

"Crossing over on those pieces of lumber, that was idiotic, Anna. You brought this on yourself."

"And yet I'm alive and well, Paolo. Don't you get it yet? I'm invincible. I have the power because the necklace rightfully belongs to me."

He scoffs. "Not for long."

I believe none of this bravado, and my insides are quivering like newly unmolded jelly, but I know this—Paolo and his family believe in curses. That means he can be controlled. "You're cursed for coveting the necklace just like Giana was."

His eyes widen and I detect a glint of doubt, but then he lets out a malevolent laugh. "My sister and mother and brother believe in that crap. Here's what I believe—you've stolen my land from me, taken my vineyards. Which means you owe me. Give me the necklace. Now!"

I laugh in his face. "How many times do I have to hear that demand from people in your sorry-ass family? First your pathetic sister breaks into my house, holds me at gunpoint, then tries to leave me in the cave for dead. Give *you* the necklace? Go ask your dead sister for it. She has it, maybe she's wearing it around the stump of her severed neck."

His face contorts with a mixture of grief for his sister and hatred for me.

"Giana also confessed to killing my mother, admitted to torturing me as a kid because she wanted the Medici Falchion so badly."

"What if she did?"

"Don't become a murderer, Paolo. Don't be like your sister."

With a confused expression, he momentarily ponders what I've said.

Meanwhile, I search left and right for something to use as a weapon. An umbrella in a copper bucket is near the entrance, but I can't reach it before he'd pull the trigger. Not unless I shove him off balance, and how will I do that to such a powerful man? And what use will an umbrella be against a pistol? Stupid idea, that umbrella.

Nevertheless. I shove him as hard as I can and go for it.

He stumbles a few steps backwards. Ah, the power of a surprise ambush—my father was right about that.

Paolo regains his balance, and like a mad dog loaded with adrenaline, barrels forward. I snag the umbrella, swing it upward, and thrust hard. Bullseye. The sharp end of the ombrello jabs hard into the delicate region of his solar plexus. He keels forward, the gun falls from his grasp. I dodge away and kick the weapon across the foyer.

"Help! Edoardo!" I shout.

Why hasn't Edoardo heard any of this?

Paolo is up again, and he's on me fast. He goes for my injured hand. I drop the umbrella and fight to free myself, punching him with my right fist, kicking him, aiming for his groin, but he expects my strikes and blocks me. He laughs in my face, enjoying his cruelty, then squeezes my left hand even harder. The pain sears up my arm, through my neck, and into my brain. He twists my wrist, the pain so excruciating that I fall to my knees.

"The police are already on their way," I say. "They'll be here any second."

"The necklace!"

I pull the Medici Falchion from my pocket and hold it out to the side. With sharp inward breaths, I rasp, "You want this, lap dog? Go fetch it." I fling the necklace across the foyer, it skitters across the slick-marble and slides underneath the coat closet door.

As he races to the closet, I scramble to my feet. He jerks open the closet only to be confronted by the figure.

"Help me, Mamma!" The eyes on the mannequin glow iridescent green.

Paolo stops in his tracks, his mouth agape as he stumbles back.

The mannequin takes a step forward. Or so it appears.

Paolo shrieks.

I grab the umbrella and jab the point of it into one of his kidneys. He keels to his side. At the close, I kick the necklace, sending it sailing across the foyer floor.

The mannequin falls forward.

I run toward the jewel.

Paolo gathers himself and follows me.

"Edoardo!" I cry.

"Who?"

"Help, Edoardo!"

"Edoardo Bortelli?" Paolo laughs as if I've told him the funniest joke ever. "We knew you were crazy, Anna. But this? Edoardo Bortelli has been dead for ten years."

I stumble, Paolo reaches me and shoves me away from the necklace.

He's gaslighting me, I know it. "You're lying. First your sister kills my mother, now you want to kill me. You're the one who's crazy. You and your dead psychopath sister."

"Your mother deserved what she got," he mocks. "Giana did the world a favor by killing her."

We both race to the necklace. He snags it up.

Edoardo enters the foyer, his gait that of a much younger man.

"Meno male!" I cry.

Paolo looks back. The older man doesn't make a sound.

"Do something, Edoardo."

Paolo freezes in shock.

I run to Edoardo.

Paolo shakes himself out of his momentary stupor. Stopping suddenly, I squat and thrust out a leg just as Paolo is on me. My leg gets caught between both of his. I yank. He loses his balance, twists, and falls toward the floor, his eyes wide with astonishment. Unable to stop the fall, his head slams hard onto the hard marble floor. Blood spills from his skull. When the necklace slips from his grasp, I retrieve it and then lock eyes with Edoardo. There's so much love between us. Love and trust.

"I love you, Anna. Remember your mother's words," he says. He steps back, and then he's no longer there. Just . . . gone.

I stumble back to the wall and slump down as two police officers arrive and thunder inside. Fulvio is right behind them.

The police are accompanied by an ambulance, which takes me to the hospital. Despite my bruises, the babies and I check out fine. Aurora, Francesca, and Antonio meet us. Fulvio never leaves my side.

We learn from a police officer that the coroner came for Paolo's body after the ambulance transported me to the hospital. And Giana's.

The authorities heard everything, all recorded on my phone after I hit the button to call emergency services. They know that Paolo tried to kill me. Still, the police interview me over the next several hours and eventually agree that I acted in self-defense. That my cries to my mother and Edoardo for help were made out of fear, and as a ploy to distract Paolo.

I wait with the Peruzzis—can I trust them after what's happened to Giana and Paolo? I don't know, but everything inside me tells me that I can. "This is a weird question," I start, "but whatever happened to the old caretaker. What was his name?"

"Edoardo," Aurora says sadly. "My half-brother. Never treated well by most of the family. I didn't treat him so well myself. He passed ten years ago; God rest his soul."

I'm not startled, not as one might be in hearing this. I think back to the first day that I arrived—the bluebottle fly that buzzed past Edoardo and me on the porch. Those flies are attracted to death. He was never interested in sharing a meal with me, either. I never saw him take one bite of food or a sip of water. And how cool the air always seemed to be when he was around. And if I'm not mistaken, we only had actual physical contact once—when he touched my forehead after I found him on the floor.

Was his presence, everything that had happened with him, only a dream? Some things can't be explained. Maybe I'll see him again in my dreams. If so, the dream will be a pleasant one, because I'm sure the bad nightmares are over.

The Peruzzis are devastated at the loss of Giana and Paolo—more so after learning how warped they were. Fortunately, I don't have to prove that I'm telling the truth; it was on the recording of Paolo trying to murder me. So many tragic answers.

A lingering question remains—what do I do with the Medici Falchion?

EPILOGUE

our years later, I have my first art show. The Galleria Borghese is hosting. My left hand is fully recovered. I'm ambidextrous now, so I use both. The critics call my work Fractured Realism.

My extended family is with me, and so are my twins—my daughter, Vittoria, and my son, Edoardo, named after my great-uncle and protector, who died many years ago.

My children bring a new little friend to meet me.

I crouch down to greet them. "What's your name, sweetie?" I ask the young girl.

"Raffaella," she says.

I start at hearing this. "You have a very pretty name to match your very pretty self. I once knew a nice, beautiful lady named Raffaella."

"I know. Vittoria and I are going to be best friends just like you two were."

My eyes flash. "Excuse me? I mean that's very nice."

"Mamma," Vittoria says. "Raffi wants to see your necklace."

I unbutton the top button of my silk blouse and reveal the jewel.

Raffaella says, "O-o, how magical."

"Told you," Edoardo says.

"You look just like a princess," Raffaella says, and leans in for a closer look. "I think I see angels inside the stones."

I hold up the bottom edge of necklace. Indeed, a thousand little angels *are* floating around inside of the stones. But only a discerning eye is able to see them. What everyone else sees are the hypnotic, dangerous sparkles from the stones.

I tried the necklace on after I returned home from the hospital the night Giana and Paolo died. I haven't taken it off since. Can't. It's part of me. I stopped trying to remove it, don't want to.

"Can I try on your necklace?" Raffaella asks.

An icy breeze sails across my neck. A reminder. I hear a lion roar. It's only in my mind.

"Oh, no," Vittoria says. "Mamma's the only one who can wear the Medici Falchion." Vittoria leans in and whispers in my ear, "Because you have just hands, Mamma." She pulls away, her eyes sparkling.

"Where did you hear that, caro?"

The three children giggle.

"Isn't that right, Mamma," Vittoria says, smiling brightly.

"So they say," I reply, buttoning my blouse.

ACKNOWLEDGMENTS

I would like to express my deepest gratitude to the following individuals for their unwavering support as *The Medici Curse* came to life. Andrew Auffenorde, Isabella Auffenorde, Michael Auffenorde, Audrey Clark, Danny Clark, Katelynn Dreyer, Maria Fernandez, Liza Fleissig, Debra Ginsberg, Ginger Harris, Eleanor Imbody, Dana Kaye, Kaitlyn Kennedy, Amanda LeConte, Will Luckman, Nathaniel Marunas, Julia O'Connell, Catherine Ottaviano, Dr. David Ottaviano, Otto Penzler, Charles Perry, Robert Rotstein, Matthew Sharpe, Katherine Smalley, Larry Smalley, Jr., my late father, Dr. Larry Smalley, Sr., Luisa Cruz Smith, Jessica Verde, and Nancy Waldron.

DACO S. AUFFENORDE is the award-winning author of *Cover Your Tracks*, which was selected as a *Suspense Magazine* "Best of 2020" Thriller/Suspense and won Action Thriller of the Year with Best Thrillers Book Awards. Her psychological thriller *The Forgotten Girl* won the Book of the Year with Best Thriller Book Awards. Auffenorde's works also appear in several anthologies, including her short story "The Virgo Affair" in *Killer Nashville Noir: Cold-Blooded*. Her debut *The Libra Affair*, a Jordan Jakes novel, was a #1 Amazon Bestseller. She is a member of International Thriller Writers, Mystery Writers of America, Authors Guild, Women's Fiction Writers Association, Alabama Writers' Forum, and Alabama State Bar.